The Curse of Samael's Grimoire©

David Dhekelia

Copyright © 2024 by David Dhekelia
All rights reserved. This book or any portion thereof may not be reproduced or used in any manner whatsoever without the express written permission of the publisher except for the use of brief quotations in a book review.

This is a work of fiction. Names, characters, businesses, places, events and incidents are either the products of the author's imagination or used in a fictitious manner. Any resemblance to actual persons, living or dead, or actual events is purely coincidental.

Other titles in this series by David Dhekelia

The Robe of Iniquity
The Pemberton Legacy
Dark Eucharist
Death Comes of Age
Sentence of a Scapegoat

Prologue

I decided in my last book *"Sentence of a Scapegoat"* to write a brief outline of the main characters and give a little background for those of you coming to this book series for the first time with no prior knowledge of my previous titles.

I'll start with the two main characters. Alan and Sue Baylock are a married couple in their mid-to-late fifties who have a daughter called Ruth. Ruth is 30 years old and married to Chris.

In my first novel, *"The Robe of Iniquity"*, we learned that Alan and Sue sold their house in order to downsize, without realising that there was something a bit odd about an item of clothing that had been left in a wardrobe in the new house. When Sue tried it on, after a long tingling sensation, she discovered that she was 30 years younger. Well who can blame a lady of mature years for taking advantage of this new vixen personae and going out to paint the town red? Oh, the broken hearts she left along the way with wild abandon shouldn't even be mentioned. There was one broken heart she left that she was truly sorry for – and that was her son-in-law Chris. Unbeknownst to him, he met Sue in a bar and let's just say one thing led to another. Since that time, Chris has seen old photographs of Sue holding Ruth as a baby and couldn't help noticing the resemblance between the younger Sue and the young woman he met at the bar. This has caused him to wonder.

Then there's Phyllis. What's not to love about dear old Phyllis? Slightly older than Sue, she was a real child of the sixties and boy did she have some fun!!! She listened to all the best music, took all the wrong drugs and generally did what people did back then. She may have put a bit of weight on and her long hair is now greying, but when she smiles, she excudes sincerity, warmth and honesty and she's intensely loyal to her closest friends, one of which is Sue. If ever an individual embodied the spirit of mother earth, it's dear Phyllis.

Robert's an interesting character. By profession, he is a clinical psychologist who lost his wife several years ago. He doesn't talk about it a lot – it's probably still quite painful for him. But his acquaintance with Sue and Alan began late one night when he was hiding in their back garden, trying to find the man who had killed a very good friend of his, Professor Ian Pemberton. Alan thought he was a burglar and tackled him to the ground. It was only when he called the police he found out that Robert Whitehead was no burglar, but according to the police just a 'meddling fool who should let the police do their work without his interference'. Since that time they have become good friends. Oh, and at one point, Robert and Phyllis almost became close but for whatever reason, it wasn't to be.

Talking of Ian Pemberton, the man was a veritable genius who created a device which could not only cause age reversal in people by 30 years (though it would only last six hours at a time), but could also read the DNA within a blood sample when injected into another person's arm who shared the same blood group. It does sound unbelievable but there has long been the idea that so called 'junk DNA' has a lot more to tell us than is presently known and Ian Pemberton always adhered to this theory. The four friends have used the device several times to 'read' DNA and discover all sorts of information pertaining to criminal activity.

Finally, we have Ophelia. A very close friend of Phyllis, she's something of an enigma. We don't know a great deal about her background, but she does have a strong connection with all things metaphysical and spiritual. She doesn't necessarily adhere to the new age movement, but she does have her own beliefs and philosophy, some of which run along similar lines to the aforementioned.

I hope this has given you some background information. I particularly enjoyed writing this book as I based it partly on a true location and event. Ten miles down the road from where I used to live, there is a village called Clophill. A lovely little village which has an old ruined church, St Mary's, that sits atop a hill which apparently fell into disuse around the 1840s. As the story goes, in 1963 some children found cockerell feathers in the ruined church and several of the graves were smashed open. It was believed that a black magic ritual had been performed there. How true this is I cannot tell for sure but the headstones were moved to the perimeter of the area so that nobody could locate where the graves were. Having visited this church several times, it is certainly not somewhere I'd want to visit during the hours of darkness, although a few brave souls have. So this book is my way of paying respects to the ruined church of Clophill and may she stand bold and proud for many centuries to come. She is now and I am sure will continue to be an enigma for many years. It was wonderful re-acquainting myself with what I feel have now become old friends and I really do hope you enjoy reading this book as much as I enjoyed writing it.

David Dhekelia

Chapter One

"Do you want me to get that Phyllis?" asked Ophelia as she heard a knock at the front door.

"No that's ok Ophelia, I'll get it. It's probably Robert."

Phyllis walked to the front door and opened it. Sure enough, there stood Robert.

"Come in Robert" she said somberly.

Robert followed her through to the lounge. "Hello Ophelia" he said.

"Hello Robert."

"Take a seat Robert, I'll make some tea" said Phyllis.

"Thanks Phyllis."

Robert and Ophelia sat in silence while they heard Phyllis in the kitchen making tea.

Finally Robert spoke. "Have either of you spoken to Alan and Sue?"

"Phyllis has" said Ophelia.

"How did they take the news?"

"Not well, although according to Sue, Alan is holding a lot in from what Phyllis said."

"Oh dear, that's going to be difficult" said Robert.

"Yes Robert, I think you're right."

Phyllis came through carrying a tray with fresh cups and her usual two pots of tea. One with herbal tea and one with normal tea. "Here you go Robert."

"Thanks Phyllis."

Robert stirred his tea as the three of them sat in silence.

Phyllis tried to put on a brave face but couldn't hold it in any longer. She began sobbing. "It's not fair" she said. "Just when she'd finally got closure for Tom, that bloody awful disease took her. She didn't deserve that."

"I know she didn't Phyllis, I know she didn't." Robert felt helpless. There was no way he could console either her or Ophelia. They'd received the news of Becky's death several days ago and even though they all knew it was inevitable, it was still a shock when she finally passed.

"It's hard to feel spiritual at times like this" said Phyllis.

"I know it's an imperfect world, but it really hits you when it's somebody you know."

"It's not just a case of knowing her, I think we all felt protective towards her" said Ophelia.

"Yes you're right Ophelia. She was like a kid sister to me. I couldn't help feeling protective towards her."

"Does anybody know when the funeral will be? Is it going to be in Cyprus or are they flying the body back to the UK?" asked Robert.

"She's going to be buried in Cyprus. That's where most of her friends lived so her last wish was to be buried there" said Phyllis.

"Apparently there's a letter on the way" said Ophelia. "Becky wanted to write us a farewell letter before she ...... before she ......"

Phyllis's phone rang and she jumped up to answer it, more as a distraction from the subject than to see who was calling.

"Hello? Oh hi Sue. How are you ...." Phyllis paused as Sue was relaying information over the phone. "Oh really? Oh that was quick, I didn't realise ......"

Robert and Ophelia both looked up attentively, although Phyllis was in the hall so neither could see the expression on her face. They could only guess what the conversation was about from Phyllis's replies to Sue.

"Oh well, yes, I can understand how you feel about that. What has Alan said? Oh not yet. Oh ok. What do you think he'll do?"

Ophelia and Robert became impatient, wanting to know what was being said. However, it wasn't too long before Phyllis ended the conversation.

"Well look Sue, why not come over later, on your own if you like. Just to give yourself time to think. Please love, I think it might help. Ok, well you know where I am. Take care."

Phyllis walked back into the living room. She could tell by Ophelia and Robert's expectant looks that they wanted the run down on the conversation she'd just had.

"That was Sue" she said.

"We gathered as much" said Ophelia, almost in the tone of somebody saying, 'no need to state the obvious'. "What did she say?"

"Well, it was a bit awkward. Apparently Alan and Becky had been emailing each other and one of her friends found Alan's email address and decided to write to him direct."

"Oh?" said Ophelia.

"It would seem that this friend told Alan that Becky had held a torch for him for years after they split up, but didn't try to contact him again because she felt ashamed for losing contact when she did."

"But we know it was because of what happened to Tom" said Ophelia.

"Yes, yes I know" said Phyllis. "But I suppose she felt it would be hard to explain. Anyway, the bottom line is that the funeral is in a week's time and they wanted to know if we wanted to fly out for it."

"A week's time? That rules me out because I've got seminars to present for the next two weeks. I'm behind my schedule and need to catch up with the paperwork and that's going to take me at least five days" said Robert.

"I can't go either" sighed Phyllis. "I promised my friend Elspeth I'd go and stay with her for a week or so because her mum died recently and I'd already cancelled on her twice. I haven't got the heart to do it again."

"I'm afraid it's the same here" said Ophelia. "I'm helping to set up the new Mind, Body and Spirit Festival. They used to run years ago but died down after a while. I've been contacted by two of the people who used to run the original ones and they told me there's been a renewed interest and they've decided to hold a few small ones locally. If they do well, they're going to expand further afield and they asked me if I'd go and give them some guidance. I promised them I would which means I'm going to be occupied for the next month at least."

"What about Alan and Sue?" asked Robert. "Will they be going?" He could tell by the expression on Phyllis's face that the answer wasn't going to be straightforward.

Phyllis sighed. "Well, I get the impression that Becky's friend is keen to meet Alan because Becky used to talk about him a lot. But the problem is ….."

"Sue doesn't want to go because she'll feel like a fish out

of water ......" added Robert.

"...... and I think there may still be a small tad of jealousy there" said Ophelia.

"Oh I don't know about that" protested Phyllis.

"Oh Phyllis, look, we're not being derisory about Sue in any way at all. It's just that I could pick up the signals quite a lot when Becky was here" said Ophelia. "Oh, please don't take that the wrong way, I know that Sue was genuinely concerned for Becky after she was nearly poisoned and fell ill, but I just got the feeling that things weren't the same between her and Alan when Becky showed up."

"But that was years ago ......" Phyllis tried to argue.

"I'm sorry Phyllis, but I agree with Ophelia" said Robert. "Just little facial tiks, expressions, looks ..... and as for Alan."

"Alan?" asked Phyllis.

"He tried to suppress it, but everytime he was near Becky he was like a little puppydog who'd found a new owner. If he'd had a tail to wag, they could have used it to power up several generators by the energy it would have produced."

Ophelia let out a little giggle and instantly regretted it. "I'm sorry Phyllis, I didn't mean to be glib, it's just that I can see exactly what Robert's saying. Couldn't you feel the energy in the room when they were in each other's company?"

"Well they didn't seem particularly sexual to me" said Phyllis.

"No Phyllis, we're not talking about sex, we're talking about two people who genuinely love each other. It was quite plain to see." Ophelia looked sadly at her friend, not wanting to disillusion her.

"Well I can honestly say I didn't pick up on anything" said Phyllis, feeling as though her psychic abilities were being challenged.

"It's no comment on your gifts at all" said Ophelia. "It's just that your loyalty to Sue blocked any unconscious signals that were being given off."

Phyllis wasn't sure she liked this observation.

"Look" said Robert trying to change the subject. "The fact is either they go or they don't go. My guess would be that Sue probably doesn't want to go and not because it's being in any way disrespectful to Becky's memory. I just think she would feel uncomfortable in that situation, and I wouldn't blame her for not going. Alan on the other hand ....."

"...... would probably give his right arm to go" finished Ophelia.

"Succinctly put" said Robert.

"Dilemmas dilemmas" said Ophelia. "What to do?"

"Well I've told Sue to pop over tonight for a chat if she wants to. I'm hoping she will. I think she needs a bit of space away from the home right now, somewhere where she'll feel free to say what's on her mind."

"Do you think she'll come?" asked Robert.

"Yes, yes I think she will" said Phyllis. "I do get the feeling she needs some support right now."

"And there's nobody better than you" said Robert, smiling at Phyllis.

Phyllis blushed. "Don't be silly Robert."

"It's just the truth" said Ophelia matter-of-factly. "Sue knows she can come to you in a crisis."

"Well just in case she does, I'll bid you both goodbye and catch up with you when we're all less busy" said Robert. "You both have my number so if anything happens ....."

"And goodness knows these days things certainly do seem to be happening" said Phyllis.

"All the more reason to keep my number to hand" said Robert.

"Thanks Robert. To be honest, I think we'll all be so pre-occupied there won't be time for any incidents to happen."

"Don't say that Phyllis" countered Robert. "That's just asking for trouble."

"Robert's right" added Ophelia.

"Ok Robert. Well don't work too hard and I hope your seminars go well. I'm sure they will."

"Thanks Phyllis. I hope your friend is ok as well. Sounds like she'll definitely need your support if she's just lost her mum. Good luck with your festivals Ophelia."

"Thanks Robert. I'm sure we'll catch up again soon" said Ophelia.

With that, Robert said his last goodbyes and headed towards his car. As the car disappeared into the early dusk, Ophelia watched the tail lights disappear. "Sooner than we think" she whispered to herself.

Chapter Two

"Come in Sue" said Phyllis.

"Thanks Phyllis."

Phyllis gave her friend a hug and definitely had the feeling that Sue was clinging on a bit longer than usual. "Ophelia and Robert haven't long gone" she said.

"Oh I hope they didn't go on my account" said Sue, concerned that they may have left to give Phyllis and Sue some privacy to talk.

"Oh no, don't be silly. They've both got busy schedules over the next couple of weeks. Robert's doing a series of seminars, Ophelia's really excited at getting these Mind, Body and Spirit festivals up and running again and ..... "

"And?" asked Sue.

"I'm going to stay with a friend of mine who's recently lost her mum. I'd already promised her and couldn't really back out" said Phyllis, almost apologetically.

"So nobody will be going to the funeral" said Sue.

"I'm sorry Sue. We really would have liked to have been there to say goodbye to Becky properly. Robert and Ophelia are both really disappointed that they won't be able to go. So am I of course but ...."

"Oh Phyllis, you don't need to apologise. It's unfortunate but life needs to go on."

"What about you and Alan? Have you decided yet whether you're going or not?"

Sue looked down. "Oh I don't know Phyll. I don't want to go ... I mean .... I don't mean that in anyway to be disrespectful to Becky but ....."

"Sue you don't have to explain, I understand."

"Do you Phyll?"

"I think so. Look, if you don't feel comfortable around Becky's friends, it's going to be awkward for you."

"The problem is that I know Alan wants to go."

"Has he said so definitely?"

"Oh he doesn't need to Phyll" said Sue. "It's just the way he looked at me when he told me that we'd been invited.

Truth is ...."

"What's bothering you Sue?" Was it Phyllis's imagination, or did Sue seem to blink back a few tears?

"Ever since .... ever since he heard the news about Becky's passing ...."

"Go on" encouraged Phyllis.

"It's just not the same anymore. You know how it used to be between us. I'd throw him an insult, he'd throw back a sarcastic remark ...... that's how we communicated. Ruth always said she'd die of shock if she came round to the house one day and we said something nice to each other. It's just that ....."

"..... that was just your way of communicating."

"Yes" said Sue, smiling feebly. "But now ......" she sighed. "I throw out a remark and Alan just looks at me with a meek smile. It's almost as if he's trying to say that he wants to respond ......"

"........ but he doesn't know how to anymore."

"That's exactly what it is Phyll. I mean look, I know we've had our problems in the past and we've always managed to resolve them somehow, but Becky showing up like that again ..... something's changed." Sue continued staring at the floor and then looked directly up at Phyllis. "And I don't think it's going to go back to how it used to be."

"Are you sure Sue? I mean it's all still very fresh. It could fade after a while."

"I'm not so sure Phyll. I've seen a real change in Alan. Ever since that first time we met Becky on the 'plane ...."

"Oh Sue, I don't know what to say."

"There's nothing you can say Phyll. It is what it is."

"So what are you going to do?"

"Well I've thought about it a lot" said Sue. "I honestly think the best thing would be for Alan and I to have some time to ourselves. I'm going to suggest to him that he goes to the funeral and I stay here."

"But would he agree to that? And what about you? You don't want to be stuck at home on your own."

"Oh I'll be fine Phyll, you know me. I can deal with anything."

"Sue, I don't want to be .... well .... direct ... but ....."

"Oh there's no need to tippy toe around my feelings Phyll. Just say what's on your mind."

"Ok, I will. You've been through so much recently and God knows you've had to deal with a hell of a lot, what with Ruth being kidnapped and then all that strange business with the child abduction case ..... but there's only so much people can take."

"You mean I might be ready to be carted off to the funny farm?"

"Oh Sue, don't say that. I didn't mean that at all."

"I know you didn't Phyll."

"I just mean that I'm not sure it would be good to be on your own right now. You'll have all that time to ruminate over everything and I'm not sure that's such a good idea."

"Well I don't know what else I can do to be honest. I mean I don't want to dump myself on Ruth and Chris. After all ......" Sue was about to let slip the fact that Robert knew about her little liaison with Chris and suddenly realised that Phyllis was most likely still blissfully ignorant.

"After all?" quizzed Phyllis.

"Well Ruth's started her new job and she'll be focussed on that ...." Sue managed to interject.

"Well, I've had an idea."

"Oh?"

"Just a thought" said Phyllis.

"Go on."

"Well I'm going up to stay with my friend Elspeth. Why don't you come with me?"

"Oh don't be ridiculous Phyllis. I don't even know the woman."

"It doesn't matter. I'm sure she'd be glad of the extra company."

"But that wouldn't be fair" Sue protested. "She's just lost her mother and the last thing she'll want is a perfect stranger in her house. It would be too much of an imposition."

"Nonsense" replied Phyllis. "I know Elspeth very well and I know she'll be glad of your company."

"Oh Phyll, I don't know ...."

"Let me call her and if she says 'no', she says 'no'. But if she says yes ..... why not?"

This was all very sudden and Sue felt uneasy about this. "Look" she said. "I'll speak to Alan and see what he says. If he wants to go to the funeral, I'll say that's fine and let him go. As for going to stay with .... with ...."

"Elspeth ..... named after Elspeth Reoch. She was executed as a witch in Scotland."

Sue suddenly felt uneasy. She knew that Phyllis and Ophelia had alternative belief systems but she'd known Phyllis for years and despite some of her more unconventional ideas, she was incredibly down to earth and had been a source of great friendship and comfort for Sue over the years. But being around witches ....

"Oh don't worry Sue, she won't put a hex on you. She's lovely. She's a bit eccentric, but she's got a good heart."

For Phyllis to say that somebody was eccentric was definitely saying something. Sue already had visions of somebody with a green face and a witches hat.

As if she was able to read Sue's mind, Phyllis said "Oh don't worry, when she flies on her broomstick she won't bash you in the head as she flies by ..... she's always very careful which direction she's going in."

"Now Phyllis, you know I don't mean that ...."

Phyllis laughed and took hold of Sue's hand. "Oh Sue, I've known you long enough to read your face ..... I can see you think she's going to have a boiling cauldron full of bones, skulls, bats wing and eyes of newt."

"Great. Could she give me the recipe?"

Both women laughed and the banter definitely helped to ease the tension that had been prevalent.

"Look, I'll do you a deal" said Phyllis. "I'll give her a call tomorrow and if she says you can come along, I'll leave it up to you to decide if you want to ok? Now I can't say fairer than that, can I?"

Sue paused for a moment. "No Phyll, you've got me there. You certainly can't."

"Deal then?"

"Deal."

For the rest of the evening Phyllis and Sue talked about the recent events, how she felt about her job and the usual challenges of everyday life.

"Oh for God's sake Sue, how long have I been telling you to quit that godawful job? Those people have made a complete mug out of you when everybody else in your team takes the piss, gets away with murder and they all do it because they know they can rely on good old Mrs Muggins to do their work for them."

"Thanks for the vote of confidence Phyllis."

"Oh come on Sue, you know I'm right. How often have you told me about that bloody middle management. A tiny bit of power and it goes to their heads. They know nothing about your job and what do they do? Fill in bits of paper all day long. As for that supervisor, don't get me started."

"Oh come on Phyllis, let's not spoil the evening."

"No Sue, I'm not trying to spoil the evening, but everything you've told me about her makes me think 'all mouth, no trousers'. She talks a lot and says absolutely nothing. Promise after promise after promise .... and when you challenge her about her lack of delivery .... she either changes the subject or disappears. You're then left to get on with it with a bunch of team mates who are too busy looking after their own interests to give a damn about whether their behaviour impacts on you. It's about time you told them where to stick that job."

"Phyllis, I've never known you to be so adamant about something."

"Sue, I've been listening to you over the years and hearing about everything that goes on there. You're working with a bunch of idiots. They're either work-shy, bone-idle halfwits, or they're so wrapped up in their own problems that they want to dump onto you and expect you to carry them while they do nothing."

"Trouble is I can't argue with you" said Sue, resignedly.

"So why are you staying there?"

"I can't retire yet. I'm not sixty."

"But you're not far off, and I thought you said that Alan had found a way to make a steady income."

"Well he has but ...."

"But what Sue? But what? Why don't you go into work tomorrow and tell them where to shove their job. You've been working there for years now and it's about time you had a change. It'll also mean the other idiots can't dump on you all the time."

"But I couldn't just sit around the house all day. I'd get bored."

"So find a hobby or something that takes your interest. The problem is you've become so institutionalised after decades of working in that crap hole that you've forgotten how to be human. Why not think about it? Life's too damn short. Look at Becky, do you think she'd care about a job if she'd been able to live?"

"To be fair, I can't argue with that" said Sue.

"Exactly. Think about it Sue. There's more to life than that lousy job."

"Graveyards are full of indispensable people as my old boss used to say" added Sue.

"I rest my case" said Phyllis.

Sue suddenly laughed.

"What's so funny?" said Phyllis.

"It's just the look on your face when you get onto your platform" said Sue. "I feel like we're going on a suffragete march and you're leading the troops."

"Damn right I am" added Phyllis. "And Sue Baylock will get the bloody vote!"

Sue burst out laughing. "Onward Christian Soldiers!"

"Er no Sue Baylock, Onward Pagan Soldiers! We will fight the good fight against the Christian invaders."

"Erm, that didn't work out to well in history Phyll."

"Oh don't you worry, we're having a renaissance. After two major world wars and God knows how many others, certain ideals are losing their appeal. People are coming back to Gaia."

"Gaia?"

"Yes, mother earth, the supreme goddess."

"Ok, well let's not get into the intricacies or pros and cons of each faith. Let's just say I need to rethink my job."

"Yes, you certainly do."

"Trouble is, even if I do decide to join you in going to stay with your friend, it might be too short notice to book the time off."

"What?" said Phyllis exasperated. "How many times have you told me about the ones who pull sickies all the time? Isn't it your turn? If you can't beat 'em, join 'em! They seem to get away with it, so why can't you?"

"I can't really argue with that Phyllis."

"There you go then."

* * * * *

"Well I'm glad you took Phyllis's advice and decided to go off sick. I still wish you'd come with me though."

"Oh Alan, I don't know any of Becky's friends and I'd feel like a fish out of water."

"But Sue, I don't know any of them either. I'm going to feel just as isolated as you."

"Yes, but at least you have the common connection of Becky. I don't."

"No, you just have the common connection of being my wife of several decades and the mother of our daughter."

"Look Alan, I would just feel more comfortable staying here."

"Yes, and I feel guilty for going."

"Well that's just plain silly. You're going to a funeral for God's sake, not spending a week in a knocking shop!"

"Even so, I got the impression you weren't very keen when you first met Becky and ...."

"Oh come on Alan, that was my first impression. When I realised what a lousy hand she'd been dealt I couldn't help but feel sympathy for the poor woman. Jesus, I wouldn't wish what happened to her on anybody."

"Even so, I still wish you'd come."

"I'd rather stay here if it's all the same to you."

"But what are you going to do? Just stare at four walls all day?"

"No. Phyllis has invited me to go and stay with a friend of hers for a week or so and I thought I might take her up on the offer."

"Oh yes, and who is this friend of hers? Another new age hippy witch no doubt."

"Oh don't be so judgmental Alan. The poor woman's just lost her mother."

"Oh lord, that's all you need. I'm going to a funeral and now you're going to stay with somebody who's lost their mother. It's hardly trading in one cheerful deal for another is it?"

"Do you honestly think Phyllis would invite me up there if she thought she was going to have a miserable time? Of course Elspeth is sad, she's just lost her mum, but Phyllis has said she's a lovely lady and has taken it quite well, despite everything."

"Well perhaps. Anyway, where does she live? In some remote part of a forest no doubt."

"There you go again. Honestly, with you everything is just stereotype on steroids. She lives in a little village about 40 miles up the A1. It's a nice quiet setting with a small community of friendly neighbours. To be honest Alan, it sounds like just the sort of thing I need right now."

"More than me."

"Alan!!"

"Ok, point taken. But I hope you don't get involved in something weird and cultish. I don't want to have to come back to find you talking to trees."

"Why not? The monarch does and nobody criticises him."

"Well they daren't. Let's face it, they'd have their heads cut off!"

"God, you are impossible. I won't dignify that remark with a reply."

"As you wish. So are you sure you want to stay here?"

"Yes, yes I'm positive."

"Ok, but you know I'm only on the end of a phone and I want you to promise me that if there are any problems you'll call me straight away ok? I can get back on the next flight to England."

"Ok."

"Promise?"

"Promise."

"Good. Now let's act like a married couple and give each other a hug. We don't seem to be doing very well in that department lately."

Sue gave Alan a hug but it didn't feel the same. It felt empty. What was the problem?

"Bring back some sunshine ok?"

"I'll try. Not sure I'll be able to fit a huge fiery ball into my suitcase."

"In the past you would have said you could – making reference to a certain part of your anatomy."

"Such filth woman. I am above such things."

"Oh I do beg your forgiveness your highness. I will try not to allow smut into the conversation in your royal presence again."

"Make sure you don't otherwise I'll have you beheaded."

"Oh I thought that was reserved for the bourgoiese. I thought common riff raff like me got hung, drawn and quartered."

"And mess up the carpet? It'll take ages to clean it out!"

"Go – and have a safe journey."

Chapter Three

"I can't think why it's taking Sue so long. She left four hours ago" said Phyllis.

"Maybe there's a traffic delay. Is she coming via the M25?" replied Elspeth.

"No, she doesn't need to go anywhere near the M25, it's straight up the A1 – it's only about 40 miles. She should have been here at least two hours ago."

"Try calling her mobile again."

"I'll try, but I've already called it three times and it just goes straight through to one of those voice mail thingies."

"It's a message answering service Phyllis."

"Yes, something like that. But I'm getting really worried now. I can't think what could be keeping her."

"Look, if it makes you feel better, let's go in my car and see if there's any hold up anywhere."

"But you don't want to drive all the way down the A1 to London, that would be silly – and we might miss her if she turns up."

"Well I shouldn't think she'd be likely to take a different route – as far as I know there's only one main road from the A1 to here. But I've got my mobile with me so we can keep calling her intermittently."

"Yes, yes, I think that's a good idea if you don't mind Elspeth. I'm sorry to be a bother, but I really am worried about her."

"Phyllis, I know you'd feel the same if it was me so it's really no trouble."

"Thanks love." Phyllis smiled at her friend but couldn't disguise the look of concern.

"Come on. Let's go."

Phyllis bent down to pick Pywackit up. "Now look sweetheart, we need to go out to look for Sue, but I promise we won't be long, ok?"

"I swear Phyllis, next time I'm coming back as a cat – and your cat. I know I'll be thoroughly spoiled."

"Ok, but don't go leaving claw marks on the back door

ok?"

The two ladies set off in Elspeth's car and followed the road leading to the A1. By now it was getting darker although there was still enough light to see fairly far ahead. As they turned the corner, they noticed police cars at the side of the road with their lights flashing. An ambulance had just pulled away.

"Slow down Elspeth" said Phyllis, her heart pounding. "I just want to see .... noooooooooo!" Phyllis let out a loud cry. "Pull over, pull over" her voice trembled.

Elspeth pulled over to the side of the road a few yards away from the police cars. One of the policeman walked towards the car when Phyllis got out and ran past him. "My God, that's Sue's car! It's Sue! What have you done with her! Where is she?"

"Now calm down madam, there's been an accident and we need to keep this area clear. Could you please ....."

"But that's my best friend's car. What's happened to her?" By now Phyllis was trembling and crying and it was clear to those present that nothing was going to placate her.

"You know this lady?"

"Of course I know her. She's my best friend. She was coming up to stay for a week. We'd just come out to see where she was."

Elspeth got out of the car and ran towards Phyllis. "Phyllis, listen to me. It's ok, let me explain to the policeman what's happened. Come on, come and sit in the car."

"But I want to know what's happened to Sue. Where is she? Take me to her now."

The policeman looked at Elspeth – possibly for reassurance that she was going to be able to calm Phyllis down.

"Phyllis" she said in her calmest voice. "Listen to me sweetheart. I want you to sit in the car and I'm going to find out exactly what's happened – and then we're going to go and see Sue, ok?"

"You promise Elspeth? I won't be able to sleep tonight. I ...."

"Listen, the sooner I find out what's happened, the sooner we can go to see her. Just let me speak to the policeman and I'll be back shortly."

Phyllis didn't appear to like this suggestion but if it

meant getting to Sue quicker, she decided it might be better to comply. She nodded her head between sobs. "Ok, ok. Please don't be too long."

Elspeth reassured Phyllis again and then went up to the policeman she'd spoken to.

"Look, please be honest with me. I don't know the lady myself but it's Phyllis's best friend and if anything happens to her I know she'd be devastated. If the worst has happened, I'll have to find some way to break it to Phyllis. But please be honest with me."

"I shouldn't actually be disclosing any information at this stage but I can see your friend is clearly distressed so I'll be brief. It's too early to tell but there doesn't appear to be any serious injury although the lady's had a nasty knock to the head. We think she may have severe concussion but they're taking her to the hospital and will probably keep her in for a few days for observation. Judging by the skid marks, we think she must have turned the wheel sharply – there's another set of skid marks a few yards ahead so we think somebody coming the other way was driving on the wrong side of the road. I'm surprised there isn't more damage to the car to be honest but the lady's had a nasty bash. Do you have any contact information for her relatives?"

"Well I don't personally but Phyllis might. I know that her husband has just flown out to Cyprus to attend a funeral so I'm not sure when he'll be back."

"Well thankfully it doesn't look like he'll be coming back to another funeral, though she was very lucky."

"Very lucky? With a lunatic driver charging towards her?" Elspeth's tone was sharp.

"I'm talking relatively speaking. As bad as it seems, it could have been worse."

"I hope you're not just saying that. It's not going to be easy convincing Phyllis that she'll be ok but I'm going to have to take your word for it. Will we be able to go and visit her?"

"Not tonight. Possibly tomorrow but I'd check with the hospital first."

"Ok, well look, here's my number. If you have any further updates or need any information from us, please call me ok?"

"Thank you miss er ... miss ..."

"It's Elspeth. Just call me Elspeth."

"Ok Elspeth. Now could I ask you to take your friend home – and possibly give her a strong brandy."

"Oh trust me – she'll need something stronger than that. Sadly I won't be able to disclose what it is otherwise you'll have us both arrested!"

The policeman looked at her and half smiled. "Then I won't ask."

Elspeth winked at him. "Mum's the word."

Elspeth walked back to the car and sat with Phyllis, explaining everything that she'd been told.

"But he might just be saying that to get rid of us. They might not let us see her .... ever again."

"Phyllis, they will, I promise. He told me she had a nasty concussion and a bit of a bash to the head, but thankfully she had her seat belt on so it prevented a more severe impact."

"I'm not so sure Elspeth. I won't rest until I see Sue myself."

"And you will see her. Look, let's go back to the cottage and I'll make us some tea. I know it's not going to be easy but if you can try to get a good night's sleep, we'll phone the hospital in the morning and find out when we can go and visit Sue."

"Ok, but my nerves are like shrapnel. I don't think I'll get any sleep tonight."

"Oh you will, believe me, come on let's go."

Elspeth managed to get a very shaky Phyllis back into the car and fastened her seat belt. The journey back to her cottage was quiet – not a word was said. When they finally pulled up by the side of the cottage, Elspeth got out of the car and walked around to help a dazed Phyllis to get out. "Come on Phyl" she said.

When they got into the cottage, Elspeth took Phyllis' jacket off. "Now go and sit on the sofa and I'll be through shortly."

Phyllis sat down on the sofa and Pywackit walked in from the kitchen and leapt onto her lap. "Oh hello darling, it's so good to see you. I've just had a nasty shock. It's Sue sweetheart. She's had an accident."

Pywackit rubbed his nose against Phyllis's and pushed his head under her chin.

"What would I do without you?" she said.

Elspeth walked in, but she wasn't carrying any cups or a tea tray. She had something wrapped in a towel as she sat down beside Phyllis. "I don't usually do this but I thought in the circumstances, it might be a little more medicinal than tea."

Phyllis looked at her puzzled.

Elspeth unwrapped the cloth and Phyllis was surprised to see several joints. "I thought we might need something stronger than brandy. Go on – take one."

"But Elspeth, I can't – I won't be any use to Sue."

"Sweetheart, you won't be any use to Sue if you don't get any sleep and your nerves are frazzled. Now go on, take one. I'll put some music on and it'll help you chill."

"Are you going to have one with me?"

"Of course I am. Do you honestly think I'm not going to indulge in some of the best grass there is? As we used to say in the sixties – this is seriously good shit man!"

Phyllis chuckled.

"That's my girl. You see, you're starting to relax already. Now go on – take one. I'll go and get the lighter."

Phyllis took one of the joints and Elspeth went to the kitchen to get a lighter. When she came back she lit Phyllis's joint and then her own.

Phyllis took a couple of drags.

"You see" said Elspeth. "You're starting to relax already."

Phyllis took a few more drags of the joint and her eyes became heavy. Her breathing grew more steady.

The two ladies sat in silence, the waft of cannabis floating in the air.

"Oh God, I've just had a thought" said Elspeth.

"What's that?" said Phyllis.

"I told that policeman that we were going to have something stronger than brandy. I hope he hasn't followed me back. I don't really want to spend the night in a police cell."

"Oh hell, don't worry, he can have a joint with us."

Elspeth chuckled. "You know, I went out with a policeman years ago .... and he always had the best shit! He used to bust people and of course he had to take their gear back to the station ..... but not before keeping a little bit aside for himself."

"What a cheeky bastard!" said Phyllis, her eyes now completely glazed over.

"Oh Phyl, they all do it. It's a perk of the job. Maybe I should have been a policewoman."

"Oh no Elspeth ..... I only like the smell of bacon when it's coming out of a frying pan!"

Both women laughed and laughed ..... for what seemed like eternity until they eventually fell asleep.

Chapter Four

When the two ladies awoke on the sofa the next morning, it took a while for them both to work out why they had fallen asleep on the sofa. Gradually they both came to and Phyllis suddenly remembered about Sue's accident, although she appeared calmer than the previous night.

"I'll make us some tea first" said Elspeth, "and then I'll phone the hospital ok?"

"Thanks Elspeth. I feel so guilty – I'm supposed to be up here supporting you after the loss of your mum and I've been nothing but a gibbering wreck."

"Oh Phyl, don't apologise. There's nothing I can do for mum now, sadly, but for Sue – there is."

Once they had had some tea, Elspeth phoned the hospital. Phyllis tried not to appear too anxious, although she was listening intently to Elspeth, trying to work out what the nurse was saying on the other end of the line. Elspeth nodded intermittently and said 'yes' now and then. Eventually she said 'thank you' and ended the call.

"What did they say?" asked Phyllis anxiously.

"Ok, well the good news is there's no serious injury."

"Oh thank God for that!" Phyllis let out a huge sigh.

"They took some x-rays of her brain just to make sure there was no internal bleeding or haemorhage. She has got a hairline fracture on the skull but they assured me it's not serious. She had a nasty bash to the right side of her head. There is severe bruising there but they've assured me it's not as bad as it looks."

"But how can they be sure?" Phyllis became anxious again.

"Don't worry Phyl, they know what they're doing. They've said they're keeping Sue in for a few days just to monitor her. She's regained consciousness but they don't want anybody to come and see her for the next few days."

"But she's all on her own, she's got nobody, she needs ...."

"Phyl, please. I know it's difficult, but we have to trust

them. I'm going to call back in a few days and we'll be able to arrange a visit. Until then, we'll just have to send out healing to her."

"Oh of course, that goes without saying. I'm still just so worried about her."

"I know you are, but she's going to be alright. Trust me."

At that moment Pywackit strolled into the lounge and leapt onto the window sill. His tail wrapped around an ornament and Elspeth gently pulled it away so that it wouldn't fall onto the floor.

"Oh that's a good sign" said Phyllis.

"What's that?" asked Elspeth.

"He always leaps up onto the window sill and wraps his tail around something when there's good news. I'm sure Sue's going to be fine."

"Well, I don't know whether to feel relieved or insulted" said Elspeth, chuckling.

"What do you mean?" asked Phyllis.

"A cat has managed to convince you that Sue is going to be ok when I couldn't. Doesn't say much for my powers of persuasion."

"Oh don't take it like that Els ....."

"It's ok Phyl. I'm only joking." She looked at Pywackit. "Now look Pywackit, you're going to have to teach me how to be more convincing .... as well as leaping up onto the window sill and wrapping a tail around an ornament without knocking it off."

* * * * *

For the next few days Phyllis was jittery, trying to be patient in waiting for the time when she and Elspeth could go and visit Sue. Elspeth managed to keep her occupied in the garden and the kitchen and couldn't help admiring Phyllis's green hands and ability to bake.

"God Phyl, I wish I had your skills."

"What do you mean? You've got a great little garden here."

"It's not bad, but you just seem to have a knack with

plants. As for your baking ..."

"Mine's not bad, but if you seriously want to taste some baking, you should try Sue's. She's amazing."

"I'm sure she is Phyl, but don't put yourself down. You're a serious trooper!"

Phyllis smiled appreciatively, feeling slightly embarrassed by the compliment.

"Now then" said Elspeth. "I thought we might go out for a walk today. I've got somewhere interesting to show you."

"Somewhere?"

"Uh-huh. Remember that old deconsecrated church I told you about when I moved up here?"

"Oh, you mean the one with all the gravestones around the edge of the perimeter?"

"That's the one. I thought we might go and take a look at it."

"Oh yes" said Phyllis. "I've heard so much about it, I'd love to go and see it."

"Come on then. It will mean leaving Pywackit on his own for a while but he can guard the cottage while we're gone."

The two women finished up in the cottage and set off, following the road that led to a footpath.

"Now it's a little bit steep so take your time" said Elspeth.

They walked up a long footpath that was guarded by trees on either side. As Elspeth had said, it was a bit of a slow steep walk, but they carried on steadily until they reached the top of the hill. They stopped to take a few breaths before heading towards a clearing in the trees. As they walked forward, Phyllis looked at the church before her. It had no roof and the lead had long been taken away. It was now mostly a ruin. Surrounded by gravestones along the edge of the wall, even in daylight it held an eerie silence and a slightly unsettling aura.

"So what was the story again?" asked Phyllis. "I know you told me when you first moved here, but I can't remember all the details."

"Well so the story goes" said Elspeth, enjoying the tale that she was about to tell, "back in the early sixties all the gravestones surrounded the church. But one day some children came up here to play and they found one of the coffins smashed open and cockerell feathers in the ruin of the church itself. The police initially thought it was some prankster but it happened several times again so they decided to move all the gravestones to the perimeter of the wall so that people wouldn't know where the graves actually were and therefore wouldn't be able to smash into them."

"Oh God, that's gruesome" said Phyllis.

"It certainly is Phyllis. There have been other stories about the place ..... rituals being held here, animal bones being discovered. All very sinister."

"But do they know if it is just pranksters trying to scare people or if it's something a bit darker?"

"I don't know for sure but I've been up here a few times and I have to say on occasions the energy doesn't feel good."

"I must admit I'm not picking up anything negative at the moment but there is an unnatural stillness."

"Exactly" agreed Elspeth. "You'll notice that despite the number of trees here, there are no birds anywhere. I don't think I've ever seen a bird up here once."

"Maybe you should do some research on the place."

"I did do a bit of research though not as extensive as I'd have liked. They believe that before it was a church, there was a leper colony here, though I don't know how accurate that is. People have seen strange things here though."

"What sort of things?"

"I know it sounds corny but ..... shadows ..... figures ...... sometimes if you go into what's left of the church, there are certain corners that feel intensely cold. I felt it myself once – it was very eerie. I have to say I didn't like it."

"I wonder why they let it go to ruin" said Phyllis. "If they'd maintained it as a church, perhaps none of the things that have happened since would have occured."

"Possibly" agreed Elspeth. "But they built a church in the village itself so that people wouldn't have to trek up the hill. I suppose elderly people found it a bit of a struggle and back in those days they didn't have wheelchairs so it would have been difficult. Even so, it's sad to see the old place in such a state."

"It is" agreed Phyllis. "Although I'm a staunch pagan I can't help but admire some of the architecture in these old churches."

"Well yes, and of course we both know that most Christian churches were built on sites that had previously been sacred to pagans."

"Here! Here!" said Phyllis.

They continued to take in the eerie silence, looking at the surrounding wall and then beyond that to the village below.

"It's so sad to learn what's happened here" said Phyllis. "It does have a strange sort of peace, though with an underlying current."

"Yes it does. That's why I don't think we should stay too long. Come on, let's go. Pywackit will be wondering where we've got to."

Chapter Five

"Oh my God Sue, I've been worried sick about you." Phyllis almost flung herself at the woman lying in the hospital bed and gave her the biggest bear hug.

"Now steady on Phyllis, the poor lady's already had one serious head injury, she doesn't need you pulling her head off" chuckled Elspeth.

"Oh I'm sorry Sue, I can't help it. I was just so worried about you."

"Thanks Phyllis. It's good to see you. Now are you going to have the manners to introduce me properly to your friend?"

"Oh I'm so sorry. Sue this is Elspeth, Elspeth ...."

".... this is Sue" finished Elspeth. She moved over to give Sue a hug, though a much lighter one than Phyllis.

"It's lovely to meet you Sue, although I wish it hadn't been in these circumstances."

"It's good to meet you too Elspeth. I was really looking forward to meeting you, but I was hoping it wouldn't be like this."

"Well hopefully you'll be out of here in a couple of days and we can make up for lost time."

Phyllis pulled up two chairs for herself and Elspeth to sit in. "Now Sue, what on earth happened?"

"To be honest Phyllis, I'm having trouble remembering. It all happened so quick" said Sue. "I had a smooth journey up the A1, no hold ups anywhere, and then when I turned off and started driving down the road towards the village, I saw this lunatic swerving over both sides of the road and he was heading straight towards me. I think I panicked and swerved to avoid him. I must have blacked out and the next thing I know, I'm here in the hospital."

"Oh my God, you could have been killed. I don't suppose you had the chance to get a look at the car or the driver?"

"No" replied Sue. "As I say, it all happened so quick. What state is the car in?"

"Never mind about the car Sue, I'm just worried about you."

"Thanks Phyllis, I do appreciate that, but when I do get out of here I'm going to need to get about."

"Well for the next few days you'll be recuperating at Elspeths" said Phyllis. "I want to make sure you're ok."

"Sue, if you've known Phyllis as long as I have, you know she loves to be the clucking mother hen and she's not going to let you out of her sight. However, if it's any consolation, we can use my car to get about until yours is repaired."

"Repaired? So it hasn't been written off then?"

"No. The policeman we spoke to said he was surprised there wasn't more damage. I'm afraid your poor head took most of the impact."

At that moment a nurse came in to give Sue some medication. "Here you are, you need to take these" she said in what Phyllis perceived to be a slightly icy voice.

"Thank you" said Sue, and duly took the tablets from the nurse. She put them in her mouth and took a sip of water to wash them down. The nurse walked away, seemingly satisfied that Sue had taken her tablets but also giving Sue an odd look.

"Good grief, what's wrong with her?" asked Phyllis. "She hasn't exactly got the warmest bedside manner, has she?"

"I think I've unnerved her a bit" said Sue in a whisper.

"Unnerved her? What do you mean?" asked Phyllis puzzled.

Sue looked towards the door to make sure the nurse had gone. She gestured for Phyllis and Elspeth to pull their chairs closer to the bed.

"I don't know what's happened, but I think it's got something to do with the concussion" said Sue.

"What do you mean?" asked Phyllis.

Sue looked over to the doorway again to make sure nobody was listening. "It's really strange Phyl. I don't know what time it was. I must have been sleeping quite a bit, but I woke up and there was an old man beside my bed. Near scared the hell out of me. I asked him what he wanted and he said he was looking for his mummy and his toy car. Well at first it didn't register, but then I realised he must have been suffering from dementia. I think the dementia ward is just further down the corridor. Anyway, I told him I didn't know where his mummy was but that the nurse at the desk might be able to help him."

"Oh?" said Phyllis.

"Anyway, I thought nothing more of it and then I turned over and went back to sleep. I don't know how long I'd been asleep but then it happened" said Sue.

"Happened? What happened?" Phyllis was intrigued.

"Well you know that thing that you and Ophelia have told me about – I can't remember what it's called now, but it's where you feel like you're floating out of your body."

"Astral projection you mean?" asked Phyllis.

"Yes, yes, that's it" replied Sue. "Well Phyllis, it was so strange, I felt this buzzing sensation and then I could feel myself being pulled out of my body. I wasn't sure if I was dreaming or if it was really happening to me." Sue took another sip of water. "I thought I would see if I could walk around. So I seemed to walk, or float, I'm not sure, but I walked out of the room and down the corridor. I could see the nurse on duty and I noticed that she was writing something – a list I think. She tore the piece of paper out of the pad and put it into the bottom drawer of the desk."

"Go on." Phyllis couldn't take her eyes off Sue.

"So the next morning, the nurse came in and gave me my medication. I told her about the old man who had come into my room asking for his mummy and toy car and she gave me the strangest look. She asked me to describe what he looked like and what he was wearing, which I did. I mean it was still fresh in my mind. So when I told her what he looked like she said that there had been a patient suffering from dementia who fit that description but that he'd died three weeks earlier."

"Oh wow Sue, that's amazing. You've actually seen a spirit."

"Well I don't know if it was that or just my imagination, but it was so real."

"It's not your imagination Sue, it sounds as though that knock to the head has triggered some sort of psychic ability."

"Well let's not jump to conclusions Phyl. Anyway, a few hours later she came in again and she was talking to one of the other nurses. She told her that she'd made a list of medication she had to pick up from the pharmacy but then couldn't remember where she'd put the list. So I told her that she'd put it in the bottom drawer. Sure enough that's where she found it. Since then she's been really funny with me."

"Oh my God Sue, this is brilliant. You're developing the gift. Just think what you can do with it."

"But I don't want it Phyl."

"What do you mean, you don't want it?"

"Look, I don't want to start seeing dead people all over the place. I mean it's really unnerved me. Seeing that old man was so real. I could swear he wasn't a ghost, or spirit, or whatever you want to call him. He was a flesh and blood human being. The nurse said he was always asking for his mummy and his red toy car."

"But you can learn so much with it Sue."

"Look Phyl, I don't want to sound like a stick in the mud, but I remember one of the girls at work talking about a couple she knew who stayed in a hotel for a few nights and they'd decided to have .... you know ...."

"Sex Sue, sex. It's not a dirty word!"

"Well yes, ok then, they decided to have sex." Sue paused. "Apparently half way through the act, the husband suffered a heart attack, keeled over and died."

"Well that's unfortunate" said Phyllis in a matter-of-fact voice.

"Unfortunate? It's bloody tragic. But that's not the point I'm making. I don't want to find myself in a hotel somewhere and wake up in the middle of the night, only to find a ghost lying on top of me trying to fuck me!"

Phyllis and Elspeth both burst out laughing.

Sue looked at both of them as if they'd gone stark raving mad. "I honestly don't think it's very funny!"

"Oh Sue, I do love you. I'm sorry, but that just tickled me pink."

"Well that's one thing we haven't got in common – a sense of humour."

"I'm sorry Sue, but you've got to see the funny side of it. You've really got nothing to feel anxious about though. Ophelia can show you how to control it. You'll be fine once you know how to train it and use it."

"I'm still not convinced Phyl. Well I don't mean to change the subject, but I'd like to focus more on when they're going to let me out of here."

"Didn't the nurse say something about the consultant coming to see you later today? I was under the impression they were going to let you out tomorrow" said Phyllis.

"Oh I hope so. I'm getting so fed up in here. I just want to get out and get on with my life. I hate hospitals."

"I know you do love, but they've got to make sure you're ok before they can release you. It won't be long now and when you do come out, Elspeth and I can take care of you."

"That's not fair though" said Sue. "I know you've just lost your mum Elspeth. The last thing you need is to worry about me."

"Honestly Sue it's fine. Of course I was sad when mum died, but she'd been suffering with bad health for such a long time that when she finally did pass, it was a blessing. She wasn't suffering anymore."

"Even so" said Sue, "I feel as though I've really put the kybosh on the next couple of weeks."

"Well don't. The three of us are going to have a great time once you're out of here. I'm really looking forward to showing you around the village and the meadows. It really is beautiful around here. So different to London."

"Well I must admit, I'm looking forward to a bit of quiet country recuperation" said Sue. "It's been a bit of a strange time recently."

"Yes, Phyllis told me about what happened with – what's the lady's name? Becky? I'm so sorry to hear the news. I understand she was an old friend of your husband's."

"Girlfriend" corrected Sue. "You don't need to be polite, they were an item years ago. I did get the impression that when they bumped into each other, the spark was still there."

"Sue, you'll only upset yourself if you ruminate about the past. I know Alan's gone to the funeral but that should bring some sort of closure to the whole situation" said Phyllis.

"Well, I'm a believer in putting your best foot forward" said Elspeth. "Whatever's happened in the past, it's over and it's better to focus on the future. You just never know what's going to happen."

Sue suddenly had an uneasy feeling. "No" she said. "You certainly don't."

Chapter Six

When Sue was finally released from hospital, the three women took the opportunity to go on country walks, exchange baking tips and generally put the world to right. Alan had called Sue to say that he would be flying home in a week or so and that he'd met quite a few of Becky's friends who he said he felt very relaxed around. Ophelia had also called Phyllis to say that the festivals were going really well and that she might consider doing more in the future. Robert was quiet but they knew he had a busy schedule.

"How much longer is he doing these seminars for now Sue?" asked Phyllis.

"I'm not sure but I think he shouldn't have too many more to do. I do think he should take a break when he's done them. He's been virtually working around the clock."

"Yes, but that's Robert though isn't it" observed Phyllis.

There was a knock on the door and Elspeth went to answer it. "Oh come in Craig" she said.

A tall man of strong stature walked into the room. "Good afternoon ladies" he said.

"Good afternoon Craig" they replied.

Craig was – as Elspeth had described him to Phyllis and Sue – a 'friend with benefits'. They had both agreed they didn't want any formal commitment but would enjoy each other's company from time to time when it suited both parties.

"Personally Sue, I don't think it's very romantic" Phyllis had confided to Sue discreetly. "I mean I know that probably sounds rich coming from me, the stereotypical burn-your-bra sixties feminist who always used to espouse the virtues of casual relationships, but as I get older I can't help feeling that people need more of a connection."

"Well Phyllis if it suits them, let them be. I mean look at me and Alan. Married for decades but I'd hardly say we have that many romantic moments. In fact I can't remember the last time we did."

"But you could do if you both worked at it."

"Whatever you're smoking Phyl, I want some of it."

"So what are you doing tonight?" enquired Craig.

"Well I haven't got anything specific planned" replied Elspeth, "but I thought that Phyl, Sue and I would have a little card reading session."

"Oh I can't read cards" said Sue.

"We'll see" said Elspeth. "How about you Craig? You could join us if you like."

"I've got a couple of jobs I've got to finish off unfortunately Ellie, but I can catch up with you later in the week."

"Sure, no problem." She smiled and winked at him. "Don't worry, we're not as scary as we look. This isn't the opening scene to Macbeth."

Phyllis chuckled. "Speak for yourself. I've got every intention of pulling out the cauldron and stirring up some mischief."

"Behave woman" chuckled Sue. "You don't need to stir it up, it finds you."

"And there was I thinking you were my friend Sue Baylock."

"Always Phyllis my darling, always."

Craig smiled and bade farewell to the three ladies. "I've got to go now but I'll call you in the week. Hope you're enjoying your stay ladies."

"Thanks Craig" said Phyllis. "If you need any spells casting, let us know."

* * * * *

Later that evening the three ladies opened several bottles of wine with both alcohol and conversation flowing freely. Feeling slightly tipsy, Elspeth looked at the other ladies and gestured to them. "Ladies, I've got an idea."

"What's that?" asked Phyllis.

"Well I'm curious" she replied.

"Curious?" asked Phyllis.

Elspeth looked at Sue. "Now I know you're not keen to explore the experiences you had in the hospital, but I can't help thinking that Phyllis was right and that something's trying to emerge."

"What do you mean?" asked Sue, unsure that she was keen to discuss the unusual occurrences she'd experienced in the hospital.

"Don't worry Sue, if you don't want to we won't do anything, but I'd be curious to see what impressions you get by looking at the cards" said Elspeth.

"Cards? What? You mean tarot cards? I can't read tarot cards."

"That's ok" said Elspeth. "Why not just take a few from the pack and see what impressions you get. If nothing comes, don't worry about it. But it might be interesting. What do you think Phyllis?"

Phyllis was only slightly tipsy but still had her faculties about her. "Well normally I wouldn't use the cards when alcohol is involved. You don't want to attract the wrong energies. But we could do a little cleanse first."

"Cleanse?" asked Sue.

"Yes, just burning a bit of sage to clear the atmosphere of any negative energies" said Elspeth.

"Oh I don't know" said Sue.

"Well don't feel pressured Sue if you don't want to" said Elspeth.

Unbeknownst to Sue, Elspeth was using a bit of reverse psychology. Feign disinterest and it tends to make the other party curious.

"Well I'll give it a go but don't expect anything amazing" said Sue.

"Amazing is off the menu tonight. Curiosity and exploration are the main courses."

Elspeth took a pack of tarot cards from her cupboard and handed them to Sue. "Just give them a shuffle and pull out a few cards at random when you feel ready."

"Ok" said Sue, who wasn't feeling particularly mystical. She shuffled the cards and suddenly had an odd feeling. She decided not to say anything but pulled three cards out of the pack. Having been instructed by Elspeth to lay them face down on the table, she turned the first card over. "Page of Cups" she said. "It looks like a male in the picture but I'm getting the image of a young girl in my mind. When I say young, I mean early to mid twenties, not a child or a teenager."

Both Elspeth and Phyllis looked at Sue with interest.

"Go on Sue, pull the second card" said Phyllis.

Sue turned over the second card. "Oh lord, I don't like that."

"That's ok" said Elspeth. "The devil can often suggest blockage, sometimes self-inflicted."

Sue shook her head. "No, no, that's not the impression I'm getting. I'm seeing a man and .... and ..."

"What is it Sue?" asked Phyllis.

"I just feel cold when I look at that card."

"Don't worry" said Elspeth reassuringly. "Just turn over the last card."

Sue turned it over and shuddered. "Oh what a horrible combination of cards to get. I know you've told me in the past that the death card can signify the end of a situation, but I'm getting quite a literal interpretation of the card."

"What do you mean Sue? Tell us what you're picking up" asked Elspeth.

"I .... I just see a young girl. Nice girl, a bit naive, easily led possibly, but a good heart. But she's either met someone or is going to meet someone and it seems to be going well but ....."

"But?" asked Phyllis expectantly.

Sue looked at Phyllis and said quite bluntly "he's going to kill her."

"Strange" said Phyllis. "Are you sure?"

"Positive" said Sue.

"Do you know where or when?"

"No, though I get the impression it's sooner rather than later. I just see some sort of argument arising. It gets nasty – out of hand, and then ..... I don't want to look at this anymore."

Sue stood up and walked away from the table.

"I'm sorry Sue, we shouldn't have suggested reading the cards" said Elspeth.

"Don't blame yourself Elspeth, I was curious, but as they say, curiosity killed the cat."

"The trouble is we're now left wondering where and when this is going to happen. If we knew, we could try to prevent it" added Phyllis.

"This is the problem in our line of work. We don't always get the full picture, only snippets. The only thing we can do is leave it for now and see if you get any more flashes of intuition Sue."

"But what if I don't? I'd feel awful if something did happen and I didn't do anything to prevent it."

"If it's going to happen, you can't be held responsible for it" said Elspeth. "Phyllis will tell you, sometimes we pick up information, a bit like a radio, but we don't always get a clear signal."

"Well that was clear enough to me" said Sue. "Too clear in fact."

"I think we need to put the cards away and change the subject" suggested Phyllis. "If we can't get any more information, there's no point in tormenting ourselves about it. As much as I'd love to solve all the worlds problems, I have to be realistic – as do we all."

* * * * *

The next few days were spent taking country walks, shopping and visiting local areas of interest. The reading that Sue had given several nights before wasn't discussed further.

"I must admit I do feel more relaxed out in the country" said Sue. "Alan and I should do it more often. It would do us good to be surrounded by greenery."

"I do find it quite peaceful" said Elspeth. "The only drawback is it plays havoc with my hay fever." She took out a tissue from her handbag and blew her nose.

"Oh no" said Sue. "Do you get it quite badly? I know Alan's brother used to suffer from it quite a lot. He always had to have an inhaler with him in case he had an asthma attack."

"Well fortunately I don't get asthma but I do get the sniffles and sneezes" said Elspeth.

"It's not fair is it" commented Sue. "You want to get out and enjoy the weather when it's good, but if you do, you suffer for it."

"Isn't that the truth." Elspeth sighed.

"Oh look" said Phyllis. "We're back here again."

"Again?" quizzed Sue. "We didn't walk this way, did we?"

"Oh sorry, I meant Elspeth and I. We came up here a

few days ago to visit the old ruined church up the hill there."

"Oh" said Sue. "I'm surprised at you wanting to visit an old church Phyllis. I thought you were pagan through and through."

"Of course I am" said Phyllis. "It's just that Elspeth mentioned the fact that the church had a bit of a reputation for strange occurences so I wanted to go and see if I could pick up anything there."

"And did you?" asked Sue.

"Not a great deal, although it did feel a bit odd. Then again, we didn't actually enter the ruin so maybe I would have felt more if I'd gone inside it."

"Interesting" said Sue. "Do you want to go and try again?"

"Well, we could do, although I'm a bit worried about you" replied Phyllis.

"Me?"

"Yes."

"Why?"

"Because of what happened the other night. You know, the reading."

"Oh that. Well I must admit I can't say it was a pleasurable experience, but if it's just an old ruin, I wouldn't mind going to have a look" said Sue.

Phyllis looked at Elspeth. "I'm not so sure. What do you think?"

"It's entirely up to Sue. If you feel comfortable giving it a once over, we could take a look. If you do start feeling a bit unsettled we can always turn around."

"Well we might as well. I can't spend the rest of my life avoiding places in case they have any bad vibes. God almighty, I face those every day when I go to work." Sue's attempt at a joke didn't seem to convince Phyllis or Elspeth, but they smiled politely as if trying to acknowledge Sue's attempt at humour.

As they walked up the hill, both Phyllis and Elspeth were monitoring Sue to see if she was ok. She didn't appear to be anxious as they continued walking so they carried on towards the top of the hill.

"Well here it is" said Elspeth. "The old ruined church. I was telling Phyllis that it's been deconsecrated for years. There have been several stories, or should I say rumours of strange things happening here. Not very pleasant things and I must admit, I did feel some strange energy when I stood inside the ruin but ......"

Elspeth stopped talking as she looked at Sue. "What is it Sue?"

Sue was staring intently towards the church, her gaze fixed on a certain point.

Phyllis became anxious. "Sue, are you ok? Do you want to turn back?"

Sue continued looking ahead but shook her head to acknowledge Phyllis's comment. She stood silently, motionless, fixed to the spot.

"Sue, what is it?" Phyllis was now more anxious.

Sue gestured as if requesting Phyllis to remain silent. She kept looking at the same spot. Finally she spoke, although it was barely a whisper. "Those poor people."

"What's that Sue?"

"Those poor poor people. They're terrified."

Phyllis darted a worried look at Elspeth and Elspeth returned the same.

"Come on Sue, maybe we should go back now."

Still Sue would not move from the spot. It was apparent that she was becoming visibly upset. "Why are they doing this? Just let them be."

"Sue, come on, you're worrying me, let's go back" said Phyllis, a little more insistently.

Finally Sue turned to look at her. "But Phyllis, they were terrified."

"Come on Sue" said Elspeth. She took Sue's hand and gently coaxed her back towards the path that led down the hill. "Let's go back and have a coffee. I'm sure Pywackit will be anxious as to where we've got to."

Sue walked silently down the hill with Phyllis to one side and Elspeth to the other. They continued walking in silence until they approached Elspeth's cottage.

Elspeth let out a loud sneeze, and then another. She tugged at her sleeve and frowned. "Oh lord, what happened to my tissue, I must have dropped it en route and I don't have another one to blow my nose."

"Here I've got one" said Phyllis, handing a clean tissue to Elspeth.

"Thanks Phyllis."

Pywackit was pleased to see Phyllis although he did swish his tail to express his displeasure about her being away so long.

"I'm sorry my love, we just got carried away" said Phyllis. Pywackit looked at her and then turned away. It was obvious to Phyllis that she would have to find some way to get back into his good books.

Elspeth had made coffee for the three companions and set the cups down on the table. Both she and Phyllis felt reluctant to broach the subject of what Sue had experienced, but they were both dying to know what had happened.

"Sue" said Phyllis gently. "If you don't want to talk about what you saw, I completely understand, but if you would like to talk about it ....."

"Of course I will Phyl. Please don't feel as though you have to walk on eggshells" replied Sue.

Phyllis and Elspeth waited expectantly.

"It was so strange" said Sue, her eyes going off into the middle distance. "I could see all these people running towards the church. Well, I thought they were running towards the church, but they weren't. They were running behind the church. I don't know why. I just knew they were terrified."

"What were they running away from, do you know?" asked Phyllis.

"I'm not sure. I get the impression it was some sort of persecution, though I don't know. I'm not even sure what time it was from, whether it was from the reformation or some time after, but they seemed to be fleeing from persecution and they were absolutely terrified."

"So they were seeking sanctuary in the church?" asked Phyllis. "Even though I'm not a Christian, I do know that people could seek protection from the church."

"No, no" said Sue. "They weren't actually going into the church, they were going behind it."

"Behind it?" asked Phyllis puzzled. "But why would they do that? If they were being persecuted, surely they were still exposed to attack from a potential enemy."

"I really don't know Phyll, I only know what I saw."

"How odd."

"I can see I'm going to have to do some more research on this church" said Elspeth. "You've got me intrigued now."

There was a knock at the door and both Phyllis and Elspeth jumped.

"Oh my God, that scared the life out of me" said Phyllis.

Elspeth went to answer the door. "Oh come in Craig" she said.

Craig walked into the lounge. "Evening ladies" he said.

"Hello Craig" said Phyllis "Have you come to join us? You weren't put off by my cauldron joke the other night?"

Craig smiled. "Unfortunately I can't stop. I've got some planning to do, but I thought I'd pop by to let you know Ellie that I took my car into the garage today to get a couple of new tyres and they said Sue's car will be ready to pick up tomorrow."

"Oh thanks Craig, that's good news isn't it. You'll be mobile again tomorrow Sue" said Elspeth.

Sue turned and looked at Craig, but said nothing. She smiled and had, what Elspeth felt was a curious look on her face.

"Well we can pick it up in the morning" she said. "The policeman said there wasn't a great deal of damage but you know these garages, they'll always find something else to charge you for."

"I wouldn't worry too much" said Craig. "They're pretty good at that garage. I've used them for years and they've always been reliable and reasonable price-wise."

"Thanks Craig. I'll give you call in a couple of days if that's ok" said Elspeth.

"Ok" he said. He gave Elspeth a quick peck and bade the three companions goodbye.

"Well that's good news isn't it Sue" said Elspeth. "Sue? Sue? I said that's good news isn't it?"

Sue looked up at Elspeth. "Sorry, I was miles away. What was that? Oh yes, the car. Good news. Good news."

Phyllis and Elspeth looked at each other, unable to hide their concern.

Chapter Seven

The following morning Elspeth was the first one to wake up. She went downstairs and the glare of the sun blinded her as she drew back the curtains in the lounge. She pottered about clearing up a few items, tidying the cups away and generally busying herself while Sue and Phyllis were still asleep upstairs. She heard a bedroom door opening and somebody coming downstairs.

"Oh morning Phyl. I'm just putting some tea on. Do you want any breakfast?"

"No thanks Elspeth, tea will be fine."

"I hope Sue's ok" said Elspeth. "Was it just me or do you think she was acting a bit off last night?"

"I must admit I agree with you. I hope she slept ok. I think we should just leave her until she's ready to get up. I am worried about what that knock to the head has done."

"Was she like this before the accident?"

"No, not at all. It does seem to have triggered something, and I'm not sure that it's necessarily positive. I wish Ophelia was here. I'm sure she'd have a better idea of what to do."

"Perhaps" said Elspeth. "What do you want to do today Phyl?"

"Well after we've picked up Sue's car, we could go into town. I think it might be an idea to do something that's not going to spook her."

"Yes, I think you're right. We're going to have to be careful and avoid anything like cards, old churches and all things otherwordly. She does seem to be picking up bad vibes."

"I know and I don't like it."

They both heard the creaking of floorboards, indicating that Sue had woken up. Shortly they could hear her footsteps coming down the stairs. She smiled as she saw them both sitting at the table.

"Morning Sue, did you sleep ok?" said Elspeth.

"Yes I did, although I still had flashbacks from the other night when we looked at the cards" she replied.

"Oh no. Was it really bad?" Elspeth was obviously concerned that Sue was still having visions that she was unable to block out.

"No, it wasn't as bad as the other night. This time I was looking at it from a more detached viewpoint, if that's at all possible. That's what it felt like anyway."

"Well if you do keep getting flashbacks, maybe we can do some energy work on you" said Phyllis.

Just then a police car flew by, followed by another and then another. The three women looked at each other with curiosity.

"Wonder what that's all about" said Elspeth. "Nothing untoward usually happens here. It's a very quiet little village."

They looked out of the window and some of the neighbours were standing in the street, talking and pointing.

"What is going on?" said Elspeth. "Excuse me ladies, I'm just going out to find out what the fuss is all about."

Sue and Phyllis watched as their host went outside and approached her neighbours. They stood talking for a while and Elspeth seemed to be getting involved in a lengthy conversation. She finally turned and walked back towards the cottage. When she opened the door she looked at both Phyllis and Sue with an expression of shock.

"You're not going to believe this" she said.

"What's the matter?" asked Phyllis.

"It's Emily – Emily Sjöberg. She's been found dead inside the ruin of the old church."

"What?" Both Phyllis and Sue looked at Elspeth in horror.

"Yes. Some kids had gone up there to play hide and seek and they discovered her lying there, lifeless."

"Oh my God" said Sue as she started shaking.

"Oh God, this is awful" said Phyllis. She could feel herself starting to tremble.

"But we were there only yesterday. How could ......"

"I don't know Phyllis. God, the thought of it makes me feel sick." Elspeth looked at Sue. "Are you ok Sue?"

"I – I don't know" said Sue. "I feel weird. I think I'm going to be sick." She ran to the kitchen sink and threw up.

Phyllis followed her and put her arms round her. "Come

on Sue, sit down. I'll get you something to settle your nerves."

"I'm ok Phyl, honest."

"No you're not Sue. I'm going to give you something to calm your nerves"

"Please Sue, let Phyllis give you something. This has come as a hell of a shock to all of us."

The three companions sat around the kitchen table, speechless. Neighbours were coming and going outside and an ambulance went by. Sue shuddered at the sight of it.

"I don't understand it" said Elspeth. "Emily wouldn't harm a fly. She's a lovely young girl. Why would somebody do this to her? Oh God, her mum's going to be devastated."

Sue and Phyllis couldn't find the words to reply. They sat there silently.

There was a knock at the door. All three women jumped.

"God, my nerves are on edge" said Elspeth. She went to answer the door. "Oh Craig, have you heard the news? It's horrendous."

Craig walked through and greeted Phyllis and Sue. "Yes" he said. "I've just heard. It's horrific."

"Is it true that they found her in the ruins of the church?"

"Apparently so. I think the ambulance has just gone up there and the police have cordoned the whole area off. It's a no go zone."

"I can't believe it" said Elspeth. "We were only there yesterday. Nothing seemed untoward at all. I just don't understand why somebody would want to kill her, she was lovely."

"Not just kill her" added Phyllis, "but why in the ruins of all places?"

"You don't think it's some sort of weird sacrifice do you?" asked Elspeth. "You know what a reputation that place has got."

"I shouldn't think so" said Craig. "I mean I've heard all the stories about smashed graves and cockerell feathers, but as far as I'm aware, there's never actually been a murder there."

"It wasn't committed there" Sue suddenly said.

"What?" asked Phyllis and Elspeth.

"I don't know" said Sue. "This is the girl I saw in the

cards, but she wasn't murdered there, I'm sure of it. She's been brought there from somewhere else."

"Are you sure Sue?" asked Elspeth.

"What do you mean?" asked Craig. "What's this about cards?"

"Well since Sue's accident, she's been having some strange experiences. We decided to pull a few cards the other night and Sue foresaw a young girl being murdered. It looks as though this is what you saw in the cards, wasn't it Sue?"

"Yes" said Sue. "She was murdered, but not in the ruins. She was murdered somewhere else. I remember there was an argument that got out of hand and ..... and ....."

"You saw the murder?" asked Craig.

"Yes" said Sue.

"Well can you describe who the murderer was? If so, you should call the police."

"No, no, I couldn't really see either of them clearly, I just picked up on the energy. The vision wasn't very strong. But I knew for certain there was going to be a murder."

"Well if you do get any flashbacks, you should let the police know" said Craig. "There's some lunatic out there and if he's not caught, it's likely to happen again."

"Oh no" said Phyllis, shuddering.

"I just don't believe it. Nothing like this has ever happened in all the time I've lived here. And to Emily of all people."

"I know and she was such a sweet kid. God knows what her mum's going through" added Craig.

"What the hell can we do? We've got to get the guy who did it – but how?"

"Maybe we can do a meditation session later" said Phyllis. "See if Sue can pick anything else up."

"I doubt it Phyl. I kept having flashbacks but the images were distorted, not clear at all. I couldn't see the murderer very well. It's almost as if ..... as if ...."

"As if what Sue?" asked Elspeth.

"I know this sounds ridiculous but ......"

"But what ...."

"It's as if the murderer was putting some sort of block so that I couldn't see them. It's weird .... I don't know how to explain it but I just got a feeling ...."

"Well maybe Ellie and Phyllis will be able to clear that block" suggested Craig. "We can't have a murderer going round the village killing people. Nobody will feel safe, even behind locked doors."

"Oh this is terrible" said Elspeth. "I feel so useless. I'm assuming somebody has contacted her mum. I wish I could do something to help the poor woman."

"It's going to shake her faith a bit. I know her husband was quite strongly involved in the church before he died and she was quite a regular churchgoer" said Craig.

"Yes, I heard that. Apparently from what I can gather it caused friction with her father as he was quite interested in all things strange and unusual. Actually, that's interesting."

"What is?" asked Craig.

"I seem to recall .... now let me think ..... wasn't he murdered a few years ago?"

"I'm not sure" said Craig. "I don't really know the family that well."

"I may have to do some research" said Elspeth. "I'm not saying there's a connection, but it does seem odd."

"An unusual coincidence granted" said Craig, "but why would somebody kill Emily after nearly a decade and a half if it was the same person who killed her grandfather? Doesn't make sense."

"No it doesn't" agreed Elspeth. "But I'll put it on the backburner for now. In the meantime, I think we need to try and put this on the backburner as well, hard as it may be. We need to go and pick up Sue's car."

Chapter Eight

Elspeth drove Sue and Phyllis to the garage where Sue's car was being repaired. As they drove along the road, Phyllis kept staring at the dashboard.

"What's wrong Phyl?" said Elspeth. "You look puzzled."

"I'm just looking at all the lights and numbers. What on earth do they all mean? Cars were a lot simpler back in the sixties."

"Well this one here" said Elspeth pointing to one of the dials "let's you know how many more miles you have distance-wise before you have to fill up again. This one measures your emissions ...."

"Oh God, how complicated. Is it really all that necessary? They seem to over-engineer everything these days. Take me back to the sixties."

"Well it's apparently all to do with carbon emissions. The climate and all that."

Sue who had been sitting quietly suddenly piped up, "you'd better not fart Phyl or the car will measure your methane emissions and report you to the climate police. They do like a good hanging, drawing and quartering before lunchtime."

"Tell me about it" said Phyl. "Life has become so complicated. I'm not surprised everybody's so stressed out these days."

"Here we are" said Elspeth. "That's your car there isn't it Sue? Looks like they've done a good job of it."

The three companions got out of the car and walked over to the person who was just polishing Sue's car. "Morning. Is this yours?"

"Yes" said Sue. "Thanks for getting it sorted out. I was afraid it was going to be a write off."

"No such concern" he replied. "The damage was really only superficial. No damage to the chassis, just a few dents. You were lucky."

"Tell my head that" said Sue. "Any good at fixing concussions?"

"Oh no, sorry to hear that. Are you ok now?"

"Yes thanks."

"Sounds like you had a near miss. What happened if you don't mind me asking?"

"Some lunatic decided to start playing silly buggers across both sides of the road and nearly smashed straight into me. I veered off sharp to the right, hence the damage to the car."

"Some bloody lunatics on the road, that's for sure."

"Tell me about it."

"Do you want to come through to sort out the paperwork? We've been in contact with your insurance company so it's all been sorted."

"Thankfully I renewed my no claims otherwise that would cost a second mortgage."

"I can't argue there. Not cheap keeping cars these days."

Sue went into the little kiosk by the side of the workshop and signed the relevant forms. She walked out with her keys in hand. "Right" she said. "I'll try and drive it back to yours before I have another accident."

"Ok Sue, if you just follow me, we can drop your car off and then go into town in mine" said Elsepth.

"Sounds like a plan to me" replied Sue. She was relieved that Elspeth had offered to drive as she still felt a bit groggy and the morning's news had left her feeling very unsettled. A trip into town might help to take her mind off things.

When they got back to the cottage, Elspeth opened the kitchen door only to be greeted by Pywackit sitting on the worktop looking directly at the door.

"Pywackit, what's the matter darling? You don't normally do this."

"What's the matter with him Phyl?" asked Elspeth.

"Well I don't know. He seems to be keeping watch on the door, though I don't know why. He's only done that a couple of times and it's usually when somebody has tried to get in. Most unusual."

"Well I shouldn't think anybody would want to get in here, especially after this morning. Most people will be more interested in traipsing up to the church."

"But I thought Craig said the police had cordoned it off" said Phyllis.

"Yes, they probably have, but you know how morbid people are. Honestly, we really haven't evolved at all, despite the advances in technology and modern living. You only need to see people rubber-necking on the motorway to see if they can spot a limb hanging out of a car or a decapitated head" said Elspeth.

"Sorry Elspeth, do you mind not saying that. I'm still feeling a bit delicate from this morning."

"I'm really sorry Sue, how stupid of me. I didn't think."

"That's ok."

"I wonder how long it will be cordoned off for" asked Phyllis.

"I'm not sure but probably a couple of days. They'll need to collect evidence and once they've finished they can take their tape down. I must admit I'm not sure I really want to go up there in a hurry."

"I don't think any of us do" said Phyllis. "Oh Pywackit, you're all on edge. It seems he's picking up on the energy, poor love. I might just give him something to settle him before we go out."

Soon the three ladies were setting off in Elspeth's car to indulge in a bit of retail therapy in order to help them take their minds off the events of the morning.

"Ooooooh Elspeth, you didn't tell me they had a crystal shop here" said Phyllis.

"Are you sure? I thought I had."

"No. Oh do you mind if we go in?"

"Of course not."

Crystals were not exactly Sue's cup of tea but she found looking at the various stones a pleasant distraction from the events of the morning.

"Now this one would be good for my healing meditations" said Phyllis. "Look at the colour."

"Very nice" commented Sue. "Though you'd need a second mortgage at these prices."

"Yes but Sue, this has got such good energy. Just feel it."

"Oh Phyllis, you know I can't feel energies."

"I'm sure you'd be able to feel the energy in this if you closed your eyes and just held it for a few minutes."

"Phyllis, I am not going to stand in the middle of the shop with my eyes closed holding a crystal. I'd feel like a total pillarck!"

"But Sue, people would understand perfectly what you were doing. There's no need to feel self-conscious."

"Even so, maybe I'll do it back at the cottage, but not here."

"Ok, come on then. I'll get this crystal and we can go for a coffee."

"But you don't drink coffee" said Sue.

"No but they'll have something I can drink I'm sure."

The rest of the afternoon was spent chatting, going in shops, wondering if it was worth buying anything before coming home.

"Well I must admit, I do feel better for a day looking at the shops although I also feel virtuous at the fact that I didn't spend any money on what Alan would describe as "useless tatt.""

"Oh don't let him bully you Sue, if you want to buy something, go ahead and buy it" said Phyllis.

Elspeth's car pulled up beside the cottage and she opened the kitchen door. There was no sign of Pywackit.

"That's funny" said Phyllis. "I can't find him anywhere. He's not in the lounge, not in my room or the bathroom, where could he be?"

"Did you try looking in mine or Sue's room?" asked Elspeth.

"No, I wouldn't have thought he'd go in there" said Phyllis.

"Well give it a try anyway, you never know."

Phyllis walked back upstairs and looked in Sue's room. No Pywackit there. She looked in Elspeth's room and sure enough, sitting in front of the wardrobe was Pywackit.

"Pywackit, what on earth are you doing there sweetheart?" Phyllis approached him and went to pick him up. The small black feline would not budge. "Sweetheart, come on. You shouldn't be in here, this is Elspeth's room. It's private." Still Pywackit wouldn't budge. Phyllis felt he seemed to be on edge. "Whatever's the matter with you?" She decided to leave him there, thinking that he would come downstairs sooner or later.

"Any luck?" asked Elspeth as Phyllis walked into the lounge.

"Yes, but it's really strange. He's in your room and he won't budge."

"That's odd" said Elspeth. "You don't think he's poorly do you?"

"No" said Phyll. "But he does seem a bit uptight."

There was a knock at the kitchen door. "Oh that might be Craig" said Elspeth. "I'll be back in a moment."

Phyllis and Sue heard Elspeth opening the door and a man's voice could be heard. Elspeth replied and the conversation seemed to be a little tense. Phyllis was curious and went to join her friend.

"Anything wrong?" she said. There was a policeman standing at the door.

"And who might you be?"

"What's it to you?" asked Phyllis, annoyed at what she deemed the policeman's impertinence.

"I'll ask the questions if you don't mind. We've been given a tip by an anonymous caller that your friend here was seen by the church yesterday evening."

"Don't say anything Phyllis" said Elspeth. What had the policeman said to her to make her so defensive?

"But what .....?"

"Phyllis, please, don't say a word."

"We found this tissue up by the church. We thought it may contain DNA which belongs to the owner. Any idea who could have discarded it?"

"Look" said Elspeth directly. "I misplaced a tissue yesterday and I was up at the church earlier that evening. If you think I murdered Emily you're out of your mind."

"Well if you don't mind ma'am, could I come in and look around."

"No you cannot! This is my property and you are not at liberty to come wandering in on a whim."

"That's all the same to me, but I can get a search warrant if you like."

"Well you're more than welcome to but you're wasting

your time because there's nothing here. I don't know what you expect to find but I can assure you, you're going to be sorely disappointed."

"That's as maybe but I will be returning with my colleagues once we've got the search warrant."

"How dare you ...." Phyllis started.

"Phyllis, please, leave it. I'll let the little toad come and do a quick search if only to send him on his way so that we can carry on with being innocent victims of somebody's malice."

"But who the hell would accuse you for God's sake? I don't care what you say Elspeth, I'm going to tell this little rind of bacon the truth." Phyllis looked squarely at the policeman. "For your information, the three of us went to visit the church last night just around dusk. When we came back I remember Elsepth saying she'd lost a tissue that she'd had because of her hay fever. Now you can't pin a damn murder on us for that!!"

"Well again, if you would oblige me in carrying out a quick search, as long as I don't find anything incriminating, I'll be on my way."

"Well of all the bloody nerve" said Phyllis.

By now Sue had joined them just as Elspeth had allowed the policeman to enter the house.

"I bet the little perv wants to look through your underwear drawer" said Phyllis in a loud voice. "Got to get his kinky kicks somehow."

Elspeth glared at Phyllis. "Phyl, that's not going to help the situation."

Shortly the policeman came downstairs with an item of clothing hanging from a pencil.

"Interesting" he said. "Your cat was standing in front of the wardrobe. Seems as though he was guarding this."

"What is it?" said Elspeth curiously.

"You tell me" said the policeman. "It certainly has blood on it. I think I may need to take this down to the station. If you don't mind escorting me I'd be grateful, otherwise I might have to radio a couple of my colleagues to persuade you to come with me."

"Now hang on" said Phyllis. "You can't just show up on somebody's door step and threaten them with kidnap. How do we even know you're a real policeman? I've heard of these cases in the States where maniacs have posed as policeman only to drag some poor victim into the bushes before raping and murdering them."

"That's fine" said the policeman. "I'm more than happy to wait here and radio through to a colleague who will turn up in another police car. I'm sure that if one police car doesn't convince you, two will."

"Well the damn cheek of it ..."

"Phyllis, cool it. I'll go down to the station and get this sorted out. I'll be back in half an hour. Don't worry."

"But Elspeth, he's just come barging into your cottage, probably planted that piece of clothing there deliberately to frame you so that he can hang a murder charge on you and wrap it all up, save him doing any real police work."

"If you continue to be disruptive, I can take you down to the station as well" said the policeman.

"Phyl, please, just drop it. There's no point in us all going down to the station. I'll see you later when this misunderstanding has been sorted out."

Phyllis was about to say something else when Sue took her arm. "Phyl, Elspeth is right. The best thing to do is remain calm. We'll get this sorted out and Elspeth will be back home before you know it." Sue didn't believe this for one minute but was trying to keep her friend calm while she processed what was happening. She didn't like it. There was something suspicious about this visit and the conveniently found item of bloody clothing.

Phyllis, although managing not to say anything else, huffed and puffed to show the policeman that she was not impressed by his attitude or his actions.

Elspeth said goodbye and Sue couldn't help noticing the anxiety on her face. They closed the door and watched as Elspeth was escorted by the policeman into his car.

Sue went into the lounge and took out her mobile. "I don't like this at all" she said. "Something's not right."

"But I thought you weren't concerned about it Sue. I thought you were ...."

"Oh I'm concerned about it alright Phyl. I just didn't want that idiot dragging us all down to the station as we'd be no good to Elspeth if we were locked up for the night. Now do you have Ophelia's number?"

"Well yes of course. Hang on a minute, I'll get it for you." Phyllis pulled out a notebook from her bag and flicked through the pages. "Here it is."

"Good" said Sue.

"Can I ask why you're phoning Ophelia in particular?"

"I believe she has Robert's number and she may even have Martin's number. We're going to need all the help we can get."

"Oh yes, good idea" said Phyl who hadn't thought about that.

Sue dialled the number. "Hello Ophelia? Hi, it's Sue. Listen, I know you're doing these festivals but I wonder if you could contact Robert for us?"

Sue told Ophelia all that had happened and emphasised that they might need a solicitor to help them. Phyllis didn't like the sound of that at all. She listened intently to the call, although she couldn't make out what Ophelia was saying.

"Ok, yes, I understand. I know you've both got commitments but if you could help in anyway, we'd both really appreciate it. Something just doesn't fit here. Ok, thanks Ophelia. Bye."

Sue ended the call.

"What did she say?" asked Phyllis.

"She had a very bad feeling about it when I explained to her what happened. She's going to phone Robert and Martin and see if they can get up here in the next few days."

"My God Sue, do you really think it's that serious?"

"Yes Phyllis, I do."

Chapter Nine

"You know Sue, you're going to think this sounds silly, but I can't help thinking that Pywackit was trying to warn us that somebody had put something in the wardrobe."

"Actually Phyl, I don't think that sounds silly at all. I don't pretend to understand the feline mind, but you did say he'd been acting strangely earlier and the fact that you couldn't budge him does seem to suggest he was trying to tell us something."

"But how did whoever did it get in?"

"Well I don't want to sound rude Phyl, but I did notice the lock on that door isn't that secure. I'm sure anybody who had the slightest idea how to pick a lock could have done it no problem."

"I must admit, I think you may have a point. Ophelia could have picked that lock in a couple of seconds."

"I've always been intrugued by Ophelia's ability to pick locks" said Sue. "A strange skill to learn for someone with her beliefs about karma."

"There are things I don't know about Ophelia's earlier life, but I get the impression she learned to pick locks out of necessity. Much as I love her, she's an enigma even to me."

Sue scratched her head and looked at the lock on the door. "I don't understand it. Even if somebody did plant that item of clothing, why would they do it to frame Elspeth?"

"I don't know. It just doesn't make any sense. I'm sure that nobody has a grudge against Elspeth. God I just know I'm not going to sleep tonight."

"You and me both Phyl, you and me both."

The two friends chatted further, pondering on the events of the past few days and trying to work out if they could do anything to solve the riddle of both the murder and Elspeth being apprehended by the police.

"If only I'd read Pywackit's signals I could have looked in that wardrobe and pulled that item of clothing out. If it does belong to the victim, we could have given it to Robert to use with his device and find out who really killed her."

"You've got a point there Phyl. I wonder if there's anyway that Robert could persuade them to hand it over. Then again, I doubt it – it's a vital piece of evidence."

"God how stupid, stupid, stupid of me." Phyllis looked at Pywackit. "Oh sweetheart, I wish I was as smart as you sometimes."

"Come on Phyl, you weren't to know. Would you honestly have looked in Elspeth's wardrobe? I'm sure you've got too much respect for her privacy."

"Thanks Sue, that makes me feel a bit better and you are right; I would never impinge on anybody's privacy."

"There you are then."

"Look, I know it's not likely that we're going to get much sleep, but we at least need to try."

"Well I'll make us a nice herbal brew – that might help" said Phyllis.

"I don't normally go for your herbal brews, but on this occasion I'm willing to give it a go."

"I'll make a sixties hippy chick out of you yet" chuckled Phyllis.

"Ah, but I was a 70s chick. Mr Bowie, Mr Bolan and friends. That was my scene."

"But I can trump you there Sue. I saw them both in the sixties when they were both starting out."

"Ok smarty pants, I'll let you have that one."

Phyllis made them a pot of herbal tea and they sat silently, saviouring the warm concoction.

Sue finally spoke. "Well I don't know about you Phyl, but I'm going to drag my duvet down here and curl up on the chair or the sofa."

"I think I'll sleep down here tonight as well. I just don't think I could sleep properly but I may nod off with any luck."

Both Phyllis and Sue eventually managed to fall asleep, although the slightest noise would cause one or other of them to wake up. As wooden staircases settled and there were no more creaks, they both fell into a deeper sleep.

Sue was standing on a path outside. If it wasn't for the light of the moon, she would have been engulfed in the pitch blackness of night. She could hear the wind and see the trees blowing dead ahead of her. She couldn't understand why, but she felt compelled to walk forward. She became more apprehensive as she approached the trees, especially as they blocked out the light of the moon. She could feel her heart thumping in her chest as the trees loomed menacingly above her. What was that ahead of her? Was it a figure standing on top of the hill or was it just her imagination? She felt compelled to continue onward even though her fear was increasing. Was the figure calling to her? She couldn't hear anything but the wind blowing and the trees rustling. The figure seemed to be signalling for her to follow. She walked slowly, steadily, listening .... but for what? The figure seemed to be more insistent, compelling Sue to keep walking. Sue continued to follow the figure until she came to the top of the hill. There stood the ruined church as the moon cast an eerie glow over it. The figure seemed to be standing by the church. What was it trying to tell Sue? It just seemed to stand there motionless for the longest time – and then it suddenly started moving slowly around the church. Sue couldn't help but follow it to see where it went. As she walked around the church, the figure seemed to disappear behind the church and into the ground. Sue was mystified. Surely the figure couldn't possibly expect her to follow them down there. She peered down to the area where the figure disappeared. There seemed to be something down there. What was it? Some sort of hatch? She recalled the other day seeing all those terrified people disappearing behind the church. Was this an escape route – an escape from persecution? Sue looked down and felt herself falling ... falling .... falling ....

"Nooooooooooooooooooooooooooooo!"

"Sue, wake up, wake up. You've been dreaming."

Sue's eyes opened and she sat bolt upright. "Oh my God, oh my God ....."

"It's ok Sue. It was just a bad dream."

"God Phyllis, it was too real to be just a dream."

"Don't talk, just relax. Take a few breaths."

"If that's going to happen everytime I drop off to sleep, I'm going to sign up to Insomniacs Anonymous. That was horrible."

"What happened?" asked Phyllis.

"I was standing on a path .... I think it was the path up to the church. I could see a figure in the distance and I began to follow them. I couldn't make out whether it was male or female. It seemed to be gesturing to me to follow it. Anyway, I eventually reached the top of the hill and I could see the church lit up by the moon. The figure was standing there .... just standing there. Then it started walking around to the back of the church. I followed it to see what it was doing. It seemed to disappear into a hatch or some sort of opening behind the church ... and then I could feel myself falling down the hole that it had disappeared into."

"That's interesting" said Phyllis.

"Interesting? It was bloody frightening!" exclaimed Sue.

"Yes, but remember the other day you mentioned a lot of people running terrified to the back of the church as if they were fleeing from something?"

"Yes, I thought of that" said Sue. "I wonder ......"

"..... if there is something behind the church. But why would this figure be guiding you there?"

"Well do you remember I said I was certain the murder didn't occur there?"

"Yes" said Phyllis.

"Well if the murderer brought the body there, it would be almost impossible carrying it up the hill, and there's also a risk they could be spotted, even at night. What if ....."

" ..... there is some sort of opening that the murderer used."

"You mean an opening leading to a tunnel?"

"I know it sounds crazy but you never know. I've heard that tunnels were built to help people escape persecution. Who's to say there isn't one behind the ruined church?" said Phyllis.

"I suppose it would tie in with what I saw both the other day and just now."

"Maybe we should go and see if there is some sort of hatch or door behind the church."

"But it's all cordoned off Phyl, we can't just go walking up there and traipsing through police tape. Besides which, the finger of suspicion is already pointed at us what with Mr Plod coming and dragging poor Elspeth away."

"Well, we could go at night."

"Oh Phyl, that place creeps me out in daylight, there's no

way I could go there at night."

"What if we had somebody with us?"

"You mean like Robert?"

"Well possibly, although there's no guarantee he's going to be able to come up."

"What about Craig? Once he finds out about Elspeth, I'm sure he'd want to do whatever he could to prove her innocence."

"Probably, but I'd rather just keep this between us for now. We don't really know him that well."

"Well what shall we do then?"

"Well the police cordon won't be there indefinitely. I think they tend to take them down after a few days once they've gathered all their evidence. We could go up during the day. I doubt many people will want to go up there."

"Won't we need to take a torch in case we do find a tunnel?"

"That's a good point."

"Do you know if Elspeth has a torch?"

"I'm not sure but I could look through her kitchen drawers. I'm sure she wouldn't mind us having a look. Otherwise we could go out and buy a couple."

"Well that will be our first job tomorrow and then we'll wait to see when the police cordon is taken down."

"Good idea. In the meantime, maybe we should try and get some more sleep."

"Easier said than done. Knowing my luck I'll probably have another nightmare."

"On the other hand, if our victim is trying to tell us something, now that they've delivered the message, they might let us get some proper sleep."

"How very considerate of them."

Sue and Phyllis tried to settle down again and eventually both nodded off to sleep. They managed to sleep for the rest of the night undisturbed. Phyllis was the first to awaken the next morning. She crept around quietly so as not to disturb Sue. Eventually Sue also woke up and noticed that Phyllis was not there.

"Phyl? Phyl? Where are you?"

"I'm just here love. Do you want some tea?"

"Oh yes please."

"Did you manage to get back to sleep after our discussion?"

"Yes thanks. Luckily no more goblins interrupted me."

"That's a relief. I do think somebody was trying to tell you something."

"Well I wish they'd do it when I wasn't asleep. I don't appreciate being woken up half scared to death."

"Yes, I can understand that."

Sue's mobile rang. She picked it up. "Hello? Oh morning Robert. Well I'm ok, no thanks to an interrupted night's sleep."

Although Ophelia had been in contact with Robert, Sue went through what she'd discussed with Ophelia to make sure he heard the story firsthand.

"Look, I appreciate you're busy so I'll understand if you can't come up. It's just that ...."

Phyllis sat looking intently at Sue.

"Ok. Thanks Robert. We really don't know where to go next. There's no way that Elspeth is responsible but the police have already got her banged to rights. Ok, bye for now." Sue ended the call.

"He's coming up?" asked Phyllis.

Sue nodded. "Yes, he and Ophelia. They're going to try and persuade Martin to come with them."

"Oh" said Phyllis.

"Sorry Phyl, I know you and he have a history but we need somebody who knows the law and hopefully he'll find more holes in their accusation than a block of Swiss cheese."

"That's ok Sue. It's ancient history and you're right, we need to get Elspeth released as quickly as possible."

"Right, how about looking for that torch?"

"Good idea. If you start looking through the kitchen drawers, I'll have a look in these cupboards."

Both Sue and Phyllis felt slightly guilty in searching through Elspeth's drawers and cupboards, but if it meant getting them closer to the killer, they would have to put their moral reservations aside.

"Ah, here you go Phyl, there's two here. They look pretty good. Let's see if they work." Sue clicked the switches on both torches. There was no light.

"Have they got batteries in?" asked Phyllis.

"Good point" said Sue. She unscrewed the bottoms of the torches. "I should have realised by the weight that they've got no batteries in them. Hang on, looks like there's some in this drawer." Sue put batteries into both torches and screwed the bottoms back on. "Presto! We have light!"

"So we're all set" said Phyllis.

"Yes" replied Sue. "It's just a case of when we go and inspect the church."

"And check to see if your theory is correct."

Chapter Ten

"Well I think today is as good a day as any" said Sue.

"Are you sure you're ok to go ahead and do this Sue?"

"Yes Phyllis. We've got to do it. We can't just sit around waiting. God knows what it must be like for Elspeth being locked up in that shit-hole."

"It worries me a bit going up there though. I can't help feeling that the police will still be sniffing around and if they see us …."

"Yes, I know what you mean, but we've got to take a chance."

There was a knock at the door. Phyllis and Sue looked at each other. Was it the police again?

"Better go and see who it is" said Phyllis. She walked to the front door. Sue could hear Craig's voice. "Oh hello Craig, come in. Have you heard any news?"

Craig followed Phyllis through to the lounge. "Morning Craig" said Sue.

"Morning Sue."

"What's the news with Elspeth? Are those bastards going to realise she's innocent and let her go yet?"

"They're being bloody obstinate and insisting it's her. We all know it's absolute bloody rot but how the hell do we prove otherwise?"

"There's got to be something we can do. While she's sitting in that place there's somebody out there murdering young girls."

"I'm just thinking" said Craig. "Did you see anybody suspicious lurking around when you went up there – or possibly on the way back?"

Sue and Phyllis both shook their heads.

"Nobody" said Phyllis. There was hardly anybody about. I can't recall anybody that stood out as unusual."

"Surely it would have been more likely to have happened later anyway?" added Sue. "I mean it was still fairly light when we were out so not exactly the sort of time you'd expect to find a murderer carrying a body around."

"And it's not as if there's anywhere to hide up there" said Phyllis. "Although Sue does think there might be some sort of door behind the church."

Craig looked at Sue surprised. "Oh?"

"Oh Phyllis, I wish you hadn't said that. It sounds silly now."

"Go on" said Craig.

Sue was reluctant to share the vision that she saw last night and so decided to play it down as just a bad dream. "Oh it's silly, I just had a bad dream and imagined that I saw somebody by the church – a ghost, I suppose. They seemed to disappear behind the back of the church and in the dream I felt as though I was falling into a hole through some sort of door. Quite ridiculous."

"Well maybe we'll have to go and check your theory out some time" said Craig. He looked at the torches on the table. "Were you thinking of doing it today?"

Phyllis darted a quick look at Sue.

"Oh, er no" said Sue. "We thought we had a power cut last night so scrabbled around to find a torch. It was only when we realised the fridge was still on that we worked out it must be the light bulb." Sue tried to make a joke – Phyllis was impressed with her quick thinking.

"Did you manage to find a bulb?" asked Craig.

"Yes" said Phyllis. "Thankfully there were a few spare ones."

"That's ok then. Look, I'm going to go and see if I can get any more information from the police. I might call around later if there's any updates."

"Ok Craig" said Phyllis. "If you do get to see Elspeth, can you tell her we're thinking of her and we'll get her out of there somehow."

"I will" he said.

Phyllis saw him to the door and Sue heard it close. When Phyllis walked back in, she looked at Sue and smiled. "That was quick thinking Sue Baylock."

"I must admit, I even impressed myself. Thing is we could have told him – maybe he would have come with us."

"I don't know" said Phyllis. "I just think that we should do this ourselves and if we find anything, then we can tell him and the others when they do turn up."

"Ok. Well shall we get ourselves ready? The only thing that worries me is if you're going to wear one of your long dresses it could be awkward getting down any potential hidden holes."

"That's ok" said Phyllis. "I can pull it up if I do need to climb down anywhere. I suppose I should buy some jogging bottoms or something. That's what people wear now isn't it?"

"Some do – others wear jeans with ruddy great holes in them – and call it fashion!" exclaimed Sue.

"It does make me feel old but sometimes I think the youth of today could learn a lot from us boomers!"

"Sounds like my grandma" joked Sue. "'Back in my day' she used to say."

"I know, we're starting to sound just like that generation – and there we were thinking they were so square."

Sue and Phyllis collected the items they felt they would need to take with them.

"Do you think those batteries in the torches will be ok?" asked Phyllis.

"I think so" replied Sue. "They were in a pack so I should think they're fairly new."

"Ok. Well let's make sure we lock the door and take the key with us … for whatever good it will do."

They set off in the direction of the hill and took their time walking up it so as not to expend too much energy. They wanted to make sure that if they did find some sort of trap door, they would have enough strength to move it. When they finally reached the top of the hill and saw the ruins of the church, they both stopped to take a breath.

"That wasn't too bad I suppose" said Phyllis. "Though I do seem to get more out of breath these days."

"Don't we all Phyllis. We're none of us getting any younger."

"Yes but you haven't got quite as much weight to carry as me."

"Give over woman. In the middle ages you'd be known as what they call a comely wench. Very desirable."

"Thanks Sue – it does make me feel better."

They began to walk towards the church.

"God it gives me the creeps just being near it" said Sue.

"If you want to back out ......"

"No Phyllis, we're here now and we've got a job to do."

They walked round to what used to be the back of the church. Sue pointed down. "This is about where she disappeared ..... and I followed her."

"Oh so it was a she?" asked Phyllis.

"Yes, I didn't know the gender when I was having the vision, but it must have been. I'm sure it was our victim."

Both Phyllis and Sue kneeled down and started groping around the grass.

"Hey, what's this?" asked Sue. "I can feel something." She began pulling at what felt like a large metal ring.

"Are you sure it's not just a tuft of weed you've got hold of?" asked Phyllis.

"No, it's a metal ring. Here, can you help me?"

Phyllis reached to feel where Sue's hands were. "Oh yes, you're right Sue. I would never have known it was there by looking at it."

Both Phyllis and Sue tugged and tugged ..... they could feel something lifting up but it took all of their strength. Eventually a whole section of the ground seemed to lift up and they pulled it up. It hung at a 90 degree angle.

"It must be on some sort of hinge that only allows it to open halfway" said Sue.

"Well what a turn out for the books. You wouldn't know it was there if you didn't look."

"It's not a very big hole – here let's get the torches." Sue took out one of the torches and shone it down the hole. "There's a make shift metal rung ladder attached to the wall. I'm going to try and climb down."

"Be careful Sue, I don't want you falling. You don't know how secure that ladder is."

"Well I'm guessing that if somebody came up here and dumped that poor girl's body here, it must have taken all their strength – and I'm assuming it was a man so I'm sure he'd be heavier than us. Here, can you hold on to this torch while I climb down?"

Phyllis took the torch from Sue and watched anxiously as she began to climb down the ladder. After a short while

Phyllis could hear her voice calling up. "I'm at the bottom Phyl. Do you want to throw the torches down and I'll catch them."

"Ok. Can you see me? I'm throwing them now." Phyllis dropped the torches down the hole, one after the other. As she didn't hear any clatter she assumed that Sue had caught them.

"Got them" Sue called up. "Do you want to stay there while I go and take a look around?"

"No Sue, I'm going to join you. I don't want you down there on your own."

"I'll be fine Phyllis, don't worry."

"No, I'm coming down." Phyllis collected the bottom of her dress and began awkwardly putting her feet on the rungs.

"Go steady Phyl. Take your time."

"Don't worry, I have no intention of falling down here. I'd probably never be able to get back out."

Slowly she climbed down the hole while Sue aimed the torch at the rungs so Phyllis could see where she was going. "God almighty, how the hell did somebody manage to carry a body up here? Surely it's not possible" she gasped.

"I should think whoever it was tied a rope to the body and pulled it up once they got to the top" replied Sue.

"Oh God, you're probably right. It's really giving me the creeps to think that I'm climbing in the same spot where there was a dead body being pulled up only a few days ago."

"Try not to think about it too much Phyl. Just focus on getting down here in one piece."

Eventually Phyllis could feel the surface beneath her feet and with a bit of help from Sue, managed to reach the bottom safely.

"God, it's quite wide down here" said Phyllis as her eyes adjusted to the darkness. "How long does it go on for?"

"I don't know" replied Sue "but it looks like there's a tunnel ahead."

"I must admit, if I'd have known it was like this I'm not sure I would have been so brave" confessed Phyllis.

"I know what you mean Phyl. It's easy to be brave when you're sitting in a cosy cottage in broad daylight. Still, we're here now so let's see what we can find down here. Here, take one of the torches."

"What about getting back? We don't want to get lost down here."

"From what I can gather the tunnel only goes in one direction so it should be pretty straightforward making our way back."

"I hope you're right Sue" said Phyllis nervously.

The two women walked slowly, cautiously down the tunnel's long passage. Sue shone her torch around the walls and the ceiling to see if there was anything they could use as a landmark.

"Nothing much down here but as I said it should be pretty straightforward getting back."

"God, I can't imagine what it must have been like for people coming down here trying to escape from something" said Phyllis, following the beam of Sue's torch. "It must have been terrifying."

"I don't doubt for one minute you're right Phyl. Hey, what's that?"

"What is it?" said Phyllis, anxious that Sue may have heard something.

"Look here, the tunnel diverts and goes in a different direction. Shall we take a look?"

"I'm not sure Sue. We don't want to get lost."

"Look, I know you're not going to be too keen on this suggestion but I'll take a quick look down this tunnel if you want to stay here. If it goes on too long I'll come back."

Phyllis didn't really like the sound of this but felt that she needed to put on a brave face. "O-oh ok Sue, but promise you won't be too long."

"I promise Phyl. I just think if you stay here, If I do get disorientated I can call out to you and follow your voice back."

"Ok." Again, Phyllis could feel the anxiety rising but tried to keep a brave face on it.

"See you shortly" said Sue and began walking down the other tunnel. Phyllis could hear her footsteps becoming more distant as the beam of her torch followed Sue. Soon there was silence. For the next few minutes she listened intently to every noise – or every imagined noise that came through the tunnel. Was it her imagination or did the small speck of light where the trapdoor was disappear? She couldn't hear anything but she was sure a moment ago she could still see the speck of light that was the outside world. She was relieved to hear Sue coming back.

"Phyl, can you hear me?"

"Yes Sue, over here" she called out anxiously. Shortly Sue joined her again.

"Any luck?" asked Phyllis.

"It went on too far, I didn't want to risk getting lost. Let's just stick to this tunnel."

"Good idea" said Phyllis. Should she tell Sue that she thought the speck of light by the trapdoor disappeared or should she say nothing? 'Oh come on Phyllis' she said to herself. 'We won't find out anything if we keep worrying about every noise and every speck of light that disappears.'

The two women continued walking down the tunnel. "God this seems to go on for ages, we've been walking a good long while now and we don't seem to be coming to any opening anywhere" said Sue.

"Well shall we give it another five minutes and head back?" asked Phyllis.

"Yes Phyll, that's not a bad idea. I know it defeats the object as we're trying to find the other entrance – and there must be one. But we can't carry on doing this for much longer."

They carried on walking for another few minutes and the beam from the torches suddenly hit a wall.

"Ah, it looks like we've come to the end" said Sue. "But where's the exit?"

They both looked around. "Look" said Phyllis. "In that corner, there's another ladder."

"Well spotted Phyl." Sue walked over to where the ladder was and shone her torch up to the top. "I can't see anything that looks like a trapdoor but I'll just climb up and take a better look. There must be something up there."

"Go careful Sue."

"I will Phyl."

Phyllis took the torch from Sue as she began to climb up the ladder. "Can you point the torch up here Phyl?"

Phyllis shone the torch in the general direction of Sue's voice.

"Hold it just there, yes, just there."

Phyllis kept the torch as steady as she could so that Sue

could see what she was doing. She could hear Sue grunting.

"It's no good" she finally said. "There's definitely some sort of door here but I can't open it by myself and there's no way we're going to get two of us on the ladder to try it."

"Oh how frustrating" said Phyllis. "I don't know what else we can do."

Sue let out a large sigh. "There's nothing else we can do Phyl. The only thing I can suggest is that we go back and when the others come, we tell them what we've discovered. Robert may be able to get it open. There must be a way if our murderer did."

"That is providing the murderer used this trapdoor. There might have been one in the other tunnel you were looking at" suggested Phyllis."

"Good point Phyl, but I've got to admit, I'm pretty tuckered out and I'm not sure I've got the energy to do any more exploring. I suggest we call it a day and go back. At least we've discovered where the tunnel is and we can show the others."

"Good idea Sue."

Sue gingerly climbed down the ladder and the two women turned back towards the direction they came. Sue continued shining the beam over the walls to see if there were any distinguishing features. They continued walking for what seemed like ages.

"I can't see the light from the entrance" said Phyllis nervously.

"No, neither can I but I'm sure we'll see it shortly" Sue tried to reassure here.

As they continued walking, Sue aimed the beam of her torch directly ahead of her and stopped. "Hang on a minute, this isn't right. There's a wall here – and there's a ladder. But there's no opening."

"Did we take the wrong turning?" The apprehensiveness is Phyllis's voice was obvious.

"No Phyl, I'm sure we didn't. I'm sure that's the ladder we came down. Hang on a minute, here, hold my torch."

Phyllis held the torch while Sue climbed up the ladder. As she reached the top she pushed what she thought was the trapdoor above her. "What the hell's happened here? I'm sure this is the trapdoor but I can't budge it. It wasn't that difficult opening it from the outside, why won't it open?"

Phyllis could feel the fear rising in her. "Sue are you absolutely sure it's the right one?"

"I'm positive Phyl" snapped Sue with more than just a tone of sharpness in her voice. "I'm sorry Phyl, I didn't mean to snap at you, I just don't understand."

"Well could it have been blown shut by the wind?" asked Phyllis, grasping at possibilities that pointed to an accidental closing.

"No, it can't have been. For one thing there was no breeze when we came up here and it's such a heavy door, you'd need to physically push it closed, it wouldn't have shut on its own." Sue regretted saying that as soon as the words came out of her mouth.

"But … but what could have happened?" Phyllis was now becoming more frightened. Sue picked up on her fear and tried to reassure her friend. "Look I'm sure we'll find some way out. Maybe we should take a walk down the other tunnel and see if there's an opening there."

"Ok" said Phyllis meekly, though she wasn't convinced. Sue climbed back down the ladder.

"It's ok Phyl, we'll find a way out of here." But even Sue wasn't convinced.

Chapter Eleven

"This is it" said Robert. "This is the address that Phyllis gave us."

Ophelia stepped out of the car and looked at the cottage. "It does seem to be the right one. It's just as Phyllis described it."

Robert got out of the car and gave his surroundings a glance over. "Looks like a nice area" he said. "Very different from London."

"Yes, you're right Robert. Seems very hard to imagine that a murder's taken place here."

"That's just what I was thinking" agreed Robert.

"When did Martin say he was turning up?" asked Ophelia.

"He should be able to come over either tomorrow morning or early afternoon."

"Good" replied Ophelia. "I've a feeling we're going to need him."

"Ok, let's catch up with Sue and Phyllis, see if they've heard any news."

Robert knocked on the door of the cottage. There was no reply. He knocked again. Still no reply. He frowned. "Strange, there's no answer."

"They must be out somewhere" said Ophelia. "Maybe they'll be back shortly."

"Odd though. They knew we were coming and they can't have gone very far as Sue's car is still here. I'll call her on her mobile." Robert tried to call Sue but there was no reply. "No reply. I don't like this."

"Hang on Robert, can you call her number again?" asked Ophelia.

"Ok" said Robert, slightly puzzled by Ophelia's request.

Ophelia pressed her head against the window of the cottage. "Robert, I can hear Sue's phone ringing out."

"Are you sure?"

"It must be. Can you end the call and try again in a minute?"

"Ok." Robert ended the call and waited a few minutes. "Here goes" he said. He typed in Sue's number again and Ophelia held her ear to the window.

"There it is again" she said. "It must be Sue's phone."

Just then a car pulled up. The driver got out of his car and walked towards the cottage.

"Can I help you?" he said.

"We're up here visiting friends of ours, but we're not sure we've got the right cottage. Do you know if Elspeth lives here?"

"Yes she does" said the stranger. "Your friends of Elspeth's?"

"Well no, not exactly" replied Robert. "We're friends of the two ladies that are staying with her. Do you know the lady?"

"Yes I do, we're close friends."

Ophelia looked at Robert with a slight frown. What did 'close friends' mean exactly?

"Well we've tried knocking at the door but there's no reply. I've just tried to call one of the ladies but it's ringing out and my friend here, Ophelia, believed she could hear it through the window. Sue's car is still here so we're a bit concerned as to where they are."

"Well they may have gone out for a walk" suggested the stranger.

"Perhaps" said Robert. "Though they were expecting us and we did tell them we'd be arriving about this time."

"That's odd."

"Sorry, we haven't introduced ourselves properly. My name is Robert and this is my friend Ophelia. Sue and Phyllis are very good friends of ours and they asked us to come up and help their friend Elspeth as I believe she's in a bit of trouble."

"Oh I see. My name's Craig. Yes, unfortunately she is in trouble. Are you a solicitor?"

"No, I'm not, although a friend of ours who is coming up tomorrow to join us is."

"Ok. I'm not sure what to suggest. I can only think to wait a bit longer – I'm sure they'll turn up."

"You wouldn't have a key would you?" asked Ophelia.

"Unfortunately not. I know that sounds odd as Elspeth

and I are good friends, but neither of us have a key to the other's property. No other reason than we just haven't got around to it."

"I see" said Robert. "Well I guess we'll just have to wait in the car until they return."

"There's a local pub you might want to have a drink in while you're waiting just down the road. It's very nice and the food is good there."

"That's ok thanks" said Robert. "We stopped to eat on the way up. We'll just wait here."

"Ok, well if you'll excuse me I'd better be going. I'm trying to see what I can find to clear Elspeth's name. It's obvious she's innocent, but the police won't believe her. I need to do everything I can to get her out of there."

"Well hopefully once our other friend turns up tomorrow we should be able to assist in any way we can."

"Thank you" said Craig. "I'm really sorry that your friends aren't here. I can't think what else to suggest."

"Don't worry" said Robert. "I'm sure they'll turn up soon."

Craig began to walk back to his car.

"Oh, um, excuse me" called Ophelia.

Craig turned around. "Yes?"

"Is there any message we can give to the two ladies when they turn up? I'm assuming you came to give them some news."

Craig paused. "Oh, um, just to say what I've told you. No other news yet, but I'm still chasing up on my enquiries."

"Ok, we'll certainly pass the message on" said Ophelia.

"Thank you." Craig turned round and headed back to his car.

Ophelia watched and waited patiently while he started the engine. The car drove off and Ophelia looked at Robert.

"That was all a bit strange" she said.

"I must admit, it was a bit odd, but I suppose in the circumstances everybody's a bit pre-occupied."

"But Robert, why was he here if he wasn't going to give them any message? I had to ask him and he seemed hesitant."

"Possibly, but I don't think we should go jumping to conclusions straight away. We need to find out what's happened here first. I can't believe that Sue and Phyllis would just disappear knowing that we were coming."

"Neither can I" said Ophelia. "I'm certainly not waiting for somebody to come back either. We need to start investigating straight away."

"How?" asked Robert. "What do you intend to do?"

"First of all, we're going to get into the cottage."

"Now hold on Ophelia, we can't just go breaking into cottages."

"Who said anything about breaking in? We're going to use a key."

"But we don't have a key."

"We have the next best thing" said Ophelia. She rummaged through her handbag and pulled something out.

"What's that?" asked Robert, although he already had a good idea what Ophelia was holding.

"It's a lock pick" said Ophelia.

"Ophelia, this is illegal. It's as good as breaking and entering."

Ophelia uncharacteristically turned on Robert. "Robert, what else do you suggest we do? Wait out here all night? Something's wrong and the sooner we look into it, the better. Now if you're not going to help me, do feel free to get in the car and stay there all night. If the police turn up I'll take full responsibility for my actions."

Robert was taken aback by this little outburst but couldn't help admiring Ophelia's fiestiness. "No, you're right Ophelia. I'm just not used to being on the wrong side of the law."

"I learned in the past that sometimes you have to be."

This was an interesting revelation coming from Ophelia. The dark horse was revealing snippets of her past that had never come to light before. She bent down in front of the door and put the pick in the lock. She moved it around several times until she could feel that familiar 'click'. "We're in" she said.

Robert looked around cautiously to make sure there was nobody around who could see what they'd done.

Ophelia turned the kitchen light on and could see Sue's mobile lying on the table. "Look, her phone's here, her bag's here. She wouldn't have just left them."

"This isn't good. Something's definitely not right. I

think we should call the police" said Robert.

"Well if you do, we need to get our story straight. I'm just going to see if Elspeth has a spare key around here somewhere. If the police ask us how we got in, we'll need to make sure we can prove that we entered legitimately."

"Good thinking" said Robert.

They both scanned the kitchen and Ophelia spotted a keyholder on the wall. There were several keys hanging up and Ophelia took them to see if one of them fitted into the lock. The first one didn't but the second one did. "Good" said Ophelia. "We have a cast iron alibi."

Robert phoned the police and explained the situation. Although he didn't expect them to be overly-interested as he believed they didn't usually follow up on a missing persons report for at least 24 hours if it was an adult, the policeman they spoke to seemed very interested.

"What do you mean they're not there?" he said, in an accusatory tone.

"Well just what I said, they're not here" replied Robert. Why was this policeman being so abrasive?

"I'll send somebody over shortly" he said. "Please don't leave the premises until somebody turns up."

Robert heard the line go dead. "Well that was odd."

"What did they say? Are they sending anybody over?"

"Yes, they certainly are – and they don't want us to leave the cottage."

Ophelia looked puzzled. "Well we've got no intention of leaving the cottage so why on earth would he say that?"

"Just what I thought" said Robert.

"Poor old Pywackit is definitely on edge" said Ophelia. "He does seem to have the knack of knowing when there's something wrong with Phyllis and he's very agitated. Trouble is I'm going to have to put a collar and lead on him for the time being."

"A collar and lead?" asked Robert puzzled. "Why? He's not a dog!"

"You'll understand shortly." Ophelia pulled out a small collar and an extendable lead and picked Pywackit up. "I'm sorry Pywackit, but it's the only way I can stop you and Grimalkin from tearing each other to pieces."

Pywackit seemed to look at Ophelia sullenly as she first put the collar on him and then the lead, tying the other end to one of the towel racks.

"I'll be back in a minute" said Ophelia. Can I have your car keys Robert?"

Robert gave Ophelia his car keys and she went out to collect the cat cage with Grimalkin inside. He looked up at her sulkily. "Come on my lovely boy, time to come inside."

When Ophelia brought Grimalkin's cage into the kitchen, Pywackit glared at it immediately and hissed. He was met with a mutual hiss from Grimalkin.

"Now Robert, can I ask you to hold on to this collar and put it around his neck as soon as I take him out of the cage. I don't want him taking a leap at Pywackit."

Robert held the collar in readiment for the emergence of Grimalkin. When Ophelia opened the cage, he attempted to sprint over to where Pywackit was but Ophelia was too fast. Robert quickly fastened the collar onto him, followed by the lead and Ophelia tied it to a hook after making sure that neither cat could get to the other one. As soon as both cats were secured, she released Grimalkin and both cats appeared to try and lunge for each other, but to no avail. They hissed and spat in each other's direction.

"It's not ideal" said Ophelia, "but at least we know they'll both be safe."

Robert looked in wonder at the two seemingly demonically-possessed cats. "Why on earth do they hate each other so much?"

"Well Phyllis is convinced that they knew each other in a previous life but I just think it's a simple case of personality clashes."

"I must admit I'm more inclined to go with your theory" said Robert.

Ophelia made some tea, if just to stay occupied more than anything else. She and Robert sat waiting for the police to arrive. They could hear a car pulling up and shortly after, there was a knock on the door.

"Good evening" said Robert. "Come in."

The policeman walked into the kitchen.

"Would you like some tea?" asked Phyllis.

"No thank you, I'm on duty."

Ophelia resisted the urge to say "I didn't think you could get drunk on tea", tempting as it was to say so.

"So I understand that two people have gone missing?" the policeman stated.

"Yes, that's correct" said Robert.

"When was the last time you saw them?"

"Well it's not quite as straightforward as that" said Robert. "We only just arrived an hour ago and were expecting them to be here. They knew we were arriving which is why it's strange that they're not here."

"So you're saying that they're definitely missing, even though you've only just arrived? How do you know they haven't gone to visit somebody?" asked the policeman.

"Well as I said, they were expecting us and it seems strange that they would just disappear, especially as they've both left their bags and mobile phone here."

"So if there was nobody here, how did you get in?"

"I have a spare key" said Ophelia. She omitted to add that she'd only just obtained the key after they'd got into the cottage. That little detail the policeman didn't need to know.

"Well if you have a key, perhaps your friends assumed you'd just let yourself in and they would join you. How do you know they're not on their way back now?"

Robert was becoming agitated with the policeman's attitude. "In light of what's happened here recently, they wouldn't have just wandered off knowing we were coming."

"Are you sure about that?" asked the policeman. There was that accusatory tone again.

"What's that supposed to mean?" snapped Robert.

"In case you weren't aware, the individual who lives in this cottage is currently in custody on a murder charge. Her two companions were told in no uncertain terms to stay here as they both went to the spot where a murder victim was found hours before. They could either be accessories to a murder or key witnesses. Either way, it doesn't look good for them if they've decided to disappear."

Robert could feel his temper rising. Ophelia shot him a look as if to say 'keep calm Robert'.

"So if they've disappeared on purpose as you seem to be

applying, can you tell me how they've done it, considering that Sue's car is still here, as are her car keys, mobile and handbag?"

"There are such things as taxis and there's a train station up the road" replied the policeman, offhandedly.

"Well then perhaps if you go and check with the train station to see if two women took a train I'm sure they'd have camera footage of it. As for a taxi, I'm sure there can't be too many taxi drivers in a small village like this, so I'm sure an interview with them would be able to clarify whether they've had any passengers fitting Sue and Phyllis's description." Robert's tone was sharp.

"Well perhaps that might be an idea" said the policeman. "In the meantime, if your friends turn up, could you please let us know as it would certainly be in their best interests to return as soon as possible."

"I can assure you that as and when they are found, if they have been held captive or harmed in any way, I shall hold you personally responsible and make an official complaint" said Robert.

"Well let's hope that they haven't but in the meantime I would appreciate it if you keep contact with us, should there be any fresh developments."

"Ophelia" said Robert. "Would you show the policeman to the door, suddenly my sense of politeness and courtesy has left me."

The policeman got up and said goodbye.

Ophelia closed the door and looked at Robert. "Well Robert, it looks like it's down to you and me."

Robert was still shaking his head. "Unbelievable. Totally unbelievable."

"I feel so helpless" said Ophelia. "They could be trapped somewhere in danger and we can't help them. I'm not going to be able to sleep tonight."

"Me either Ophelia" said Robert. "I wish Martin was here. He might have a better idea of what to do."

"Well let's hope he gets here as soon as possible tomorrow. Earlier rather than later" said Ophelia.

Chapter Twelve

Despite the fact that neither of them felt as though they could sleep, they decided to try and catch 40 winks so that they would be in good form for the following morning. However, Pywackit seemingly had other ideas. Almost as soon as they'd settled down, Ophelia on the sofa and Robert on one of the chairs, Pywackit starting howling. Initially it was just the odd 'meow', but after a while it got louder and louder and he kept pulling at his collar.

"Oh Pywackit, I know you're missing Phyllis but we can't do anything tonight" said Ophelia.

It seemed as though Pywackit was completely oblivious to Ophelia's protests. He continued to howl constantly, whilst tugging incessantly at the lead.

"Oh God Robert, I don't know what we can do to settle him. He just seems to be hell bent on howling all night. If this carries on we'll get no sleep and we'll be no use to anybody tomorrow."

"I must admit" replied Robert, "although I'd never harm an animal, Pywackit is testing my patience at the moment. I know he's fretting over Phyllis but this isn't helping anybody. Haven't you got any suggestions that might help him settle?"

"Not really. If he was unwell I could probably give him something to settle him, but he's just too wired at the moment. Maybe if I just take him out in the garden for five minutes it might help."

"Not a bad idea, but for goodness sake keep him on the lead so he doesn't wander off."

"Don't worry, the last thing I need tonight is to look for a cat in the dead of night." Ophelia stood up and went to untie the lead from the towel rack. "Come on Pywackit, let's get a bit of air."

As soon as Ophelia took hold of the lead, Pywackit leapt forward like an overly-excited dog. "Calm down Pywackit, we're going out now." She unlocked the door and Pywackit pulled forward on the lead more frantically.

"Robert, can you come out here please?" called Ophelia.

Robert went into the garden to see what Ophelia wanted. "What is it Ophelia?"

"He seems to be hell bent on getting out. I know he's fretting for Phyllis but I'm just wondering if something else is going on."

"What do you mean?"

"Well I know it sounds crazy and I wouldn't normally think about doing something like this at such a late hour, but I've heard instances where families have moved and left their pets behind. Sometimes it can be a case of thousands of miles."

"Go on" said Robert, already anticipating what Ophelia was going to suggest.

"Well I'm just wondering if Pywackit has some sort of sixth sense as to where Phyllis could be."

Robert paused a while. "Yes, I have heard of similar stories, although at this time of night I must admit it wouldn't be my first choice to go wandering off after a cat."

"I know it sounds preposterous, but I can't help thinking we should give it a try."

"Possibly" said Robert. "Hang on though, before we do decide to go on a wild goose chase, I've got a torch in the boot of my car. I'll just go and get it."

Robert collected his car keys from the house and went to fetch the torch. He then went back to the cottage. "Have you got the key to lock the door?"

"Yes, here it is. I suggest we pick up our jackets, it's not that warm out here and we don't know how long we're going to be. I'll go inside and get them."

Ophelia picked up their jackets and locked the door of the cottage. She left a light on for Grimalkin and Robert handed the lead back to her with the incessant Pywackit pulling on it.

"He seems pretty determined" said Ophelia. "Let's see where he takes us."

Pywackit was trying to run across the road but Ophelia had a firm hold on the lead so that he couldn't run off.

"I can't believe we're following a cat in the dead of night" said Robert. "If my colleagues could see me now, they'd be laughing their heads off."

"Don't worry, what happens in Horseshoe Hill stays in Horseshoe Hill."

"I'll hold you to that" said Robert.

Pywackit continued to head towards the hill where Sue and Phyllis had walked only a few hours earlier. Robert pointed the beam of the torch towards it. "It looks like he wants to take us up there" he said.

"I must admit, it wouldn't be my first choice at this time of night, but in the circumstances ..... onward and forward."

Pywackit continued to head up the hill, with Ophelia and Robert following close behind. Eventually he reached the top of the hilll and there in front of them, outlined by the moon, was the old ruined church.

"Oh my God" said Ophelia. "This must be where the girl's body was found." She suddenly felt a cold chill all over her body. "I don't like this at all Robert. I hope to God nothing's happened to them."

"I know exactly how you feel Ophelia – I feel exactly the same" agreed Robert. "The trouble is we need to continue. We need answers."

Ophelia paused for a moment, despite the fact that Pywackit was still pulling at his lead. She let out a deep sigh. "Ok Pywackit, go ahead."

Pywackit led them straight over to the ruined church, walking round to the back. Just in front of them was a headstone lying flat on the ground. He walked directly up to it and sat on it. He then looked up at Ophelia.

"Why on earth is there a headstone at the back of the church lying flat on the ground?" said Ophelia puzzled.

"I don't know but Pywackit seems to think that there's something here."

Ophelia stumbled slightly.

"Are you ok Ophelia?" asked Robert.

"Sorry Robert, I feel a bit dizzy. I'll be ok in a minute."

Robert waited for Ophelia to recuperate.

"Ok Robert, I'm feeling a bit better now. Let's carry on."

"Well I'm not sure quite what Pywackit wants us to do. Hang on, let's see if I can shift this headstone." Robert kneeled down and began to push the headstone.

"Here let me help you" said Ophelia. They both pushed the heavy stone until the area it covered was completely clear.

As soon as they had moved it, Pywackit promptly sat down on the grass mound where it had been.

"I don't understand it. Why's he sitting here? There's nothing there" said Robert.

"Are you sure Robert?" asked Ophelia. "Let's just check." She began feeling around on the ground. Her hand went over a ring pull handle initially without noticing it, but the second time her hands scanned that part of the ground, she suddenly noticed it.

"Robert!" she exclaimed excitedly. "There's something here."

"Are you sure?" said Robert.

"Yes, here. Take a look."

Robert started prodding around the area where Ophelia had been investigating. "I think you're onto something Ophelia. Hang on, can you hold the torch a minute?"

Ophelia took the torch and Robert continued to poke and prod. "Here it is, it's some sort of big ring pull handle. Hang on a minute."

Robert began to pull at the handle. It was a struggle at first but he persisted and gradually he could feel something lifting up. "I've got it Ophelia."

"Hang on Robert, let me help you." Ophelia also grasped the handle and they pulled it together. Gradually the trap door lifted.

"Presto!" exclaimed Robert. "Give me the torch Ophelia."

Ophelia handed the torch back to Robert. He shone it into the darkness below.

"Hello. Is there anybody down there?" At first there was silence. Pywackit sat on the edge of the hole and Ophelia made sure she had a tight hold of the lead in case he decided to take a leap.

"I don't understand it Robert. Unless ...."

" .... try not to think about it Ophelia. There's a set of rungs here. I'm going to go and investigate."

"Be careful Robert. I'm saying it as much for myself as I am for you because I don't relish the idea of walking back to the cottage on my own."

Robert smiled. "Don't worry, I'll take it slowly."

Ophelia watched as he climbed down the rungs. She waited patiently, nervously looking around at the surrounding trees, expecting something or somebody to leap out at her any minute.

Robert reached the bottom rung and then felt his foot hit solid ground. He cautiously looked down and held the torch steadily. He took in his surroundings, listening for any sound.

"Is there anybody here?" he called out. "If you can hear me, please let me know."

Still there was silence. He sighed. "I'm beginning to think that cat has led us a merry dance."

"Can you see anything Robert?" Ophelia called down.

"No I can't. I think we just have a case of an excited cat with an overly-active feline imagination."

"I don't understand it. Why would he have led us here unless there was something specific?"

"I don't know" Robert called up. "But I'll take a bit of a look around and I'll come back if I don't find anything. It looks like quite a vast tunnel so it might take a while. Do you want to come down and join me rather than staying up there?"

Ophelia didn't like the thought of being sat there on her own with Robert out of earshot and decided that she would join him.

"Yes, I think I will but I'll have to be careful as I've got Pywackit."

"Do you want me to come up and get him?"

"If you don't mind."

Shortly Robert's head appeared again. "Here, give him to me."

Ophelia handed over an apprehensive Pywackit. "It's ok Pywackit, Robert's got you."

Robert climbed down the rungs again, carefully holding Pywackit with one hand while gripping onto the rungs with the other. "Ok Ophelia. Now take it steady. I'll shine the torch up for you."

Ophelia began climbing down the rungs. She was grateful for the light from Robert's torch. As she neared the bottom, Robert reached out to help her down.

"Oh my God, I didn't realise how big the tunnel was down here" said Ophelia. "How far does it go?"

"I'm not sure" said Robert. "Let's take a look."

They continued walking steadily along the tunnel. Pywackit had started tugging at the lead again. At one point Ophelia loosened her grip and Pywackit took the opportunity to pull free, running along the tunnel.

"Oh for goodness sake, Pywackit come back!" Ophelia had tried to be patient with him but he seemed to be behaving like a petulant child. "Robert, can you see where he's gone?"

"Hang on, let me see if I can pick him up in the torch beam." Robert shone the torch around the floor of the tunnel but Pywackit had gone.

"I'm sorry Robert, I let my grip loosen slightly and he took advantage of it."

"Don't beat yourself up Ophelia, I'm sure he can't go far. We'll find him eventually."

They continued walking down the tunnel.

"God I wonder how old these tunnels are" said Robert. "It'll be interesting to see what the story is behind them."

"I think Phyllis said something about people using them to escape from whoever was trying to persecute them."

"Yes, it would make sense. Civil war, reformation, who knows. Certainly there was ..... hang on, what was that?"

"What?"

"I thought I heard something."

"Did you? I can't hear anything."

"Hang on, there it is again."

Ophelia frowned as she strained to listen. "Yes, yes, I can hear something. Come on, let's keep going."

As they carried on walking down the tunnel, the sound became clearer. Was it the sound of a woman sobbing?

"Hello? Is there anybody there?" Robert called.

"We're here" called a faint voice.

"Did you hear that Ophelia?"

"Yes I did. Come on."

They both started to run down the tunnel, calling out as they went.

"Robert, is that you?"

"Yes it is. Is that you Phyllis?"

"Yes, we're here."

Eventually Robert and Ophelia could see two figures

crouched on the ground. He shone his torch at the first figure and Phyllis blinked in the light of the torch.

"What on earth are you doing down here?" exclaimed Robert.

"It's a long story Robert. We didn't think anybody would ever find us. We thought we were going to die down here. How did you find us?"

"You can thank your favourite feline for that" said Robert.

Pywackit was purring loudly as Phyllis held him tight. "What do you mean?"

"He wouldn't stop howling and pulling on his lead so Ophelia took him out into the garden to see if that would help him settle. He just became more frantic and Ophelia came up with this insane idea that he might be able to sense where you were. Ridiculous idea – but it looks like she was right."

"What? You mean Pywackit led you here?"

Ophelia smiled at Phyllis and nodded. "Yes, he led us directly to you."

"You see Sue" said Phyllis, sobbing and smiling at the same time. "I told you he was special. He's just saved our lives."

"Well I can't argue with you there Phyl" said Sue.

"Look, I think we need to get you two back to the cottage. How long have you been here?"

"We set out earlier to come and investigate when we found the tunnel. We walked right down to the other end of it but the trapdoor was blocked. When we came back the other trapdoor was blocked and we couldn't get out. We thought maybe the wind had blown it shut, but we just couldn't get it open again."

"Well I hate to tell you this" said Robert, "but it wasn't the wind that blew it shut."

"What do you mean?" asked Sue.

"When we got here, there was a headstone covering the trapdoor. It looks like somebody deliberately shut you in."

"What????" said Sue.

"Yes, unfortunately I'm afraid so."

"But how did anybody know we came here – and why?"

"That's what we need to find out" said Robert.

"Right now though, we need to get you two back to the cottage. Come on. Here let me help you up Phyllis" said Ophelia as she reached out for Phyllis's hand.

"Here Sue, take my hand" said Robert.

Both Phyllis and Sue were stiff and tired and glady accepted the help that Ophelia and Robert offered them. Phyllis was quietly apprehensive, afraid that somebody had closed the trapdoor again and now all four of them were trapped, but as Robert shone his torch on the rungs, they could see the opening.

"I think I should go up first" said Robert, "and I can help each of you to get out at the top. Here Phyllis, let me take Pywackit."

Phyllis was reluctant to hand over her precious feline but Robert insisted. "It'll be easier for you to climb up the ladder with both hands." He climbed the ladder steadily and when he reached the top, he called down. "Ok, Phyllis, you first."

Phyllis began to climb the ladder. She stumbled slightly at first but once she got her balance, began to climb steadily. Robert reached down to pull her out and she managed to grip hold of his arm as he guided her safely onto the grass. "Oh, that air is so good" she said as she took in large gulps.

Sue followed shortly and she managed to pull herself onto the grass without any assistance. Finally Ophelia followed, climbing deftly up the rungs. She managed to pull herself out but stumbled a little, so Robert helped to guide her out.

"Right" said Robert. "I'm going to pull this headstone back over the trapdoor so that whoever put it there assumes that you're still down there."

"It's a good idea Robert, but it could present a problem" said Ophelia.

"What's that?" said Robert.

"Well whoever did this clearly wants Phyllis and Sue out of the way. If they realise that they've managed to get out, they could come after them again."

"That's a good point Ophelia. I'm not sure how we're going to keep you two hidden out of the way. Right now though let's just focus on getting back to the cottage."

Robert closed the trapdoor and replaced the headstone in the same position that he had found it in. "That should do it."

The four walked quietly back down the hill with Sue

explaining to Ophelia and Robert how she'd seen a ghostly figure in her dream guiding her to the tunnel.

"Interesting" said Ophelia, who was listening intently to Sue. "And you say these visions only started after you had the accident?"

"Yes" said Sue. "First of all there was the elderly man in the hospital, then there was the nurse putting the list away in the bottom drawer of the desk and finally, the ghost. I'm sure it was the girl who's been murdered."

"Very interesting. I think we need to discuss this further in the morning."

"Well don't forget Martin's coming tomorrow and we need to furnish him with the facts as we know them before anything else" said Robert.

"I understand Robert" said Ophelia. "I do wonder how this all ties in though."

"Well there's no guarantee that it does, though I must admit it's a strange coincidence that you found that tunnel and it would seem like a good choice for a murderer to transport a body without being seen."

"Yes it does. It'll be interesting to see if we can find out where the other trapdoor is" said Ophelia.

"Trapdoors" said Sue.

"Trapdoors?" asked Ophelia.

"Yes, there was a second tunnel which I initially decided to look at but it went down quite a way so I gave up. I'm pretty sure there will be another trapdoor at the end of that tunnel as well."

"Perhaps you can see if you have a vision of the end of that tunnel in your dreams Sue" said Robert jokingly.

"Well you never know" said Ophelia. "You just never know."

Chapter Thirteen

The following morning Ophelia awoke first, followed by Robert. As Ophelia arose from the sofa, Robert awoke in the chair he'd been sleeping on.

"Morning Robert, did you sleep ok?"

"Not bad thanks Ophelia, a little unsettled but for the most part ok. How about you?"

"Same here. I think I heard Phyllis calling in her sleep once or twice, but I managed to get back to sleep eventually."

"Yes, I can understand she's probably still anxious after being trapped in that tunnel."

"Exactly. I'd like to know who put that stone across the trapdoor so that I could put a curse on them." Ophelia's tone was curt.

"The only thing I would say is that we must be pretty much over the target if they felt that Sue and Phyllis were getting too close."

"Yes, I think you're right. But that's what worries me. How can we keep them both safe? If we pretend that they still haven't been found, the murderer will expect us to put out a big announcement about it, but if we come out and say they're ok, that could put them in danger all over again."

"A valid point in both cases" noted Robert. "I don't know what the best thing is to do. All I can suggest is we wait for Martin to get here and see if he can put a fresh angle on it."

"I would agree but I don't think Phyllis or Sue would be very happy if they felt that they had to be cooped up here for however long it takes to find our resident psychopath."

They both heard stirring upstairs and after a few creaking floorboards going back and forth, Phyllis traipsed downstairs.

"Morning Phyllis, how did you sleep?" asked Robert.

"Not too bad Robert, but I did keep having strange dreams about being trapped in a tiny cavern."

"I'm not surprised to be honest" commented Robert. "It's going to take some time to feel comfortable again after what you went through."

"It just proves we need to find where the exit is to the

end of the tunnel. Do you think it will really lead us to our suspect?"

"Well he must have thought so otherwise he wouldn't have tried to trap you down there."

"Trouble is, he could come after us again if he finds out we're still alive."

"Ophelia and I were discussing that very possibility. We do need to think about what we're going to do to keep you and Sue safe."

"Well apart from locking us in a room hidden away from the outside world, I can't think of what else would work" replied Phyllis somberly.

"Unless you both go home" suggested Robert.

"While Elspeth is still in custody?" remarked Phyllis. "Robert, you have got to be kidding me!"

"I didn't think you'd agree to that suggestion, but just thought I'd put it out there."

"There's no way I'm going to leave her rotting away in there and desert her. She needs us now more than ever."

Robert heard his phone buzzing. He picked it up. "Oh that's a surprise. Martin decided to set out early as he heard there may be some congestion due to roadworks on the M25 and thought it might help him avoid it."

"Well I know Elspeth could certainly use his help. I can't believe it. Robert, do you honestly think they can hold her much longer? You know as well as I do that she's innocent. I can't believe they honestly think she could be capable of such a thing."

"As much as I'm certain she didn't do it Phyllis, I don't have the legal expertise to pick their story apart whereas Martin does. I'm sure he'll be able to get her released."

"I hope so" said Phyllis. "It's bad enough that she's just lost her mum, although she does seem to be taking it quite well. Even so, she doesn't need a murder charge on top of that."

"No, I shouldn't think she does. Martin does seem to be quite astute though so I've every confidence he will clear her name."

"Oh yes" said Phyllis. "He always was very good with detail." Was that a look of remorse on Phyllis's face?

"Well we need as much help as possible with this case

before anybody else gets harmed."

The creak of floorboards indicated that Sue had just woken up.

"I was hoping she'd have a bit more of a lie in" said Phyllis. "I'm still worried about the after effects of the accident."

"Yes, I didn't get to the bottom of what you were talking about last night" said Robert. "You said the accident seems to have given Sue some sort of ability? What exactly do you mean?"

"Well honestly Robert, there's no way we would have found the trap door or the tunnel if it hadn't been for Sue. She followed this figure in her dream who led her right to the trapdoor itself. Now I can't believe that's just coincidence. And then the two incidents in the hospital."

"Interesting" noted Robert. "It does seem to defy logical explanation."

"Well you know how Ophelia and I view these things. There's more to life than what the eyes and ears can see and hear."

"I'm still on the fence in that field Phyllis, but I try to keep an open mind."

Sue walked down the stairs, although the look on her face certainly indicated that a few more hours sleep wouldn't go amiss."

"Sweetheart, why didn't you have a lie in?" said Phyllis.

"I'm ok Phyl, honestly. Admittedly I didn't get a great deal of sleep but it was a hell of a lot better than sleeping in a cold dark tunnel, that's for sure."

"I can't argue with you there" agreed Phyllis.

"If I could find the bastard who put that headstone over the trapdoor I'd like to put it over his head – from a great height" said Sue.

"You and me both my love" said Phyllis.

"When did Martin say he would turn up?" asked Sue.

"He shouldn't be too long now. I've just received a text message from him saying that he's on his way. He wanted to avoid the traffic so he set out earlier" said Robert.

Sue looked at Phyllis with concern. "How do you feel about him being around Phyl?"

"Oh I'm fine Sue. It was a long time ago."

"Maybe, but it was also a long time ago with Alan and Becky, but let's be honest, he was like a little boy when she was around."

"Oh don't be ridiculous Sue" countered Phyllis.

"Phyllis, you're my friend and I love you to bits, but you don't need to try and convince me otherwise. He still held a torch for her – and the feeling was definitely mutual."

Phyllis wanted to change the subject and thankfully Ophelia interjected for her.

"Well with all due respect ladies, I think we need to put our respective histories on the back burner at the moment and deal with the situation in hand. Elspeth needs every bit of help we can give her."

"Yes she does" agreed Phyllis.

Ophelia set about making tea and generally looking after everybody. Poor old Grimalkin and Pywackit couldn't understand why they had been tied up and looked sulkily at the four friends who didn't seem to show any concern for their incarceration.

"I don't like Pywackit being tied up" said Phyllis. "Cats aren't supposed to be held captive."

"I don't like it any more than you do Phyllis, but I'd rather keep them like that than let them tear each other to pieces" said Ophelia.

"I know Ophelia. I just wish they would sort out their differences and realise that they are both infinite consciousness."

"Well I don't know about infinite consciousness" said Sue, "but Pywackit is definitely an infinite hero after guiding you two to the church last night. If it hadn't been for him we'd probably be half dead by now."

"Of course I knew he'd find us" said Phyllis. "I've always known he's an advanced being. It's just that other people don't realise it."

Robert and Ophelia looked at each other and smiled. How could they possibly argue with Phyllis – and why would they want to? He'd saved her and Sue's life and deserved a bit of praise for his efforts.

The four friends spent the next hour discussing the events of the week and looking for solutions to the problem of

Elspeth's incarceration. They heard a car pulling up outside.

"Is that the police again or is it Martin?" wondered Ophelia.

Robert looked out of the window. "It's not the police so it must be Martin."

Sure enough, Martin emerged from the car and from what he was carrying, it looked like he meant business. He was carrying a briefcase and had a look of seriousness on his face. As he walked towards the kitchen door, Robert went to greet him.

"Thanks for coming Martin. We really appreciate it. We're definitely going to need your help."

"My pleasure Robert. It's nice to see everyone, although it always seems to be in very tragic circumstances."

Robert took his jacket and briefcase. "Take a seat Martin. Would you like a tea or coffee?"

"A coffee would be nice please Robert."

"Have you had anything to eat? We could fix you some breakfast."

"I'm ok thanks. I had some toast before I came out."

"How was the journey?"

"Not as bad as I thought it was. A few idiots on the M25, but that's nothing new."

"Trust me, there are idiots out here too Martin. One of them nearly ran me off the road."

"Oh yes" said Martin. "How are you feeling now? I hear it was quite serious."

"Well they didn't manage to finish me off just yet. If I didn't know any better, I'd say it was Alan trying to cash in on my insurance policy."

"Oh Sue, that's not even funny" protested Phyllis.

"Oh Phyllis, I'm only pulling your leg. A car accident would be far too messy and no guarantee. I'm sure he'd use poison!"

"Sue Baylock, stop it!"

Sue let out a laugh. "Oh Phyllis, you're too easy to wind up. You must stop taking the bait so easily."

"Here you go Martin" said Ophelia as she put his coffee down on the table.

"Thank you Ophelia." A little smile passed between

them – thankfully out of Phyllis's sight.

"So can you give me an overview of what's happened" said Martin as he opened his briefcase and pulled out a laptop.

"Well, where to even start?" said Robert. "So much has happened, I'm not sure where to begin."

"Well how about we start with the details of this poor unfortunate girl's murder" suggested Martin.

Sue and Phyllis told Martin the story of how they'd gone out for a walk and visited the old ruined church at the top of the hill. They explained how Elspeth had dropped her tissue and how the policeman had come round to search the cottage and found the bloody item of cothing in Elspeth's bedroom wardrobe as well as the tissue. Martin fiercely tapped away on his laptop, stopping now and then to clarify particular details.

"And you say he received a tip-off from somebody. Most unusual."

"Well that's what we thought. Why on earth would anybody want to frame Elspeth? Everybody knew she had no quarrel with Emily."

"What's this you mentioned about the victim's grandfather being murdered a few years back? It's probably just a coincidence but definitely a strange one" asked Martin.

"Yes. We don't know a lot about that to be honest" said Phyllis. "All we know is that Emily's mother was married to a man of the cloth and she clashed a bit with her father as he was interested in unusual books."

"Unusual? In what way unusual?"

"Not exactly sure but I got the feeling possibly occult books, black magic – that sort of thing."

Martin frowned as he continued to tap away at his laptop.

"Then there was the incident yesterday" said Phyllis.

"Incident?" Martin raised his eyebrows. "What incident."

Both Sue and Phyllis told Martin about Sue's dream, or vision – and how they'd decided to go and investigate to see if there was any tunnel behind the church.

"And you discovered there was" he interjected.

"Yes, and if it hadn't been for dear Pywackit here, we'd probably be dead by now" said Phyllis.

"Well I'm not sure we'd be dead Phyllis, but we certainly wouldn't be in great shape" said Sue.

"Oh come on Sue, how long could the oxygen last down there. We could have been gasping for breath for hours."

Although Sue was definitely not overjoyed about the experience they'd gone through, she felt that Phyllis was being a bit dramatic.

"Well I think the oxygen might have lasted a little longer than you think. It was a vast tunnel. Even so, I'm certainly grateful to Pywackit for rescuing us." Sue had made sure to add the last caveat so that Phyllis didn't feel she was being undermined.

"Well I still believe he saved our lives didn't you darling?" she said, looking down at Pywackit with great affection.

"Talking of em, Pywackit – that's his name is it? Is there a particular reason why he and the other cat are tied up? Slightly unusual for cats" observed Martin.

Before Phyllis had the chance to come up with a metaphysical theory about past lives, reincarnation and previous relationship dynamics between them, Sue cut to the quick.

"Well it's to stop them tearing each other to pieces. Basically they hate each other."

"Oh Sue it's not like that" said Phyllis.

"Phyllis, let's be honest, if you let them anywhere near each other, you'd end up with a floor full of chicken chow mein."

"Oh Sue, that's horrible. Besides it wasn't cats that used to be used for chow mein, it was ..."

"I know it wasn't Phyllis. I'm just being descriptive to give Martin an idea of what the problem is."

"Ok, well let's get back to the facts as we know them" said Martin, trying to veer the conversation back onto the topic in hand.

"Well the problem is we need to decide what to do about Phyllis and Sue" said Ophelia. "The murderer probably assumes they're still trapped down there and well, you know ...."

"Believing that they're slowly dying down there" added Martin.

"Well I wasn't going to put it quite like that" said

Ophelia.

"I'm sorry Ophelia, I'm a solicitor, I need to deal with facts."

"Yes, of course. I understand."

"And now we have the dilemma of whether we allow people to see you out and about and know that you're still alive as that will no doubt alert the murderer."

"Yes, that's what Robert and I were discussing this morning" said Ophelia.

"The only other alternative ...." started Robert.

"..... is for us to stay hidden, locked inside this cottage for God knows how long" finished Sue.

"I wasn't going to put it quite that bluntly" said Martin.

"You're a solicitor, you deal with facts" said Sue. "I've worked for a law firm for years, I know the set up."

"You work for a law firm?" said Martin. "So you must get some pretty interesting cases."

"Oh no, it's all corporate, so not that interesting." She was going to mention her experience with her previous boss and how she'd tied him up and exposed him naked to a waiting conference of lawyers, but decided that it wasn't appropriate in the current situation. The wry smile on her face suggested to Martin that possibly she hadn't disclosed everything about her job.

"We do have a problem though" said Martin. "I would strongly suggest you both go home, probably at night when nobody can see you but ...."

"Not going to happen" said Phyllis firmly. "We've already gone down that road and I am NOT leaving Elspeth in her hour of need. I'd rather die first."

From Phyllis's tone, Martin could tell she meant it. "You always had a feisty spirit, Phyllis Brewer" said Martin. "I think that's why I ended up being stripped naked and thrown into a fountain."

Phyllis blushed. "I am sorry about that Martin, I was ...."

"No need to apologise Phyllis, it was a long time ago."

This made Phyllis blush even more.

The sound of a car pulling up caught everybody's attention. "Who's that?" asked Sue.

Robert looked out the window. "It's that chap Craig, he

came here the other night. He's a friend of Elspeth's. I wonder if he has any news."

"Well let's see what he has to say" said Sue.

"Hang on Sue" said Robert, apprehension in his voice. "I know it sounds as though I'm being overly-cautious as I know he wants Elspeth released as much as we do, but we did say that it might be better if the whole village still thinks you're missing. I'm not saying he would deliberately go out and tell the village you've been found, but it could slip up in conversation and get back to our murderer. I suggest you both go upstairs quickly."

"But Robert, that's ridiculous, I'm sure ...."

"I mean it Sue" said Robert, a sharp tone in his voice. "Could you please go upstairs now."

Both Phyllis and Sue were taken aback by Robert's curt remark, but decided it might be best to take his advice.

"Quick, let's hide their tea cups. We need to make sure there's no evidence of them being here" said Ophelia. She took the cups and saucers and put them in the dishwasher. She quickly scanned around for any evidence of Sue and Phyllis's presence. It looked as though they'd never been there.

Craig knocked on the door. Ophelia opened it.

"Good morning Craig, is there any news about Elspeth?"

"No, not at the moment. Have you had any luck finding your friends?"

"No, sadly not at the moment, although we had a very rude policeman here last night when we reported them missing, suggesting they'd disappeared of their own volition."

"But that's ridiculous" said Craig. "Why on earth would he think that?"

"Guilty by association" said Ophelia. "As they assume Elspeth is guilty of committing the murder, they have it fixed in their minds that Sue and Phyllis were her accomplices."

"Oh for God's sake, they seem to want to hang it on the first person they can" said Craig.

"Although they did find some evidence in the cottage I believe" interjected Martin.

"Sorry, we haven't met" said Craig.

"My name is Martin Smithson. I'm a solicitor. I said I'd come and offer my help."

"Well Elspeth does have a solicitor but thank you for the

offer" said Craig.

"I'm happy to be of assistance if she needs another pair of ears." Martin's smile was polite but still formal.

"Well they do seem to think she's guilty because they found that bloody blouse in her wardrobe but I know Elspeth well enough to know she's not capable of such a thing."

"I'd be happy to go and have a word with her if you like" said Martin.

"Martin's a very good solicitor" Ophelia assured Craig. "He helped to convict a man of a double murder recently, as well as exposing a major drug ring in Cyprus."

"Very impressive credentials indeed" said Craig. "Well you might want to speak to her solicitor. I'm not sure they'd give you direct access but there's no harm in asking."

"Craig, when you next see Elspeth, can you tell her we're fighting her corner and doing everything in our power to clear her name" said Ophelia.

"Thank you. I will. What about your friends? How are you going to go about finding them?"

"Well it certainly won't be with the police's help" said Robert curtly. "The policeman who came last night made it quite clear that as far as he was concerned, they were two felons and that as soon as they were found, would be brought in and locked up. For all we know, they may have gone into hiding somewhere."

"But surely they would have contacted you to let you know wouldn't they?" asked Craig.

"You'd have thought so" said Robert. "Then again, Sue is a bit of a detective programme buff and probably knows that mobile phones can be tracked so decided to leave it here. I hope that's the case. I'm still worried though."

"The policeman also suggested they could have gone home though I think it's highly unlikely" added Ophelia.

"Well I hope they turn up soon. I thought this was such a quiet little village when I came here all those years ago. Nothing usually happens here and then within a week all of this happens. Do you think it could be connected somehow?"

"Possibly though I don't see how" said Robert. "Sue and Phyllis didn't know this young woman so it doesn't make sense."

"Does anything ever make sense with a murderer?" asked Craig.

"Well no, that's true, but the MO is different. I mean with the young woman, he was quite happy to leave her dead body on display for all to see. But so far ......"

"...... let's not talk about it Robert. Let's hope they do turn up soon" said Ophelia.

"Well likewise, if I can be of any help, let me know" said Craig.

"Thank you Craig" said Ophelia.

"Look, I've got to go but I'll touch base with you tomorrow."

"Ok. Goodbye Craig. Until tomorrow."

Craig left the cottage and headed towards his car.

"Well that was quite a performance" said Martin. "Had I not known better, you would have had me fooled. I don't know whether to label you as first rate actors or blatant pathological liars."

"Oh I'll stick with the actors label" said Ophelia smiling. "If I'd been the latter I might have gone into politics."

"Very good Ophelia" said Robert smiling.

"Joking aside though" said Ophelia. "Where do we go from here?"

"Well first thing I'd like to do is speak to her solicitor though I'm not sure they'd be keen to do that and I'd also like to look at the police report" said Martin.

"That's definitely going to be a challenge because I don't think you're allowed to have visitors whilst you're in custody, is that right Martin?" Robert began.

"Yes, that's usually the case. It's just a shame we don't know who her solicitor is."

"Couldn't we make enquiries" asked Ophelia.

"We could, but I shouldn't think he or she would want to discuss the case with us" replied Martin.

"There's got to be something we can do." Ophelia felt deflated. It seemed as though they were being blocked every step of the way.

"Hadn't we better tell Sue and Phyllis that Craig has gone? I don't think they'll want to be cooped up there all the time if possible" said Martin.

"Oh of course" said Ophelia. "I was just so focussed on Elspeth. Hang on I'll go and call them."

Sue and Phyllis came back downstairs and they were given an update on the latest situation.

"Well if we can't do anything to help release Elspeth, we need to start elsewhere" said Phyllis.

"What do you mean?" asked Robert.

"Surely can't we find out who Emily's mum is and go and ask her some questions about who might have wanted to do this?"

"That's tricky Phyllis" cautioned Robert. "We wouldn't be acting under legal supervision and she might not appreciate people prying into Emily's private life."

"But we've got to start somewhere" said Sue. "I don't think it's a bad place to start. She might be able to give us some information."

"I don't know" said Robert. "Let's see what the solicitor can do first and if we don't feel as though any progress is being made, we can pursue that line of enquiry."

Chapter Fourteen

"Well that was the strangest phone conversation I've ever had" said Robert frowning.

"Oh? What did they say?" asked Sue.

"It doesn't seem as though the solicitor is going to be representing Elspeth anymore, that's what the policeman I spoke to said."

"What????" Sue looked at Robert in disbelief.

"Apparently so. His wife phoned the station and said that he'd had some sort of breakdown."

"Breakdown? Strange. Overwork maybe?"

"I don't know – I suppose so. Does seem odd though – even they seemed puzzled by the news. They said he seemed perfectly ok a few days ago but from what his wife said, he had several nights where he woke up screaming and every time he tried to settle down again and go to sleep, it would keep recurring. He's been put on strong tranquilizers and told to take a couple of weeks off to recuperate."

"Well, as horrible as it sounds, this might be an opportunity to go down there and offer my services" said Martin.

"That's just what I was thinking Martin, although the solicitor's firm may have somebody else to take over the case."

"Well it wouldn't hurt to try" replied Martin.

"No it wouldn't" said Robert.

"Ok, so we need to set up a plan for today" said Ophelia. "May I suggest that Robert and I try to find out where Emily's mother lives so that we can go and speak to her. Martin if you go and see if you can visit Elspeth and try to represent her, perhaps you can find out some information."

"But what about us two?" asked Sue. "I feel guilty just sitting here all day doing nothing while everybody else is trying to find our murderer, not to mention being totally bored."

"The only thing I could suggest" said Robert, "is making some phone enquiries to the local authorities to see if they have any idea about those tunnels. They might not be able to tell you directly about them, but they might be able to point you in the right direction."

"The land registry might be able to help out there as well" said Martin.

"Ok" said Sue, although her tone wasn't overly-enthusiastic. "I can't imagine it will take that long though, but if it means doing my bit for the war, I'll give it a go."

"Just in case they ask for your identity Sue, I would give them my name" suggested Ophelia. "Remember, you and Phyllis are still supposed to be stuck in a cold dark tunnel."

"Ah yes" said Sue. "Slowly starving to death in the dark. What a lovely way to die."

"Thanks to Pywackit we were saved" said Phyllis, a big beam on her face.

"I can't argue there Phyl" said Sue.

"Right, well I suggest we go and see what we can find out" said Robert. "Martin, you've got my number if you need to call me. Likewise if we find any information that might be useful we'll let you know."

"In the meantime the two redundant old hags will remain here, festering away in their dungeon" said Sue.

"Now Sue, that's not the case and you know it. You'll be providing vital evidence for the troops" said Robert, smiling.

"Aye commander" said Sue, a tone of sarcasm.

"And don't forget, if anyone asks, you're name is Ophelia, not Sue."

"Lordie, I won't know who I am by the end of the day" said Sue.

* * * * *

It didn't take long for Ophelia and Robert to find out who Emily's mother was and where she lived. A visit to the local newsagent and striking up a general conversation with the lady behind the counter gave them both the information they needed. Robert couldn't help admiring Ophelia as she used her charm to coax the information out of the newsagent.

"So dreadful what happened to that poor girl" said Ophelia. "I can't imagine what her poor family must be going through."

"You're not wrong there. I think the whole village is

still in shock. Why on earth would anybody want to do that to poor Emily? Such a lovely girl."

"I feel so sorry for the parents" added Ophelia. "It's a parents worst nightmare – nobody is supposed to outlive their children."

"Well sadly her poor father is no longer with us. He was the vicar here years ago but sadly died of a respiratory condition. Not quite sure exactly what it is but he'd had problems for years. Lynette is absolutely heartbroken. She lost her father years ago and now Emily. It's positively tragic."

"That's terrible" said Ophelia. "Had he been ill for a long time?"

"No" said the newsagent, consternation in her voice. "He was murdered as well! Two people in the same family murdered. It's just wrong I tell you, wrong!!"

"Murdered?" said Ophelia. The shock in her voice wasn't totally feigned. "Who on earth did that?"

"They never found out" said the newsagent. "Complete mystery and the police never solved it."

"But why would anybody want to kill him?" asked Ophelia. "Surely a man of the cloth ...."

"Oh no, he wasn't a vicar." The newsagent smirked. "Almost quite the opposite."

Ophelia frowned? "Sorry I don't understand."

"Lynette's father used to own an antiquarian bookshop. Had all sorts of weird and wonderful books and was interested in ... well .... you know ...." her voice lowered, "all things related to the occult."

"Really?" Ophelia was now genuinely shocked.

"Oh yes, I mean don't get me wrong. Very nice man – would do anything for anybody, but he did have a fascination for all things strange. Caused a bit of a rift between him and Lynette when she met her husband, the vicar. He was just going into the ministry at the time and Lynette tended to follow his advice rather than her father's."

"Oh I see" said Ophelia.

"Between you and me, I think the old man and the son-in-law probably had a few run-ins and poor Lynette was caught in the middle. One thing was for sure – she didn't like her father showing his books to Emily."

"But surely he didn't ....."

The newsagent nodded. "Oh yes. He and Emily were very close and he loved telling her all sorts of stories about wizards, fairies and goblins. Lynette didn't mind at first but as time went on, she started to clash with her father. Didn't like any of it – said he was corrupting Emily's mind."

"Well I suppose she was only thinking what was best for her daughter" agreed Ophelia.

Robert had to turn away and hide a smirk. Hearing Ophelia talking about such matters in a way that sounded disapproving would usually come across as hypocritical, but he knew that she was only using this as a ruse to gain more information.

"I honestly don't think she had anything to be concerned about though. Emily turned out just fine. Never in any trouble – never any bother to her parents. Developed into a beautiful young lady and then this. God, it doesn't bear thinking about."

"Does her mother live locally?" asked Ophelia.

"Oh yes" said the newsagent. "Used to live in the vicarage years ago but when the new vicar and his wife took over, she moved to Derwent Road."

"Well I hope for her sake she hasn't moved in to number 13" said Ophelia. "It does sound as though she's had a lot of bad fortune, poor lady."

"Oh heavens forbid. I don't even know if there is a number 13. No, she's number 8. No chance of her moving into a house with that number."

"Relieved to hear it" said Ophelia.

Another customer walked into the shop at this point. "Well we'd best not keep you" said Ophelia. "I do hope they find the person who committed this horrendous crime."

"Oh so do I" said the newsagent. "I've heard they've got somebody in custody but they aren't allowed to disclose who it is in case a mob comes after them, though they damn well deserve it. I'd personally stick them up on a pole and let them hang there for the birds to peck at!"

"I'm sure the police will find the monster" said Ophelia. With that, she and Robert left the shop.

"You really are a cunning old fox Ophelia, I have to say. All that rot about the mother thinking about what was best for her daughter."

Ophelia looked at Robert with a semi-smile. "When in Rome Robert, when in Rome."

"I have to admire the way you coaxed the lady's address out of her though."

"You see, if you watch and study, you'll learn a trick or two."

"If this was the middle ages, you'd be burned at the stake I shouldn't wonder."

"Oh no, I would have escaped long before they came for me."

"Yes, I should think you would."

They found the address and Robert turned the engine off. "Ok so what tactic are we going to use so that she doesn't slam the door in our faces?"

"Leave it to me Robert" said Ophelia.

They walked up the path and Ophelia knocked on the door. There was no answer initially so Ophelia knocked again. They heard shuffling inside. Eventually a middle aged woman with greying brown hair came to the door.

"Yes?"

"Hello. I'm very sorry to bother you but we're here from a group called Friends of Jesus. We heard about the horrendous death of your poor daughter. We wanted to offer our sincerest condolences" said Ophelia.

"Oh thank you" said the lady. "I don't really want to see anybody at the moment to be honest. I'm still not coping very well with it."

"I understand" said Ophelia. "I was just so horrified when I heard the news that I wanted to do anything I could to help. Believe me, we want to find the monster who did this to your poor daughter and just wondered if there was any way you could give us any guidance so that we can help the lord bring this person to justice."

"Thank you, but I believe the police have somebody in custody so they are dealing with it."

Ophelia put on her most sombre expression. "Yes, I understand the police have somebody in custody but to be honest, we're very concerned that they're not giving it their full attention. I mean – they're not really used to dealing with crimes of this magnitude. We just want to help in any way we can. You know, glean any information that might be useful."

Robert felt that Ophelia was stretching it a bit and that at any minute, Emily's mother was going to close the door on them. However, he underestimated Ophelia's powers of persuasion.

"Do come in, but there's nothing I can tell you."

"Thank you" said Ophelia and they both followed Emily's mother into the house.

"By the way, my name is Ophelia and this is my colleague Robert."

"My name is Lynette. I haven't seen you in church before."

"We don't attend in this parish. We're visiting a friend who advised us of what happened."

"Your friend – does she go to this church?"

"Not for a while, not since her husband died. Alice is her name."

"Oh I know Alice. We haven't seen her for years. Yes, poor dear, she does tend to keep herself to herself since Frank died."

"Well she asked us to pass on her condolences as well."

"That's so sweet of her. Please give her my regards when you see her."

"I will" said Ophelia.

Robert didn't know where to look. How did Ophelia know this Alice? She'd never been here before.

"Do take a seat. Would you like some tea or coffee?"

"No thank you" said Ophelia. "We just want to try and understand what happened. Alice assured me that Emily had no enemies. She can't understand why anybody would want to do this."

"Nobody can understand it. I know I'm biased because I'm her mother but everybody loved Emily. She didn't have one enemy – it's just beyond comprehension."

"How was she the last time you saw her?"

"She was fine, absolutely fine. I mean she'd split up with her boyfriend a year before but they parted on fairly amicable terms and she moved back to the village. They'd bought a house together but sold it so she was able to buy a flat here, though I told her she was more than welcome to come home. She told me she was going to meet somebody the night that it happened but she didn't say who it was. The next thing .... well ..... you know the rest."

"Very strange" said Ophelia. "I hope you don't mind me asking but I understand your father died some years back."

"Yes. You must have also heard the circumstances around his death as well. Our family does seem to be cursed."

"Did they find out who did it?" asked Ophelia, though she already knew the answer.

"No, they had no idea. Again, he had no enemies. Got on with everybody. Nobody had a bad word to say about him."

"I know your late husband was a vicar, God rest his soul. Did it run in the family?"

"My father?" Lynette gave Ophelia a look of contempt. "Not a chance. He owned an antiquarian bookshop, but it wasn't just old books generally that he was interested in."

"No?" Ophelia feigned a look of innocence.

"The occult, black magic, supernatural, everything strange, weird and ungodly. Horrible books. He tried to get Emily interested in them. I put a stop to that. I wasn't going to allow him to take my daughter down the wrong path. We made it quite clear to him that we did not want Emily looking at any of those books. I wouldn't go anywhere near the shop. It gave me the creeps."

"So you didn't get on with your father?"

"Our relationship was ok but when I met Justin, let's just say we didn't exactly meet eye-to-eye anymore."

"Do you think he could have been killed by somebody who didn't like his ... erm ... interests."

Lynette sighed. "No. People knew that he was interested in that subject, but he didn't usually mention it to people and they just thought he was a bit eccentric. I honestly don't think it would have led anybody to kill him though."

"And you don't think the two murders could be connected?" added Ophelia.

"I doubt it" said Lynette. "My father died about 15 years ago. Why on earth would there be any kind of connection?" She sighed. "No connection, just a horrible sick coincidence."

"I really am sorry but believe me, we want to bring your

daughter's killer to justice as much as you do and we will be doing everything we can to make sure he's caught."

"But surely they already have somebody in custody. I don't understand."

"They do but we have some information that suggests further work needs to be done. That's why we're here. We won't bother you any further. God bless you and may he keep you in his heart."

"Thank you. I do hope they find who did this. My daughter didn't deserve this. I want justice for her."

"Believe me, so do we."

Ophelia and Robert said goodbye and walked back to the car. When they were out of earshot Robert shot a look at Ophelia.

"How on earth did you manage to pull out the name Alice?"

"Oh Robert, there's always somebody called Alice who goes to church."

"I'm sorry Ophelia, I don't swallow that for one minute. Where did you get that information from?"

"Ok, I'll level with you. Phyllis told me about a conversation she once had with Elspeth. Apparently Elspeth had a bit of a tiff with this woman called Alice who was a regular church goer. Her husband had just passed away and this Alice accused Elspeth of putting some sort of curse on him. All totally ridiculous of course, but this lady knew that Elspeth was interested in tarot and wicca and when her husband died, she wanted to find somebody to blame."

"So she picked on Elspeth."

"Exactly."

"Sounds like the middle ages all over again" said Robert.

"Exactly. But there's something bothering me Robert."

"Oh? What's that?"

"Even though Emily's mother doesn't believe there's any connection between the death of her father and Emily, I can't help feeling there is."

"But that was years ago Ophelia. Surely it is just a coincidence. A horrible one granted, but neverthelss, just a coincidence."

"I'm really not sure Robert, I'm really not sure."

Chapter Fifteen

"So what did you free spirits find out whilst you were galavanting about outside?" asked Sue.

"Not as much as we would have liked" said Robert. "We spoke to Emily's mother but she has absolutely no idea who could have killed her daughter. She knows the police have somebody in custody but obviously they can't disclose that just yet, so she has no more idea as to who the murderer is than we do."

"She did mention that her father was interested in similar things to Phyllis and I, although I get the impression his interests veered more towards the darker side of magic than we do."

"Oh? And do you think there's a connection?" asked Phyllis.

"I do Phyllis" said Ophelia, "although Emily's mother didn't seem to think so."

"But so many years apart?"

"Yes, it doesn't sound as though there should be but something's niggling me – I can't ignore it."

"Well I wouldn't worry too much about it. Just see if you get any flashes of intuition."

"How about you two? Did you find anything out about the tunnel?"

"I made some enquiries with the local council and they didn't really know. They did advise me to call the local library as one of the librarians there is quite up on the history of the place. She was actually very helpful. She said they had a book in the library that went into the history of the village and that we might like to come and take a look at it. I told her that we wouldn't be able to go over there today but said that we could possibly come over tomorrow. She's kept it aside. I told her my name was Ophelia, so you might want to pop over there tomorrow whilst we jailbirds sit here in our cocoon."

"Good work Sue but don't worry, I'm sure the more we find out, the closer we'll get to the truth and then you and Phyllis can wander outside to your heart's content."

"I hope so" said Sue. "It's only been a day and already

I'm climbing the walls."

"I'm sorry Sue, I'm just thinking of your safety."

"I know you are Robert, but it doesn't make it any easier."

"Oh is that Martin's car pulling up?" said Phyllis.

They all looked out of the window, Robert more for concern that it might be Craig or a policeman returning. He was on the alert and wanted to make sure that Sue and Phyllis were being protected. He needn't have worried as it was indeed Martin's car.

"So what's the latest?" asked Robert when Martin came in and sat down.

"It's a complete and utter joke!" he said, contempt in his voice. "They're absolutely clueless!"

"Do tell" said Robert.

"Well I showed them my credentials and managed to speak to Elspeth."

"How is she?" asked Phyllis anxiously.

"She's ok, though she's looking very tired."

"It's not fair. She's just lost her mum and she' now dealing with this. It's ...."

"Phyllis, I don't mean to sound unkind, but can we just concentrate on what Martin's found out first?"

"Of course. Sorry Robert."

"Go on Martin."

"I spoke to the solicitor who had been taking the case over the phone. Something is definitely wrong there – he just wasn't making a lot of sense. He did say that the police had his report on file and gave them permisson to let me see it. All I can say is I'm surprised anybody could make any sense of it. There were some salient points in it, but I can only assume he was having a breakdown of sorts when he started writing it. I did manage to point out to the police that it was completely ludicrous to assume that because they'd found a garment from the victim in the cottage, it automatically made her a murderer."

"Well I suppose I can see it from their point of view Martin" said Robert. "You find a vital piece of evidence in somebody's house that belonged to the victim and ......"

"And nothing Robert" Martin almost snapped. "Look, I've represented some very undesirable people in my career.

People who were obviously guilty and who made damn sure that they hid as much incriminating evidence as possible. Usually it's due to meticulous detective work that they find a shred of evidence but more often than not, the criminal has cleared their tracks so there's no trace leading back to them."

"I'm sorry Martin, I don't follow."

"Think of it logically. Let's just say for one moment that Elspeth committed this murder, which we know she didn't. The police come round and ask to search her property. She tells them no so is then told they will get a search warrant. Then she agrees to let them come in and do the search. What self respecting criminal would allow the police to enter their property knowing full well there was damning evidence hidden away? The first thing she would have done was tell them to go and get their search warrant and in the meantime, ran hell for leather up to that wardrobe and get rid of that garment faster than you can say 'Jack Robinson'."

"I haven't heard that expression for years, but yes, I see your point. It would be a bit stupid wouldn't it."

"Stupid. It would be downright ridiculous! The fact that they found a tissue belonging to Elspeth proves nothing either. Then there's the other not so small matter of Elspeth's size. She's actually one inch shorter than Emily and yet she was supposed to have dragged her body all the way up to the hill on her own. The sniffer dogs didn't get any scent of it anywhere on the path leading up to the hill. It's a total farce. I've actually put in a formal complaint about police incompetence. I'm actually going to send an email to the Inspector today outlining all of this and asking, no, demanding that he release her."

"Well my goodness, you've certainly done your homework Martin. I just hope he agrees with you and let's her go."

"Well if he doesn't I will be writing directly to his superiors."

"At least it seems as though we've made some progress today. Unfortunately Ophelia and I didn't really get very far."

Robert told Martin what they had learned from Emily's mother and Sue also mentioned her chat with the librarian.

"Well I wouldn't fret too much Robert. It's another piece of information that may come in useful. As for the tunnel,

I strongly suggest that you and Ophelia go to the library and see what you can find out about it. I think it could be important."

"Do you think we should tell Craig about the latest developments?" asked Robert.

"Oh he was already at the police station when I got there. I told him that Elspeth's arrest was on a very spurious premise and that with any luck, we should have her release date forthcoming."

"I'm sure he'll be relieved about that."

Martin said nothing but just looked away.

"I don't think we can do any more today" said Robert. "Ophelia, you and I will go to the library tomorrow. Martin, I'm not sure what else you can do right now but ...."

"Well one thing I'll need to do is book in with a bed and breakfast."

"Oh don't be ridiculous. There's plenty of room here."

"There can't be with four of you sleeping here. Don't worry I can ..."

"Nonsense" said Phyllis. "Look, Sue and I currently have separate rooms but as Elspeth's room is not being used we can change the bed and two of us can sleep in there. Two can take the single rooms which means one person will need to sleep downstairs."

"I'm more than happy to sleep down here" said Robert. Ophelia and I slept on the sofa and chair respectively. It's quite a comfortable sofa."

"I could sleep on the sofa Robert ....."

"No Martin, you can take one of the bedrooms. Honestly, I'm fine."

"May I suggest that Phyllis and I share the bed in Elspeth's room? I say that only because that way Pywackit can sleep with us, Grimalkin can go in with Ophelia so we don't have cat fights waking us up in the middle of the night."

Phyllis was a little taken aback by Sue's comment but nevertheless could see the sense in it. "Yes, that sounds like it would be the most practical thing."

The five companions discussed the case a little further, then allowed themselves to relax for the rest of the evening. Sue and Phyllis took charge of the kitchen, preparing a meal, while Martin and Robert talked more about the investigation in general.

"If you do find any more information about those tunnels" said Martin, "I'd like to go and see for myself where they lead."

"You and me both" said Robert.

As Phyllis and Sue were in the kitchen and out of earshot, Martin whispered "I don't understand why the killer would trap them in there. What did he have to gain? Surely he didn't think they had any idea of who he was?"

"But they must have been close to the target to make somebody do that" said Robert. "I wonder if we'll have more of a clue when we find out where those tunnels lead."

"Dinners up" said Sue. She laid the table and Phyllis helped her put plates of food down on it.

"Well I had heard about your culinary abilities Sue, and I must say they live up to your reputation" said Martin.

"Well when you have a slave driver like Alan chaining you to the kitchen sink for decades, you have to do something."

"Sue has a dry sense of humour Martin."

"You do make him sound like a tyrant Sue. I'm sure he's not."

"Well, he does let me off my lead once every six months or so" she said.

Phyllis laughed. "Don't listen to a word of it Martin. Sue Baylock is nobody's fool and certainly nobody's servant."

"Phyllis, how am I supposed to gain any sympathy if you're going to tell everyone that I'm not a downtrodden wife?"

"As if" added Robert.

"And whose side are you on Mr Whitehead?"

"Well as you've made such a delicious meal, I'll be on your side for the time being."

"You see Phyllis, men are all the same. Ruled by their stomachs."

"Don't mention the other one Sue" added Phyllis quickly.

"Perish the thought!"

Eventually, everybody decided to turn in for the night. Robert settled down on the sofa and turned off the light. He heard the others shuffling around in the bedrooms above, preparing to get a good night's sleep. However, it wasn't to be.

There was silence throughout the house as the clock struck 3 in the morning. Then did Phyllis imagine it or did she hear moaning? What had woken her up? She got up and listened. She definitely heard moaning. She continued to listen as it seemed to grow a little louder. But where was it coming from? She gently got out of bed so as not to disturb Sue and went to the door. She opened it as quietly as she could and heard the moaning get louder. As she did so she noticed that the door opposite her was opening. It was Ophelia.

"Can you hear that?" she whispered across.

Ophelia nodded. "It seems to be coming from Martin's room."

"Do you think he's ok?"

"I'm not sure."

The two women continued to listen, growing more concerned about the moaning. Then suddenly out of nowhere they heard a horrendous shout of terror coming from Martin's room.

"What the hell is that?" said Phyllis as she and Ophelia rushed to Martin's door. They opened it and switched on the light. Martin was writhing on his bed in terror. "NO, NO! LEAVE ME ALONE! GET AWAY!! GET AWAY!!"

"Martin, Martin, wake up, it's us!"

Martin seemed to lash out, totally unaware that Ophelia and Phyllis were in the room. He fell off the bed and crawled to the corner of the room. His head was tucked in his arms as he tried to hide himself from .... what?

The noise woke both Sue and Robert who both came rushing in.

"What's going on?" asked Robert. "What's happening?"

"We don't know Robert. We just heard this moaning and got up to see what it was. When we opened the door, Martin was writhing around on the bed and then fell off and crawled into the corner. I don't understand it." Phyllis sounded frightened.

"Robert, help me" said Ophelia. She went over to Martin and took hold of his arm. He lashed out but Robert managed to catch his arm before it struck Ophelia.

"Martin, Martin! Wake up, it's Robert! It's Robert!"

Martin lashed out a few more times and then seemed to

stop. His eyes opened and he looked first at Robert and then Ophelia. The look of terror on his face alarmed both of them.

"I don't like this Robert. Can you hold him a minute. I'm just going to my room, I'll be back in a minute."

Robert managed to contain Martin who by now was starting to calm down a bit. He had no idea what Ophelia was up to so just tried to keep Martin as calm as possible.

Ophelia returned and took some oil from a small bottle and rubbed it on Martin's forehead. She massaged the tincture in gently and applied several more drops. Martin started to breathe more regularly and eventually seemed to be his usual self. He looked at Ophelia and Robert confused.

"What happened?" he said.

"You must have had a terrible nightmare" said Robert. "You were trying to hide in the corner, God knows what from but you looked pretty damn scared."

"Can you all leave the room please?" said Ophelia. Her voice was firm.

"But we need to ....." Robert began.

"Can you all leave the room now please!" It was almost a command.

Phyllis, knowing Ophelia as she did, gestured to Robert and Sue. "Come on, Ophelia knows what she's doing."

Sue and Robert looked at each other, totally puzzled. What on earth was happening?

They stood outside Martin's room waiting while they heard Ophelia muttering something. After several minutes she came out.

"He'll be able to sleep peacefully now but we have some serious work to do tomorrow."

"What do you mean Ophelia, what's going on?"

"I'm afraid you have a couple of tasks and I won't be able to go with you to the library tomorrow."

"Why not? Ophelia, what's going on?"

"Sorry Robert, I can't say too much now but in the morning I want you to drive me to the train station as early as possible. I need to get the first train home that I can. I then want you to go to the library and find out what you can about the tunnel and then I want you to get the other solicitor's phone number and speak to his wife. I want you to ask her exactly what's happened to her husband. I've got a feeling it's something similar to what's occurred tonight."

"Ophelia, you're speaking in riddles, you're not making any sense. I don't under ..."

"Please Robert" said Phyllis. "I've known Ophelia long enough now to know that she's onto something and it's best to let her follow it through."

"Thank you Phyllis, and I'm sorry Robert, but I must insist we carry out my instructions."

Robert looked totally flummoxed but nodded his head. "As you wish Ophelia, as you wish."

Chapter Sixteen

The following morning everybody arose as if nothing had happened. Martin looked tired but didn't seem to be too shaken about the previous night's activities. Ophelia collected all the things she needed and Robert took her to the train station as she'd requested.

"I'll return tomorrow and I'll call you from the station when I arrive" she said.

"Do you have any idea which train you might catch?" asked Robert.

"I'm not sure Robert but I don't want to keep you hanging around so it's best I call you when I'm here. That way you can carry on with what you need to do."

"Ok. Well, safe journey and we'll see you tomorrow."

"See you tomorrow Robert. I'm sorry if I was a little curt earlier, it's just that I need to make sure we're dealing with this properly."

"I won't pretend to understand Ophelia, but I'll take your word for it."

Ophelia walked towards the platform, turned her head to say one last goodbye to Robert and then went into the ticket office. The train pulled into the station shortly afterwards and Ophelia walked out of the ticket office and went into one of the carriages. Other people also got on and off the train and after five minutes the whistle blew and the train started to move away from the station.

When Robert returned to the house the four companions discussed the plans for the day ahead.

"First I need to go to the library and look at this book" said Robert. "I don't suppose they'll let me take it away if I don't have a membership card but they may have a photocopier there in case there's anything useful in the book."

"I'll give the other solicitor a call and see if I can speak to his wife. I don't know how keen she'll be to speak but I want to find out if he had the same experience as me. The trouble is, if he did, what can we do about it and what the hell is causing it?"

"Are you sure you've never had nightmares like this before?" asked Sue.

"Never. I can honestly say it was the most terrifying experience I've ever been through – and I don't want a repeat of it."

"What did you see?" asked Sue.

"It wasn't so much what I saw as what I felt. It's very difficult to explain but I honestly felt as though I was losing my head and this feeling of absolute terror was like something tangible."

"Did you drink anything at the police station?" asked Phyllis.

"Nothing. One thing that this job has trained me to do is be very cautious if somebody offers you a drink – even if you're representing them. You don't know what can get slipped into it."

"And how about what you ate?" Sue frowned as she tried to think what could have happened to Martin.

"Again, only what I had here. Before that, the toast I had before I left home."

"Well look" said Robert. "Why not phone up the solicitor first; I'm sure his wife will answer and ask her exactly what happened. In the meantime, I'm going to go to the library. Do I need to bring anything back foodwise?"

"Could you bring back some milk, coffee and bread please Robert. Apart from that I think we're ok foodwise for a couple of days. Elspeth did manage to get a good stock in for us."

"Coffee, bread and milk. I should be able to remember that. Ok, I'll see you soon."

With that, Robert left. As he got into his car and started the engine, he checked to see whereabouts on the map the library was. Soon he was off. Even though everything seemed to be chaos at the moment, the morning sun felt pleasant as it beamed through his window. He opened it to let the breeze in and it had a calming, cooling effect. The flowers at the side of the road danced around in the wind, almost as a celebration of the day. The library wasn't that far away from Elspeth's cottage and Robert couldn't help feeling disappointed that the journey hadn't lasted longer. He parked his car and walked towards the entrance. There were not many people in that morning and he went over to the desk with a lady sitting behind it.

"Excuse me" he said. "A colleague of mine by the name of Ophelia phoned you yesterday making enquiries about some tunnels that run under certain areas of the village. She was advised by the lady she spoke to that you have a book that tells the history of the village and the possible location of such tunnels. Would it be possible to see the book?"

"Hang on, that's probably Barbara who she spoke to. She's just over there re-shelving some books if you'd like to go and have a word."

"Thank you" said Robert. He walked over to the lady who had a pile of books in her arms and introduced himself, explaining why he was here.

"Oh yes" said the lady. "I remember the phone call." She put the books down on a nearby table. "If you'd like to follow me."

Robert followed the lady who bent down and reached into the drawer of a desk. "Here it is. I've made a note of the pages that will probably be of particular interest. There's a reading area over there if you'd like to take a seat."

Robert took the book from the librarian. "Thank you, especially for making those references. That will help a lot."

She smiled. "You're welcome." She walked off and proceeded to re-shelve the books she'd been holding.

Robert took a seat, pulled out his notepad and pencil and opened the pages on the piece of paper. He skimmed through them initially to get an idea before going back and reading them more carefully. From what he could gather there was a long tunnel leading from the old ruined church down through the village and off into the next village along. Halfway along the tunnel, there was a fork to the right. This one went to an old priory that was still standing to this day and had been taken over by an organisation who had spent money renovating it and keeping it in good structural order. It was now used as a museum and teaching centre for young students. There was a debate as to when the tunnel had originally been built. Some theories claimed it was built in the 12th century, others were torn between the 15th and 19th century. The author of the book veered more towards the theory of the 15th century as he claimed it was used to escape from religious persecution, especially by monks who feared that were they caught, they would probably be executed. The tunnel had originally stopped where the fork now was but apparently had been extended forward because the authorities knew that somehow people were able to get between the two locations undetected, although they were not aware of the tunnel itself. The tunnel was then extended so the monks could go into the next village and escape, possibly into the next county, possibly to the coast and onto the next boat out of England. Robert turned the page. Where was the exit? The author continued to reveal that it was originally under a drinking tavern that was next to the coach house but whoever built it feared that as there were so many people who frequented such an establishment, there was a risk of being spotted and reported to the authorities so it was extended further under somebody's house – somebody who sympathised with the monks. Robert made a note of the area and also an old illustration of the house – one that was made long before the age of photography. He looked up to see if anybody was watching. Not that anybody would become too militant about photographing a page illustration, but better to be safe he thought. He took several pictures with his phone and also wrote down the title, the author and the ISBN number of the book. He walked back over to the librarian and handed her the book.

"Thank you" he said.

"Was it of any help?" she asked.

"It was very helpful indeed."

She looked at him and moved closer so as to speak in a lower voice. "You do know that one of the exits to that tunnel is by the old ruined church where that poor girl was found."

"I do indeed" said Robert.

The librarian seemed taken aback by this. "Do you .... do you think there's any connection between the young girl being found there and the tunnels?" she asked nervously.

"Possibly" said Robert. "I'm exploring that possibility but keeping it very quiet so I'd appreciate it if you didn't say anything to anybody."

The librarian nodded. "Oh yes – I understand. I believe the police have somebody in custody."

"Yes, I believe they have" replied Robert. He thought it

would be best just to agree rather than to disclose that they had the wrong person in custody as it would not only cause mass panic if people believed the real killer was still on the loose, but also alert the guilty party who may then disappear forever. "Thank you again, you've been a great help."

"My pleasure" smiled the librarian who possibly felt as though she had in her own way contributed to the eventual conviction of the killer.

Robert looked at the picture of the house and also the general area. He decided to drive into the next village to see where the house was. Could it be possible that the killer owned the house? It would be a bizarre coincidence if he did. Remarkably handy for disposing of bodies undetected. It made Robert wonder if this had been his first victim. The thought was not a pleasant one.

As he drove into the village, he slowed the car down as he was unfamiliar with the environment and wanted to make sure he didn't take a wrong turning. He looked at the notes he'd made, following the road signs and street names. As he continued, he drove along the main road through the village and noticed a pub which he believed was once the coach house. There sitting next to it was a small bakery that used to be the old drinking tavern. A few yards along was the house. Robert looked at the photo he'd taken of the illustration and the house as it now stood. It had definitely had quite a make over, but geographically speaking, it stood in the very spot where the original house was. So this was definitely the right house. The problem was that he didn't want to arouse suspicions by gawping at the house, only for the killer to see him looking. As well as that, if he started asking around the village who lived there, that could also arouse suspicion. There had to be a way to find out. He could sit in his car along the street watching to see who came in and out, but that could take all day. Time was of the essence and he would have to think of something else. In the meantime, he remembered that he needed to get some provisions for Sue. What was it again? Milk, coffee and bread. There was a local supermarket that he'd passed as he came into the village so he decided to turn around and head back the way he came. He managed to find the supermarket, buy the items he needed and head back to the cottage.

When he arrived he saw a car outside the cottage. It was Craig's. He was walking out just as Robert pulled up.

"Morning Craig, are there any updates on Elspeth?"

"I was just coming round to ask Martin the same question" said Craig. "The police don't seem to be too helpful so I thought Martin may be able to give me an update. I wondered if he'd made any progress as we don't seem to be any further ahead."

"Well it's still early days so I wouldn't be too dispirited. He's a good solicitor. Give him a bit of time and I'm sure he'll get Elspeth released."

"I hope so. It's not doing her any good cooped up in that place. As far as they're concerned, it's a done deal. They've all but thrown the book at her already. In the meantime we're not getting any further."

Robert was about to tell Craig what he'd discovered this morning when he saw a face peering out of the upstairs window. It was Phyllis. Craig noticed him looking but fortunately as he turned round to look, Phyllis's face had disappeared.

"What's the matter?" said Craig. "Seen something?"

Robert realised it would seem strange if he denied that he'd seen anything as Craig had obviously caught him looking. "I don't know – whether it's a lack of sleep, investigating this murder or a combination of the two, but I could swear I just saw a face up at that window. That's the last thing I need, to sleep in a haunted house. You don't know if there's anything odd about this house do you?" Of course it was a hypothetical question – he was asking it merely to distract Craig's attention.

"Not that I know of" said Craig. "These cottages are quite old though, so I wouldn't be surprised."

"It's bad enough sleeping with two cats that constantly want to have a go at each other. All I need is a ghost floating down the stairs wailing at silly o'clock in the morning." Robert was trying to make light of the situation and Craig seemed to take the bait.

"Elspeth's never mentioned anything to me and she's interested in that sort of thing, but then maybe ghosts only make their presence felt by people who don't want to see them."

"Just my luck" said Robert.

"I've got to go now but if I hear anything I'll let you

know and likewise if Martin makes any progress, I'd appreciate it if you could let me know as well."

"Of course" said Robert. "All hands are on deck at the moment so we're bound to make a breakthrough sooner or later."

"Ok, bye for now."

"Bye Craig."

Craig walked to his car and Robert waved one last time before going into the cottage. He watched the car drive off. "PHYLLIS! GET DOWN HERE NOW!" It sounded like an angry parent chastising a naughty child.

Phyllis plodded slowly down the stairs as if she knew what to expect. Actually, she did.

"Phyllis you nearly blew it there! I couldn't help but to look up when I saw you peering out of the bedroom window and Craig saw me. Thankfully I acted quickly and told him I thought I'd seen a ghost. Luckily I think he believed me but for God's sake don't do that again!"

"I'm sorry Robert" said Phyllis, her head hanging low. "I thought he'd gone already. I didn't realise he stopped to talk to you."

"Well if he comes round again can you just make sure you don't go near the window until one of us gives you the all clear."

Phyllis kept her head bowed. "Sorry Robert" she said again.

Immediately Robert felt guilty for his outburst. Phyllis had very nearly blown their cover and had Craig spotted her, he would no doubt have started to ask some awkward questions. The problem was that Phyllis had no malice in her and telling her off just seemed slightly unfair.

Sue came down the stairs shortly after Phyllis. "Go easy on Phyl Robert. It's not easy being cooped up in this damned cottage all day long. It's starting to get to both of us and I can't help feeling the overwhelming need to look out onto fields and grass and open spaces. We're both starting to feel like a pair of bloody convicts!"

"I'm sorry Phyllis, I shouldn't have reacted like that. I think it's just that we're all getting under each other's feet and we're all frustrated that we haven't made any real progress."

"Does that mean you didn't find anything out about the tunnels at the library?" asked Phyllis despondently.

"Actually I did" said Robert. "But before I talk about that, I'd like to hear what news you have about the other solicitor Martin."

Martin had been sitting at the table during the last few minutes. "Well" he said, "I spoke to his wife and she says he's under heavy sedation at the moment. They're not sure if he's had some sort of breakdown but he's not displaying the usual symptoms. The one thing that's proving very difficult is trying to get him to sleep. He's absolutely terrified – and I can't blame him if he experienced exactly the same thing as I did. I have to say I'm not looking forward to tonight."

"But you don't need to worry Martin, Ophelia has left strict instructions with me" said Phyllis.

"Instructions? What instructions?"

"Well I don't know how much you remember of last night after we er .... discovered you, but Ophelia rubbed some oil onto your forehead and that calmed you down."

"Oil? I don't remember that" said Martin.

"Well you were in a fairly agitated state so I'd be surprised if you did remember" said Phyllis. "But whilst Robert was holding you down, Ophelia rubbed some of the oil onto your forehead and it definitely calmed you down."

"What oil was that then?" asked Martin, not sure if he actually wanted to know the answer.

"To be honest, I don't know" said Phyllis. "Oh don't worry, it won't be illegal or harmful. Ophelia just has a vast knowledge of plants and their healing properties. She's quite the expert and I can assure you her remedies work wonders."

"Well I'm not sure I'd want her to use it again" said Martin.

"Oh but you must Martin. Ophelia has left a couple of vials here for me. She wants me to make sure that you rub some on your forehead tonight."

"Look Phyllis, I appreciate the gesture but I'm not going to start rubbing things onto my forehead if I don't know what they are."

"Well ok Martin, suit yourself, but if you want to have another screaming fit tonight like you did last night, go ahead.

Don't worry too much that we won't get any sleep either. We'll just wait until it's over."

"That was a bit to the point wasn't it Phyllis?" said Martin taken aback.

"Your choice. I guarantee it will happen again tonight."

"I just had a bad dream. I'll be fine tonight."

"Just a bad dream – you mean like the other solicitor who is having to be heavily sedated so that he doesn't go totally off his head."

Martin was about to say something when Robert interjected.

"I hate to admit it Martin, but Phyllis has a point. It seems a strange coincidence that you and the other solicitor have had a very similar experience, an experience that neither of you have had before."

"What are you trying to imply Robert?" said Martin, a slight irritation in his voice.

"I don't know what I'm trying to say Martin and that's what worries me. Something strange is happening. I mean first with Sue seeing ghosts wandering over hills leading her to secret tunnels and now this. Look, we're both men of logic. Your job is very much about applied logic and although mine is slightly different, I still look for patterns of behaviour. I still look for connecting influences – things that make people behave in certain ways. But in this instance I can't put my finger on anything – and to be honest, it scares me."

Those last few words made both Sue and Phyllis feel uneasy. Martin didn't give away any expression but sat in silence.

"Look Martin, I don't think it would hurt just to put some of that oil on your forehead before you go to bed tonight. For all we know it may just be a placebo, but God, after what I saw last night, it even scared the hell out of me."

Chapter Seventeen

The following morning Robert headed towards the train station. Ophelia had called him to let him know which train she was catching and when it was due to arrive. Robert had arrived in plenty of time and checked his watch. The train should be due in the next 10 minutes.

Robert waited and waited. He waited a bit more. "Good God, they can send satellites into outer space and probes to explore other planets but can they get a train to run on time? Can they hell!"

Just as he said that, in the distance he could see a train approaching. Was it Ophelia's train? There was an announcement over the tannoy system to say that it was indeed the late running train. "Hallelujah!"

Robert watched as it slowed down and pulled into the station. Many people alighted and Robert struggled to see if he could spot Ophelia. Eventually he saw that slim, tall, demure figure approaching his car. He could swear that even if she'd just survived a nuclear holocaust, a hurricane, a tornado and an earthquake, she'd still look immaculate, not a hair out of place.

"Good morning Robert, how is everybody? Did you all sleep alright?"

"Good morning Ophelia. Yes, we slept fine. Don't worry, we managed to persuade Martin that he should let Phyllis apply your mystical tincture. Fortunately he had a good night's sleep and as far as I'm aware, your concoction didn't send him to some far off astral plane with pink elephants and psychedelic donkeys."

"No need to mock Robert, I know what I'm doing."

"I'm sorry Ophelia, I didn't mean any harm. I'm just curious as to what's in that potion."

"It's one that took me a lot of trial and error to get right, but rest assured, it's very safe and it's very effective."

"Well Martin definitely seemed to have a more settled night last night, that's for sure."

"I'm pleased to hear it" said Ophelia. "However, tonight we have much work to do."

"Ophelia, I do wish you would let down this mystical front once in a while and just tell us what is going on."

Ophelia looked at Robert directly. "Robert, I understand that you and Alan don't really believe in some of the philosophies that Phyllis and I adhere to. You think it's all airy fairy pie in the sky nonsense."

"Now hang on Ophelia I never said tha ......"

"Robert, you don't have to explain and I don't expect you to understand. I appreciate that due to the jobs that you and Alan both have, you have to use your left hemisphere analytical minds and that's perfectly fine. We would be in a total mess if we relied solely on our right brain, but when it's working at it's peak, miracles can happen – quite literally."

"Let's just respect each other's differences and leave it at that shall we?" said Robert.

"Ever the diplomat Robert" smiled Ophelia.

"Anyway, I'm not trying to change the subject, but did you find what you'd gone home for?"

"Oh yes" said Ophelia.

"Interesting tone there" said Robert. "Should I be afraid?"

"No, you shouldn't, but somebody should .... very afraid."

"That last statement almost sent a shiver down my spine" said Robert. "I do hope you're not going to do something that you might regret."

"I never do things without proper thought and consideration Robert, you should know that by now. What I have in mind will hopefully solve two problems." Ophelia paused. "I was going to say 'kill two birds with one stone' but didn't feel that was appropriate in the context of the present situation."

"You are very hard to read sometimes Ophelia. How long have I known you now but sometimes I still feel as though you're a complete stranger."

"I don't try to be mysterious Robert. I just don't over-share, which everybody seems to think is the thing to do these days. Don't get me wrong, feelings have their place, but everybody wants to cry at the drop of a hat now. I come from a long line of people who knew how to stand strong in adversity.

I look forward to the day when that comes back into fashion."

"I completely understand what you're saying and I share your sentiment Ophelia, believe me."

"So you see, you understand me more than you realise."

Robert laughed. "Well, maybe. I may have to take a rain check on that one."

They drove back to the cottage, most of the journey in silence. Phyllis had broken the golden rule of not looking out of the window as the car pulled up.

"Phyllis, you know Robert will have a go at you if he sees you at the window" said Martin.

"But it's ok Martin, it's his car and Ophelia's back." Phyllis was jumping up and down like a little puppy dog, over excited to see her friend return.

Ophelia opened the door and got out of the car. Martin and Sue almost had to restrain Phyllis from opening the door and running out to greet her.

"Phyllis, just hold on, she'll be here in a minute" said Sue.

Sure enough, Ophelia walked through the door only to be bamboozled by an overly enthusiastic Phyllis. She smiled and gave her crazy friend a big hug. "I've missed you too Phyllis, and I owe you a big thank you for carrying out my instructions on Martin. No doubt it wasn't easy persuading him to let you apply the oil."

Martin looked at Ophelia's almost accusatory stare. "Now Ophelia, I can assure you I took my medicine just as mummy told me to. I didn't have to go and sit on the naughty step."

Even Ophelia laughed at this remark. "Well I'm glad to hear it, although you might not be so keen on what I have planned for tonight. But enough of that for now. What's the latest situation regarding the other solicitor, oh and not forgetting the tunnel?"

Robert and Martin in turn told Ophelia what they had discovered. Ophelia seemed to be very impressed with the information they shared.

"I think I may need to pay a visit to this solicitor and I would like to go and pay a visit to that house Robert." Her voice had a determined tone to it, as if nothing was going to prevent her from doing what she intended to do.

"Well I'm not sure about the solicitor Ophelia, we can't just go round traipsing all over other people's privacy" said Robert.

"If it means giving that poor man some peace of mind, I'm afraid we very much will have to" said Ophelia. "I'm not budging on this one Robert. It's too important. You have no idea what we're dealing with here. I have work to do and the sooner I get on with it, the better." There it was again. That 'don't mess with me' tone.

"Well I can't stop you Ophelia, but if you do insist on paying him a visit, would you please use your 'Friends for Jesus' personae so that he doesn't feel as though he's met the devil incarnate!" said Robert.

"Robert, you know me – iron fist in velvet glove. Works every time."

"Yes Ophelia, I know exactly how you operate. God help the poor man."

"He will indeed get the help he needs. But first, when do we get to see the house?"

"Steady on, we've only just got back."

"But Robert, there's no time to waste."

"The problem is it's going to be very difficult to find out who lives there unless we sit in a car all day waiting for the occupant to go in and out."

"But that's how we found Tristran Eldridge."

"Very true, but let's just say for arguments sake that we do see the occupant. We can't exactly go up to them and say 'excuse me, we believe you've commited a murder and used a tunnel under your house to dispose of the body. Would you mind awfully if we come in and take a look around?'"

"Touché Robert, Touché! I see your point, but perhaps we'll need to use stealth."

"Stealth?"

"Yes, go there at night and see if there's anybody in. If not ....."

"Now Ophelia, no more lock picking. Look, I didn't mind you doing it here, but this is somebody else's house. For all we know, it could be alarmed and even if it is in darkness, who's to say somebody isn't asleep in bed."

"Granted you've made some valid points but there's room for negotiation here. I've a feeling we need to get inside that house."

Robert turned to Martin. "Martin, would you do me a favour?"

"What's that?"

"In the future, if I find any information relating to ANYTHING, please feel free to tell me to keep my big mouth shut!"

Martin chuckled.

"I'm just saying Robert ....."

"I know what you're saying Ophelia, but my risk aversion antennae tends to twitch long before yours does."

"Risk aversion is one thing, knowledge of the situation is quite another."

"Right, well if you two want to continue back-and-forthing all day long, some of us would like to get some sort of plan together so that Phyllis and I don't feel like life long jail birds" said Sue.

"Good point" said Martin. "We need to think realistically about what we can actually do."

"Well Sue and I found the exit in the tunnel. Would it be possible for you two to go and open it?"

"If it's a hefty trapdoor Phyllis, it would probably make a hell of a racket, thus alerting the occupant to our presence. Even I have to admit that Ophelia's lock-picking idea would be better."

Ophelia smiled.

"Look" said Sue. "Why don't you call this solicitor and arrange for Ophelia to visit him. Get that out of the way and then we can focus on this house."

"Not a bad idea" said Ophelia. "Would you call him Martin?"

"I feel odd calling again – what am I supposed to say. 'Hello, we have a magic potion for your husband, can we pop round?'"

"Just call the number and give me the 'phone" said Ophelia, matter of factly.

Martin looked at Robert and Robert nodded. "Go ahead Martin."

Martin dialled the number and handed his phone over to Ophelia. He whispered "the name's Jenkins."

Ophelia could hear a woman's voice over the phone. "Hello, is that Mrs. Jenkins? Hello, you don't know me but I'm acquainted with a colleague of your husband who is very concerned about him." There was a slight pause. "Yes, yes, I understand he's not been well at all and that he's been advised to take a much needed rest." Another pause while the lady at the other end responded. "My friend, that is your husband's colleague, reached out to me as he knows I have much experience in dealing with stress-related conditions. He asked if I would help your husband. I said I would only be too happy to come over and see him, gratis of course. No, it's no trouble at all. I owe my friend a favour and it's the very least I can do. Yes? When could I pop over? I'm free most days. Well later would be fine – about 4 o'clock? My pleasure, don't mention it. Please make sure he gets plenty of rest until then. Thank you Mrs. Jenkins."

Ophelia pressed the 'end call' button.

Robert looked at her and shook his head. "Butter wouldn't melt. Talk about silver tongue! You don't happen to have any ice cubes you could sell to this Eskimo?"

"Inuit Robert, Inuit."

"I do beg your pardon. Well how about those ice cubes? Any to spare?"

"No, but I would be much obliged if you could take me to see Mr. Jenkins this afternoon at 4 o'clock."

"Martin, why do I suddenly feel that you should address me as Parker and Ophelia as Lady Penelope."

"Know your place Robert, know your place."

The following hours were spent discussing plans to access the mystery house without breaking the law amongst other topics. The time quickly passed and it almost slipped Robert's mind that he agreed to drive Ophelia over to the house of the other solicitor.

"Time for us to go now Robert" she said.

Robert looked at the clock. "Oh yes. Well hopefully we won't be too long."

"I hope it goes well Ophelia" said Sue.

"It will" she said.

Chapter Eighteen

Several hours later Ophelia and Robert returned. Phyllis in particular looked eagerly at Ophelia. "How did it go?"

"It went very well Phyllis, very well indeed. He'll be fine after a few days."

"A few days?" said Martin. "The poor guy was a gibbering wreck from what I've heard. It'll take more than a few days."

"He'll need plenty of rest but he's fine, believe me" said Ophelia. "I'm very happy with how it went."

"What exactly did you do?" asked Martin.

"I rebalanced his equilibrium. He won't have any more nightmares."

"Robert, could you put what Ophelia just said into plain English for me please" protested Martin.

"Oh that I could my dear chap, oh that I could."

"It worked didn't it?" said Phyllis, a big smile on her face.

"Beautifully Phyllis, beautifully."

"Now they're talking in riddles. It's time to give up" said Robert.

"Did you use some of that oil?" asked Sue.

"No, no need" said Ophelia.

Now even Sue was curious. "Well come on Ophelia, spill the beans. I'm intrigued."

"In good time Sue, in good time."

As Sue was trying to work out what was behind Ophelia's magic touch, a car could be heard pulling up outside.

"Oh bloody hell, I think it's Craig" said Sue looking from behind the net. "Come on Phyllis, the two naughty school girls have to go to their room without any supper."

"Here, I'll clear away the cups" said Ophelia, springing into action.

Shortly they heard a knock on the door. Ophelia opened it. "Hello Craig, how are ....."

"They're going to press charges. They're actually going to formally start proceedings for a trial."

"Not on my watch" said Martin. "I've seen the report, it wouldn't hold water in any court. Don't worry Craig, I'm going to see her tomorrow. I'll get this cleared up."

"But what can we do? They've got the blouse, they've got ....."

"They've got nothing" said Martin. "Trust me, I've dealt with more criminal cases than I care to remember and this one is laughable. It's clear that the evidence was planted. The lock on that door could be picked by any criminal worth his salt. That's just the start of it. Don't worry, by the time I've finished with them, they'll be left looking totally incompetent – which they are!"

"I hope you're right" said Craig. "Elspeth hasn't slept a wink over the last few nights."

"We'll get it sorted out Craig" added Ophelia.

"I wish I shared your confidence" said Craig. "I honestly don't know where to turn."

"Look Craig, why don't you go home? I know it sounds hard but try to relax. We'll give you a call tomorrow after Martin's spoken to the police" said Robert.

Craig sighed. "Ok, but if you could let me know as soon as you hear anything I'd appreciate it."

"We will, honest."

Craig said goodbye and drove off in his car.

"This makes it even more necessary for us to get into that house" said Ophelia.

"We could be totally barking up the wrong tree Ophelia. We're assuming that the murderer actually lives there. It could be just a coincidence that the tunnel lies underneath it."

"So how do you explain getting the body up to the ruined church?"

"Oh I don't know, we seem to be going round in circles here."

"We forgot to tell Phyllis and Sue to come down. Poor old Phyllis wouldn't dare to show her face after the way you chewed her out Robert."

"Thanks for reminding me of that Martin" said Robert. He called up the stairs. "Sue, Phyllis. It's all clear."

Sue and Phyllis both walked down the stairs. Phyllis looked particularly anxious. "Is it true they're going to take it to trial? This is horrendous. Martin, you've got to do something."

"Don't worry Phyllis, I'm going to see her tomorrow."

"Be honest with me Martin, she will be ok won't she?"

"Phyllis, if I was seriously worried I'd be going down to that police station tonight."

"Ok, but please don't let them send her to prison. She's innocent, totally innocent."

Martin continued to reassure Phyllis that Elspeth would be fine, although they were still concerned about the stumbling block of the house and how to gain access to it. They decided to drop the subject eventually and as the evening wore on, the days events had made everybody feel tired. Everybody that is except Martin. Sue noticed it at first. Ophelia noticed it. Robert and Phyllis also felt that he was acting a little strange.

"Maybe you should go to bed Martin" said Ophelia. "I think you're going to have your work cut out for you tomorrow."

"Yes, maybe I will." He shuffled restlessly in his seat. "Strange though, I don't feel tired."

Phyllis and Ophelia looked at each other and Ophelia nodded.

"If you're not feeling tired, I can do a light hypnosis on you to help you sleep" said Ophelia.

"No, I'll be ok, I just need to .... um .... "

"Come on Martin, you look tired."

Martin seemed listless. Sue and Robert looked at Ophelia with concern. Were they going to have a repeat of what happened the other night? Martin seemed to stand up and start walking around aimlessly.

"Come on Martin, this way" said Phyllis.

At first he seemed reluctant to go, but Phyllis guided him to the stairs. Ophelia seemed to be muttering something under her breath. Phyllis walked in front and Ophelia followed behind.

"What the hell is going on?" whispered Sue to Robert.

"I have no idea, but I don't like it" said Robert.

"Shall we follow them?" asked Sue.

"No, I don't understand it, but Ophelia seems to have everything under control."

As Sue and Robert continued to wonder what was going

on, Phyllis opened Martin's bedroom door. She gently coaxed him to sit down on the bed.

"Help him to lie down Phyllis" whispered Ophelia.

By now Martin didn't seem to know what was happening and it was relatively easy for Phyllis to help him settle.

"Here, take this" said Ophelia as she handed Phyllis a small jar. "Now when I indicate, gently sprinkle it around the bed."

Phyllis nodded. Ophelia continued to speak almost in a whisper. She made various gestures with her hand. Martin became slightly agitated but didn't move. Ophelia nodded to Phyllis who proceeded to take some of the contents from the small jar and sprinkle it around the bed.

"Now Phyllis, the response."

Ophelia muttered some words, paused for a few seconds and Phyllis offered a response. Ophelia muttered a few more words and Phyllis again gave a response. This went on for ten minutes, in which time Martin's body went into jerks and spasms. His breathing became erratic but Ophelia continued reciting particular words. She then turned away from the bed, walked forward and sat in front of it with Martin's feet just inches away. Her head went down as she continued reciting words and Phyllis sprinkled more of the contents around the bed and now just above Martin's head. Suddenly Ophelia flung her arms out. "BEGONE SPIRIT! GO BACK TO THY MAKER AND POUR ON HIM TENFOLD THE CURSE HE HAS USED! SO MOTE IT BE!"

Sue and Robert looked at each other alarmed as a mighty wind seemed to sweep over the cottage.

"What the hell caused that?" asked Sue.

"God only knows."

Upstairs Ophelia got up and turned around. Martin seemed to be very calm. Ophelia gave him a little prod but it would seem as though he'd gone to sleep. She looked up at Phyllis and smiled.

"Thank you blessed sister." Phyllis responded with the same. They gave a small ceremonial bow to each other and then quietly left the room, turning the light off and closing the door behind them. They walked quietly down the stairs.

"Did you hear that wind?" asked Robert.

Ophelia said nothing but smiled.

"Ophelia, what just happened?" Robert wasn't sure he wanted to know the answer but asked the question nevertheless.

"A cure Robert, a cure."

"A cure? What do you mean? Is Martin ok? He looked really agitated and I've never seen anybody act so strange."

"He's fine Robert, trust me. He's absolutely fine. He's fast asleep. Nothing will disturb him tonight."

Robert knew better than to ask Ophelia what had happened upstairs. She would no doubt start talking in riddles and he was in no mood for cryptic puzzles. "Dare I ask if you did the same to Martin tonight as you did to Mr. Jenkins?"

"I did indeed" said Ophelia. "Though it was easier this evening as I had Phyllis to help me."

This didn't really answer Robert's question as he would have liked but he knew that he should be content with this answer ..... for now.

"Now all we have to do is wait" said Ophelia.

"Wait?"

"Yes" replied Ophelia. "For the universal law to unfold. I wonder who it will be."

Chapter Nineteen

The following morning Sue and Ophelia woke up first. They gingerly walked down the stairs in an effort to not disturb Robert who was sleeping on the sofa in the lounge. They went to the kitchen and Sue proceeded to make some tea.

"Look Ophelia, I'll be the first to admit I don't have the first clue about some of the things you and Phyllis believe. Most of the time I just listen to Phyllis talking about this crystal or that pack of tarot cards and I don't really take it all in. I won't pretend to have any interest in it. But what happened last night has completely puzzled me. That sudden gust of wind blowing up out of nowhere – I won't pretend it didn't freak me out a bit."

"There's no need to be scared Sue. All I did was send back a psychic attack."

"Psychic attack?"

"Yes. It's a lot more common than you think. You've heard of the idea of somebody having the hex put on them haven't you?"

"Well yes, but I can't say I believe that actually happens."

"Well that's where you're wrong, because it does."

"Really?"

"Yes, really."

"So are you telling me somebody put some sort of hex on Martin .... and the other solicitor and that's why they had those nightmares?"

"They weren't nightmares, they were astral entities sent to quite literally terrify them out of their minds."

"But why?"

"Think about it Sue. They both represented Elspeth and from what I can gather, the murder charge is totally flawed and both Martin and Mr Jenkins knew that. They could both easily clear Elspeth's name."

"So .... so ..... you're saying that somebody's trying to thwart their efforts?"

"Precisely."

"But who .... and why?"

"Oh Sue, don't pretend to be so ignorant. You know why – so that Elspeth takes the wrap for this murder. As for the who ..... well it's going to be interesting finding out the answer to that question."

"But how can we do that?"

"Easy. We wait."

"Wait?"

"Yes."

"For what?"

"Sue, in many religions, philosophies, belief systems there is a law that says if you send energy out to somebody, be it good or bad, it can be returned ten fold. You've heard of karma haven't you?"

"Yes, isn't that where if you do bad things in your life you come back as a rat in your next?"

"Well, that's one idea, but the general philosphy is that if you send bad thoughts or wishes out to somebody, it can bounce back on you with more force."

"So you're saying that Martin and this Mr Jenkins were hexed or cursed – and that whoever did it is going to get it back?"

"You could put it like that."

"Well if that's the case, how will we know?"

"Just wait – I'm sure it will become obvious."

"If it does work, remind me never to get on your wrong side" said Sue.

Ophelia laughed. "You have nothing to worry about there Sue. Whoever did this did it with malice and intent. They wanted to make sure that Mr Jenkins and Martin were sent permanently off the case."

"But that's just plain ridiculous. I mean the only thing that will happen is they get another solicitor to represent Elspeth. Whoever's doing this can't go around cursing everybody that comes along surely?"

"Perhaps, but if enough people get wind that this is happening, it may put them off, and in the meantime the police go ahead with preparing for trial."

"Good God there are some nasty people in this world."

"Sadly you're right. That's been the same throughout

time immemorial."

"Oh what a cheerful thought to have with your morning cuppa."

They heard noises coming from the lounge. Robert had woken up and walked into the kitchen.

"Morning Robert. Would you like some tea and toast?"

"Thanks Sue, but don't worry. I'll get it."

"It looks like Martin slept through last night" she added.

"Thank goodness for that." Robert deliberately avoided Ophelia's gaze. He didn't need a look that said 'I told you so' this early in the morning.

Phyllis walked downstairs. "Morning everyone" she said.

"Morning Phyl. We're about to make a fresh brew. Take a seat."

They sat around the kitchen table, discussing the plans for the day ahead. Eventually Martin woke up and came to join them.

"How are you feeling Martin?" asked Ophelia.

"I know this sounds strange, but I haven't felt this good in years."

"Glad to hear it. What time are you meeting with Elspeth today?"

"11 o'clock. I'm just going to run through my notes and then I'll go over to see her. I'm looking forward to shredding their so-called evidence to pieces. I do enjoy a good tear down of the other side when they clearly haven't got their facts right."

"Easy tiger" said Phyllis. "At least have the courtesy to barbecue your victims before you eat them. Raw meat's not good for your digestion."

Martin laughed. "I always did like your sense of humour Phyllis."

"I was being serious."

"What about the rest of us? What can we do?"

"Well" said Robert, "I was thinking that you and I could go back to the library today Ophelia and have another look at that book. I did manage to get quite a bit of information from it but I may have missed something."

"I think that's a good idea Robert" agreed Ophelia.

"Well Phyl, I wonder what wall we should stare at today.

I feel the wall in the lounge might be quite fascinating although if I get too excited I'm not sure I would be able to contain myself. How about we start with the wall in the hall?"

Phyllis decided to join in on Sue's act. "Well I don't know about that Mrs. Baylock, I mean a girl can only take so much excitement in one day and I just know I'd probably fart or dribble if I got too excited!"

"OR BOTH!" said Sue.

"Now look you two, I feel bad enough as it is that you're having to lay low, but I promise you we'll get this case solved once and for all, and then you can go and stare at blades of grass in a big open field for eternity" said Robert.

"Ooooh, did you hear what the nice man said Phyllis? He said we can go and join the cows in the field and have fun looking at the blades of grass."

"Sarcasm is the lowest form of wit Sue Baylock and if you carry on, I'll give up on this case altogether and leave you here forever."

"You're all heart Mr Whitehead, all heart. Being walled up here forever sounds like such a joy."

"Actually that reminds me" said Robert. "When I was reading that book the other day it mentioned the fact that in the old priory one of the monks got a nun pregnant and they walled the poor woman up."

"What?" said Phyllis indignantly. "You mean the monk got to dip his wick and get the poor woman pregnant and she alone paid the consequences for it. Why wasn't he walled up?"

"Well maybe whoever did it didn't fess up" said Sue. "What a bastard!"

"Ok, before we start getting into a debate about toxic masculinity, I need a shower, then I'm going to get dressed and then head on out to the library if you'd care to join me Ophelia. I give you my word I won't wall you up in the library."

"In that case I shall accept your offer."

Ophelia, Martin and Robert proceeded to get ready to go out while Sue and Phyllis cleared the table. "It can't be much longer Phyl" said Sue.

Ophelia walked into the kitchen at the tail end of the conversation. "Don't worry Sue, it won't be long now at all. I know it won't."

"I hope you're right Ophelia. I really hope you're right."

Before long, Robert and Ophelia were setting off to visit the library and Martin was going through his notes before he also went off to meet up with Elspeth.

"I have to say Robert, there's some nice countryside around here."

"Can't argue with you there Ophelia. Nice little villages scattered around."

"I know you don't want to Robert, but I really would like to just go and take a look at that house today."

"Well once we've finished in the library I don't suppose it will do any harm, as long as it doesn't look obvious that we're giving it a once over."

Robert pulled over to the side of the road. "The library's just over there."

He and Ophelia got out of the car and walked over to the main entrance. Robert could see the lady he spoke to the other day and managed to catch her eye. "Good morning, I'm back again. This is Ophelia, the lady you spoke to the other day." It was a little white lie as it was in fact Sue, but that was a mere detail.

"Good morning" she replied.

"I was wondering if we could look at that book again" asked Robert.

"Yes of course" said the librarian. "Hang on, I put it back on the shelf after you looked at it so it'll be in the local history section." She walked over to the shelves that housed the books on local history. "Well that's odd, it was definitely here. Let me check again." She searched through the books but to no avail. "Hang on, I'll check with my colleague to see if it's been taken out." She went over to the main desk and asked the woman sitting there to check on the system to see if the book had been taken out. It was obvious just by looking at their mystified expressions that it hadn't. She walked back over to Robert and Phyllis. "I don't understand it. I only put it back the other day. It hasn't been checked out either. I wonder if it's fallen below the trolley." She bent down to check underneath but Robert and Ophelia already knew instinctively that it wasn't there. Somebody had obviously taken it. "Well I don't understand. I'm really sorry. I'll keep checking if you want to come back later."

"Ok. Thanks for your help though."

Both he and Ophelia walked out of the library and headed back to the car. "That's very strange Robert. It's almost as if somebody knows we're onto them. But how? We haven't mentioned this to anybody."

"I know. We need to start stepping up a gear. It's beginning to feel as though the suspect is ten steps ahead of us."

They drove towards the second village without a word. Robert pointed out the house to Ophelia as the car was still some distance away. Two women were standing directly in front and making gestures whilst pointing to the front door.

"That's odd" said Ophelia. "Wonder what's going on there?"

"I don't know but I think my curiosity is going to get the better of me and cause me to throw caution to the wind" said Robert. He pulled in on the other side of the road. He opened the window to see if he could eavesdrop on the conversation. He only caught a few words.

"Totally manic .... flung open the door .... eyes were like nothing I've seen ..... scared the hell out of me."

"Something's obviously happened" said Ophelia. "We need to find out."

"I've had an idea" said Robert. "I'm not usually somebody who likes to fabricate the truth, but on this occasion ...... wait here." He grabbed a notepad and pen from his glove compartment and walked across the road.

"Good morning ladies. Sorry to disturb you but I'm from the local press and want to find out more about what happened." Ophelia heard Robert's spiel from the car and smiled.

"Nice one Robert. You're learning."

"It was like nothing I've ever seen" said one of the women. "We were coming out of the pub as it had just gone 11 and we were walking down the road when he just ran out screaming."

"Who ran out screaming?"

"Well the man who lives there of course" she said pointing to the house.

"Do you know his name?"

"No. He's lived there for years but doesn't really speak to anybody. A bit stuck up if you ask me. Thinks he's better than the rest of us. But last night, my God, he was acting like a man possessed. Came running out of the house shouting, his eyes were like golfballs and the look of sheer terror on his face. Well we were terrified. We thought there was somebody else in the house who was trying to murder him and they were going to follow him out any minute. We all but ran over to the other side of the road. Anyway he ran right into the middle of the road, fell down and started scratching at the tarmac. A few guys in the pub came out when they heard all the racket and wondered what was going on. They tried to pick him up and calm him down but his arms were going everywhere. He was screaming until his voice was hoarse. We got somebody to call an ambulance but it seemed like the longest wait I've ever experienced. It took eight men to hold him down. When the ambulance finally arrived they gave him some sort of sedative and once he'd calmed down, they put him on a stretcher and took him off. I'll never forget the sound he was making though. It gave me nightmares."

"Had anything like this happened before?" asked Robert.

"No, I mean he's lived there for years and as I say, never talks to anybody. Then all of a sudden this."

"Did the ambulance crew have any ideas of what may have caused it?"

"Well they did say the only thing that they think may be responsible was some sort of hallucinogenic, like that drug they took back in the sixties ..... what was it called now ...."

"LSD?" offered Robert.

"Yes, that's right. Why on earth anybody would want to take something like that if it's going to do that to you, I haven't a clue."

"Did they say how long he may have to stay in hospital?"

"No, they didn't say anything, they were too busy trying to keep him calm and get him onto the stretcher. It's really unsettled my nerves. I won't feel safe walking down this street at night again, and I've lived here all my life."

"Is there anything else you can remember about the incident?" asked Robert.

"Not really. It all happened so suddenly. I can still see his eyes .... " The lady shuddered.

"Well thank you for your time" said Robert.

"Will it be in the papers then?" asked Robert's informant.

"It all depends. I'd need to get a name and do a bit more research but what you've told me has been very helpful. Thank you."

Robert said goodbye and walked back to his car.

"Did you hear all of that?" he asked.

"Most of it" said Ophelia. "And I can tell you now Robert, this is the house where the murderer lives .... and I wouldn't mind betting it's the house where the murder occurred."

"Well let's not run before we can walk Ophelia."

"Robert, who needs to run or walk when you can fly? I'm telling you, this is the house."

"Go on ...... what are you suggesting?"

"We come back here tonight and get in."

Robert put his head in his hand. "Why did I just know you were going to say that?"

"Robert, it could be the only chance we get. He could be back home tomorrow. What else do you suggest?"

"I don't know but I don't like it."

"They're going to take this to court if we don't do anything."

"The emotional blackmail card. Nice move Ophelia."

"Robert, I'm not trying to blackmail you, I'm just pointing out the simple truth. This may be the one and only chance we get. We just HAVE to take it."

Robert sighed again. "Look, let's just go back to the cottage for now and think about it."

"Very well, but think we must."

They drove back to the cottage in silence. When Phyllis opened the door, she looked slightly worried.

"What's happened Phyllis, is Elspeth ok? Is Martin ok?"

"It's nothing to do with them. We just had some crazy woman here."

"Crazy woman? What do you mean?"

"Sue and I were sitting in the lounge when a car pulled

up and somebody walked up to the door and started hammering on it. She was screaming for somebody called Darius and saying that she knew he was here and that she was going to get him. Well of course we didn't answer the door because nobody knows we're here. She was doing this for about ten minutes before she went away again but she seemed pretty livid."

"How weird" said Ophelia.

"I'm sure she had an Australian accent" said Phyllis. "I'm surprised she didn't knock the door down."

"Has Martin returned yet?" asked Robert.

"No not yet" said Phyllis.

"Things are getting weirder and weirder round here" said Robert.

"I'll say" said Ophelia.

"Anyway, did you two get any more information from that book in the library?"

"It wasn't there."

"What, you mean somebody else has borrowed it?"

"No, I just mean that it hadn't been checked out and it wasn't on the library shelf."

"Are you sure?"

"Positive. The librarian who showed it to me the other day couldn't understand what had happened to it. She said she would have another look for it but Ophelia and I are both of the opinion that somebody has lifted it."

"But surely nobody knew you were looking at it?" Phyllis had a puzzled look on her face.

"That's what we thought Phyllis, but obviously somebody does."

"So we're no further forward" said Sue.

"Oh but we are Sue" said Ophelia, a smile on her face.

"What do you mean?"

"We decided to drive over and look at this house and we noticed two women standing in front of it pointing to the door. Well I must say I was quite impressed with Robert because he actually threw himself into the role of a journalist and started asking them questions. They had quite a story to tell as well."

"Oh go on." Sue was all ears.

"Apparently the occupant of the house suddenly ran out screaming in terror and started clutching the tarmac on the road.

Several men had to come out of the local pub and try to contain him. They called an ambulance and the paramedics finally managed to sedate him but by all accounts it caused quite a scene."

"So you were right Ophelia and the spell worked!!" Phyllis was clapping her hands in pure glee.

"It certainly did Phyllis. I knew it would."

"Whoa, whoa, whoa. Will you two slow down and tell me and Robert what on earth you're both talking about?"

"Ok Sue, I'm going to be completely honest with you. Robert, I know you're going to find this hard to believe but I'm going to tell you anyway."

Robert looked at Ophelia with a slight look of concern. She proceeded to ignore him.

"I just knew instinctively that something was wrong when Mr Jenkins, the first solicitor, had a breakdown and then Martin did. I knew it wasn't coincidence. That's why I went back home to get one of my books."

"Oh, that's why you went home" said Sue. "Which book was that?"

"It's a book about psychic attack. Remember what I was telling you this morning? Well this book has a lot of information about psychic attacks and how to return them to their senders. That's why Phyllis and I took Martin upstairs last night. We performed a very powerful little ritual that I found in the book. It's very old and all I can say is that whoever sent the original attack knows about magic."

"You mean like black magic?" said Sue.

"I would call it old magic, but yes, some of it definitely has darker elements to it."

"So what you're saying is that you sent this psychic attack back to the originator and it caused them to run screaming out of their house."

"Precisely Sue, precisely, and it just so happens that the individual came running out of the very house that we believe lies over the tunnel."

"Well it would all seem to tie in" said Sue. "But the problem is you have no proof. Trust me, when you've worked for a law firm as long as I have, you need to make sure you dot all your 'i's and cross all your 't's.

"That's why we're going back there tonight."

"Tonight??!"

"Yes Sue. Whilst the occupant is still in hospital we need to get in there to look around."

"But what are you hoping to find? I mean let's be honest, even if they did commit the murder there, they're hardly likely to leave knives and bits of bloody cloth lying around the place."

"No, but even so. We need to go and see if we can find anything that will give us a clue as to why they committed the murder."

"The problem is Ophelia that these days people don't need a motive to kill somebody. Some psychos do it just for the sheer hell of it."

"Very true, but it's the way the murderer deliberately took the body up to the church that makes me think it wasn't just a random killing. I think there was a reason behind it."

"So you're definitely going to go then? Isn't it a bit risky?"

"There's always going to be a risk, but I'm sure it won't take long to pick the lock and get in, hopefully before somebody sees us."

Sue turned to Robert. "Are you ok about doing this?"

Robert looked at Sue with what appeared to be defeated eyes. "I can't say I'm pleased at the prospect of doing it, but Ophelia has a point when she says it might be the one and only chance we get."

"Well for God's sake be careful if you do."

"The thing that concerns me though" said Robert, "is if that woman comes back and starts trying to break the door down."

"Well I'm sure Martin will be back by then so there'll be three of us" said Sue.

"Oh yes, I forgot about that."

Chapter Twenty

Martin arrived back at the cottage two hours later.

"How did it go?" asked Robert.

"It went very well" said Martin. "I literally tore their argument to pieces, told them to come back here and we could demonstrate how easily this lock could be picked, asked them if they'd checked the blouse for DNA, to which they said they hadn't, at which point I chewed them out for their sheer incompetence and negligence. I told them it was vital we have the blouse checked straight away for any specs of the murderer's blood."

"But do you think there'll be any on there?" asked Phyllis.

"Well there's only one way to find out. At a guess, it looked like a pretty violent death so I wouldn't be surprised if the victim fought back and caused some injury to the murderer. With any luck she did."

"I've just had a thought Robert."

"I think I know what you're thinking Ophelia ...... would it involve Ian's device?"

"Great minds think alike."

"Trouble is I don't have it with me."

"Well I don't wish to sound pushy, but don't you think in the circumstances it might be worth going home to get it?"

"I could do. It would have to be tomorrow though if we're going to commit this burglary tonight."

"Hang on, what are you talking about? What device?" asked Martin.

Robert looked at Martin. "Look Martin, erm, is there any way you could get a blood sample from the victim's blouse for us? It would have to be dissolved in water only, no solution."

"I'm not sure they'd allow it and why on earth would you want it anyway?"

"Even if we tell him, he's not going to believe us" said Ophelia.

"Believe what?" Martin looked slightly concerned.

Here was a man who had been a criminal lawyer for years, working with facts and evidence. How were they going to tell him firstly, that Ophelia had successfully sent a psychic attack that had been projected towards him back to the sender and then discuss how they could use a device to read the DNA from a blood sample which would contain the equivalent to a video recording of somebody's last moments?

Robert and Ophelia looked at each other as if to say "he's not ready for this yet."

"Just try if you can Martin, if not we'll have to use other methods."

Martin sat looking at both of them puzzled.

"I thought you didn't like riddles Robert, but now you're using them on me."

"Not exactly. I just need to make sure I pick the right moment to explain certain things."

They went over the last few days events until the evening came and the light was fading.

"I think we need to start preparing Robert" said Ophelia.

Robert reluctantly started to check through the list of the things they would need.

"Right" he said as he and Ophelia headed towards the car. "Wish us luck, and if we're not back in a couple of hours, bring a pie with a file into the police station as we'll probably need it."

"Don't even joke about things like that Robert" said Sue. "You'll be fine. Just keep a cool head and make sure one of you stays watch."

"Trouble is we won't be able to take a good look round and keep watch at the same time" he replied.

"I've got an idea" said Sue.

"What's that?" asked Robert.

"Why don't I go with you?"

"What????!!"

"Why not? Look, it's dark, I can sneak out to the car and nobody's going to see me. If I stay by the window in the front of the house I can keep watch while you and Ophelia take a good look around."

Robert frowned. "No, I don't think that's a good idea."

"Well I do" said Sue.

"Actually Robert, Sue may have a point. If we're both looking at different rooms we could get the search done a lot quicker."

"It makes perfect sense to me" added Phyllis.

Robert shook his head, more out of frustration than anything. "Why do I let myself get talked into these situations?"

"I take it that's a yes then?" said Sue.

"Ok, but make sure you stay quiet and out of sight. We don't want to draw any attention to ourselves."

"Oh what a shame Robert, I was going to wear my best Paris cat walk gown and do a little dance down the stairs in front of the house."

"I'm being serious Sue."

"Oh for goodness sake Robert, you don't think I don't realise how serious this is? Of course I'm going to keep quiet."

"Come on then."

"Break a leg ..... oh, not literally of course, you know ...." said Phyllis.

"Thanks Phyll. We know what you mean."

The three set off in Robert's car. Both Ophelia and Sue had butterflies in their stomach, thinking about what might happen in the next hour or so. Robert was trying not to think about it.

The time passed quietly as the car drove through the first village and then the second one. The car pulled over to the side of the road about 100 yards away from the house.

"Ok Ophelia. You go first. We'll keep watch while you open the door. Once you've got it open, give us a slight wave. Sue, you then follow and I'll come shortly after."

"Right" said Ophelia and proceeded to get out of the car. She walked down the road towards the house looking all around her. It was quiet and there was nobody in sight. She went up to the front door and took out her lock pick. A few prods here ... a few twists there ... a small click ... a slight turn and ..... presto, she was in. She looked around to see if anybody was in sight. Nobody. She waved towards the car. Sue got out and walked quietly down the road. She crept quietly up the steps to the front door. Now it was Robert's turn. He opened the car door and got out, closing the door behind him as quietly as possible. He felt paranoid that 1,000 eyes were watching him, when in fact most people were more interested in watching their TVs. He walked into the house and took a look up and down the street before closing the door. He had his torch on and walked into the lounge. Ophelia and Sue were sitting on the sofa.

"What are you doing?" he almost hissed. "You could leave DNA on the sofa."

Ophelia looked at him, a little shaken. "I'm sorry Robert, but I had to sit down. I suddenly came over all dizzy and queasy."

"Sorry Ophelia, are you alright?"

She nodded. "I'm ok, it's just that ..... it's just that .... I could pick up the sensations of what happened here."

"What do you mean?"

"This is the very room where the victim was murdered."

"Are you sure?"

"Positive. I can feel it. There was a struggle. I don't know what happened because at first everything seemed to be calm. They were getting along fine and then .... something happened to change that."

"You mean he attempted to rape her?"

"No, that's what surprises me. He didn't. I'm sure if you ask for the autopsy report, there'll be no signs of sexual assault."

"Well what then?"

"I don't know. I need to focus. Sue, would you be a dear and keep an eye out at the window?"

"Of course I will Ophelia. Are you sure you're going to be ok?" Sue was genuinely concerned.

"I'll be fine once I get over the initial shock. It was so powerful when I first walked into the room, it just took me by surprise."

"Ok, well I'll keep watch while you two go and investigate."

Ophelia and Robert searched each room of the house methodically, leaving the lounge till last. "There's nothing in any other room of the house Robert. It all happened here."

"The thing is I can't see any real evidence."

"Hang on, shine your torch down here."

Robert pointed the beam of his torch onto the carpet where Ophelia pointed.

"I'm sure these are blood spots."

Sue was still looking out the window but looked quickly over at Ophelia. "You need to use luminol Ophelia."

"Luminol? What's that?"

"They use it in these forensic detectives documentaries all the time. It detects trace amounts of blood which lights up when they use a blue light after spraying it. Apparently it reacts with the iron in hemoglobin and shows up."

"Interesting Sue" said Robert. "Trouble is, how do we get the police to come round and carry such a test out? How would we explain the fact that we think there could be blood evidence here?"

"Good point" said Sue. "It was just a suggestion."

"Can I have your torch a minute Robert?" asked Ophelia.

"Of course." Robert handed her the torch.

She proceeded to walk around the room inspecting the carpets and the furniture. The torch skimmed across a bookcase. "Hello" she said. "Looks like there are some interesting titles in here." She knew that she should be looking for clues but she couldn't help having a quick nose at some of the titles in the bookcase. She suddenly stopped. "What's this?"

"What is it?" asked Robert. "Found something?"

Ophelia remained silent. She took something out of the bookcase. "Surely it can't be ..... surely ......"

"What is it Ophelia?"

"Sorry Robert, just give me a minute."

Robert waited, trying to be patient, but he could feel himself getting agitated.

"I must admit I'm getting slightly nervous" said Sue. "Any idea how long you're going to be Ophelia?"

Ophelia looked up and blinked, as if coming out of a trance. "Sorry Sue, I got a little distracted there. I think we've seen all we need to see here but we definitely need to ask Martin to get a blood sample for us. I think we've got most of the pieces to the jigsaw puzzle, but a blood sample will give us the missing piece, I'm sure of it."

"Ok, come on then. Let's just make sure it's all clear. Sue, you go first, then you Ophelia, and I'll follow you after. Here, take my keys so you can get into the car."

Sue quietly opened the front door and looked up and

down the street. All clear – she walked carefully down the steps so as not to trip and then slowly towards the car in case anybody was looking. She didn't want to arouse any suspicion. She opened the car door and got in. Ophelia followed shortly, slinking down the stairs and quietly towards the car. Robert took an extra cautious look before closing the door behind him and walking back to the car.

"Right, back to the cottage" he said as he started the car.

When they arrived back at the cottage, Martin answered the door. He shouted upstairs. "It's ok Phyllis, you can come down. It's Sue, Robert and Ophelia."

Phyllis tromped downstairs, obviously pleased that she didn't have to remain quiet whilst sitting upstairs. "How did it go?" she said. "Did you find anything?"

"Find anything?" said Ophelia. "Phyllis, you won't believe what I found."

"Oh?"

"Some solid evidence then?" asked Martin.

"Oh-er no, not quite, although I'm sure I saw some blood drops on the carpet."

"The trouble is how do we explain to the police that we found it without admitting that we broke in?" said Robert.

"Good point" said Martin. "And I'm afraid I'd have to deny all knowledge of what you did otherwise I could kiss goodbye to my career. I'd be struck off immediately."

"Mum's the word Martin" said Ophelia. "I do know for certain that the victim was murdered in that house though."

"Well, blood spots are a pretty good start, but let's not get ahead of ourselves. They're not conclusive proof unless DNA samples are tested" said Martin.

"I don't mean that. I mean the impressions I picked up when I walked in. It was horrible. I could feel what happened. It wasn't pleasant at all."

"Oh Ophelia, that's awful. Do you want me to give you some healing?"

"That's ok Phyllis, I'll be fine. But there is also something else I found, something that I believe is very significant."

"What's that?"

"Phyllis you won't believe it, but I was skimming the beam of the torch across a book case and some of the titles looked quite interesting. I took a closer look and you'll never guess what I found in there."

"Go on, tell me."

"A print of Samael's Grimoire."

"What??????? Surely not. It can't be. I read somewhere that there were only two copies in existence and one of them was in a German national library."

"That's right" said Ophelia.

"But how on earth did he lay his hands on that? It's one of the rarest Grimoire's ever printed."

"Grimoire? What's this about a Grimoire? Sorry ladies, what are you talking about?" asked Robert. He was completely lost.

"It's an ancient book of spells. But this isn't just any old Grimoire, it's one of the most powerful texts ever in the world of the occult. As Phyllis rightly says, there are only two of them in print, and one is indeed in a German national library. It's an extremely rare book and most people I know in our circles have heard of it, but nobody's ever seen it."

"Are you sure it's not some sort of fake?" asked Robert.

"I can assure you Robert, I had a quick look through some of its pages, and it's definitely not a fake. I had to be careful as the pages were so fragile. But my goodness, what a find. It explains everything."

"Explains everything? What do you mean?"

"The attack on Mr Jenkins and on Martin. The person who lives in that house obviously has extensive knowledge of ritual magic and they used a very powerful spell out of that book to send a psychic attack to both men. Luckily my book had a good counter-attack spell and we were able to return it to source and that's why the person who lives in that house ran out of it screaming the other night. Frankly it serves him right for being so evil."

Martin and Robert looked at each other. Ophelia caught their expressions.

"You two can be as cynical as you like. I don't expect you to believe me but I know it's true. I should think whoever sent that spell will be having quite a few sleepless nights for the next week or so."

"But if you're right and the ambulance took them to hospital, they might be heavily sedated in order to help them sleep."

"Oh sedation might help, but they are going to feel the fruits of their own evil in the next few days believe me."

"Well in the meantime" said Martin, wanting to change the subject, "we're no nearer finding the murderer."

"Oh but we are Martin" said Ophelia in a matter of fact voice. "It's the same person who lives in that house. All we need to do is find out who it is and then try to persuade the police to take him into custody."

"Yes but Ophelia, if you start telling the police about casting spells and psychic attacks, I don't wish to sound disrespectful, but do you honestly think they're going to take you very seriously? I wouldn't be surprised if they tried to take you straight to the funny farm."

"That's why you need to get the blood sample from that blouse Martin. Even a cold hard fact-lover like Robert knows that we'll get results from that. Isn't that right Robert?" Was Ophelia looking to Robert for support?

"Ophelia's right Martin. It will give us results. We've used it quite a few times before and it's never been wrong."

"I still can't get my head around the fact that some sort of device can read the DNA from a blood sample. It sounds completely ludicrous."

"If I were in your shoes, I'd feel exactly the same way" agreed Robert.

"But you're not in Martin's shoes" added Ophelia. "That's why you can show him that what we're saying is true."

"Baby steps Ophelia, baby steps."

Chapter Twenty-One

"I feel like I'm on tenterhooks waiting" said Sue. "There's got to be a way he can get a sample from their autopsy lab."

"Yes but Sue, solicitors aren't normally given access to blood or tissue samples. That's more the police's line" said Robert.

"But we've come so far, we only need that one little piece of hard evidence and I'm sure we'll solve the murder."

"Sue, I feel exactly the same way as you, but we can't go around trying to steal vital forensic evidence. It was bad enough that we broke into somebody's house last night."

"We didn't break in Robert, I just used something other than a key to open a door" said Ophelia. "Besides which, we were entering the house of a murderer, so I don't feel as though I've broken any sort of moral or legal code."

"Well whether we like it or not, we certainly broke a legal code. As for the moral one, that's open to debate."

"Open to debate?" said Ophelia indignantly. "How can you possibly say that?"

"Look Ophelia, whether you like it or not, we don't even have circumstantial evidence. Somebody running out of their house screaming is no proof that they're a murderer. And let's be honest, people can cut themselves accidentally at any time and leave bloodspots on a carpet. We're making far too many assumptions and the only way we can clarify if it is the murderer's house is to use the device with a blood sample."

"Well I still think you should go and get the device now in readiness just in case Martin does manage to get hold of a blood sample."

"And if he doesn't it would be a total waste of my time."

"I'm with Ophelia on this one Robert" said Sue. "We're just sitting here waiting for Martin to contact us and in the meantime, if we got the device, we'd have it in readiness."

"It's not just down the road Sue, it's a 100 mile round trip. I don't mind doing it but I want to make sure I'm doing it for good reason."

Robert's phone rang. "Hello? Oh hello Martin."

Sue, Phyllis and Ophelia all looked at each other. Was this the news they were hoping for?

"Uh-huh. Uh-huh. Ok. Oh really? Strange. I wonder why. That does seem odd. What about Elspeth. Oh, oh. Oh that's ridiculous. Well ok. Alright, I'll see you soon." Robert ended the call.

"Translation please?" said Sue.

"They're running the DNA tests and should have the results back in the next few days."

Sue rolled her eyes. "More waiting."

"Hang on Sue. Martin managed to speak to one of the forensic team and he explained that he wanted a blood sample as part of his evidence. Not quite the truth, but not exactly a lie. So hopefully in the next few days we will have our blood sample."

"Oh that's great news!" said Phyllis.

"Hold on Phyllis. Don't get too excited. We don't know what blood group Emily was yet so we have to make sure we know that the person running the DNA genetic memory module has the same blood group."

"Well hopefully that shouldn't be too difficult" said Sue.

"Hopefully not, we'll just have to wait and see."

"You mentioned something being strange. What was that about?" asked Ophelia.

"Well Craig hasn't been down to the police station in days. He usually goes down a couple of times a day to ask for any progress and to see if Elspeth needed anything. But she hasn't heard anything from him."

"You don't think he's had an accident do you?" said Phyllis.

"I could try giving him a call" said Robert.

"Go ahead Robert, give him a call" said Ophelia.

Robert took his notebook out of his pocket and typed in the number Craig had given him. He looked at the others and shook his head. "Nothing. It's just going through to his voicemail."

"I hope the murderer hasn't got to him" said Phyllis.

"I don't think that's likely Phyl" said Sue.

"But how do you know? I mean if the murderer was

willing to send a psychic attack to both the first solicitor and Martin, who's to say he's not willing to kill somebody, especially somebody so close to Elspeth?"

"No Phyllis, I think we can rule that out" said Ophelia. "There's got to be a good reason."

An hour later Martin returned to the cottage.

"Hi Martin" said a very deflated Phyllis.

"Oh dear, what's happened here?" he replied.

"Oh nothing, it's just that we seem to be waiting all the time and not really getting anywhere. It's starting to get so frustrating. We don't seem to be moving any further forward."

"Well I'm doing my best Phyllis and it looks as though I am going to get that blood sample so all isn't lost."

"I know but we've got to wait days before we can actually pick it up. I'm really starting to suffer with cabin fever."

"I understand Phyllis. I do think that it might be best if you and Sue went home. That way you wouldn't have to be cooped up in here all day."

"No Martin, I can't just leave Elspeth. She's got nobody. Looks like even Craig has deserted here."

"It does seem strange that he hasn't been around for the last few days. It's not like him at all. I hope he's alright."

"Well he may turn up soon. He may have just had things to do."

"Still seems odd" said Phyllis.

"Talking of odd" said Martin, "I saw the strangest thing today."

"Oh?" said Robert.

"I'm sure it was outside the house you broke into the other night."

"We didn't break into it Martin" corrected Ophelia.

"Ok, well the house you 'gained access' to the other night" he said.

"What about it?" Ophelia looked at him with interest.

"Well as I was driving past it, there was a woman banging on the front door, shouting loudly. I stopped to see what was going on and she was really ranting at the occupant to come out and get his just deserts. I'm sure it was an Australian accent. Anyway, some of the neighbours came out to see what the commotion was. I think they must have told her that he was taken away in an ambulance a few nights ago as she seemed to calm down a bit, but my God she looked absolutely livid."

"That sounds exactly like the woman who came round here a few nights ago doesn't it Sue?"

"Yes it does. Did you hear who she was calling for Martin?" asked Sue.

"I didn't quite hear the name but she was threatening all kinds of curses on him."

"And you said she definitely had an Australian accent?"

"Yes, I'm sure of it. I didn't stay around too long as I didn't want to draw any attention to myself but she looked pretty riled up, that's for sure."

"This is just getting stranger and stranger. Robert, I really think you should go home tomorrow and pick the device up" said Ophelia. "We need some answers and we need them fast."

"It's a shame you didn't speak to that woman Martin" said Sue. "You could have asked her what business she had with this guy. We may have learned something."

"To be honest Sue, she was so angry, I honestly don't think any sort of reasoning would have calmed her down. Even the neighbours were keeping their distance as they were talking to her. I think they were worried that if they got too close, she'd probably start attacking them. She might not have been quite the full picnic."

"You mean she had nothing between her two bits of bread?"

"That analogy would fit perfectly."

"On the contrary Martin, I get the feeling she knew exactly what she was doing" said Sue.

"I do too" said Ophelia. "I wish I'd been there. I'm sure I could have tried to reason with her."

"To be honest Ophelia, after the visit we had from her the other night, I was quite relieved she didn't break the door down" said Phyllis.

Chapter Twenty-Two

Several days had passed and Robert had finally decided it would be a good time to go home and pick up Ian Pemberton's device. He collected several items that he would need for his journey and bade the others a farewell until he returned tomorrow. He decided to drive at night as he thought the traffic might be better. Ophelia and Martin waved at the gate as he drove off in his car. Sue and Phyllis wanted to come and wave him off as well, but he insisted that they stick to the plan of keeping out of sight.

"I wonder if he was a jailer in a previous life" said Phyllis. "If I didn't know any better, I could swear he's enjoying our incarceration."

"Oh don't be unkind Phyl, he's just trying to keep us safe, although in some ways, if we were visible it might bring the murderer out of his hiding hole."

"You mean use us as targets?" asked Phyllis.

"Well, I didn't quite have those words in mind but ....."

"But open targets we would be."

"Probably."

Ophelia and Martin returned to the cottage.

"I hope he has a smooth journey. I don't think there are any roadworks but they keep putting them up everywhere."

"Oh yes" replied Martin. "Cones running along the carriage for miles and miles and miles, and not a workman in sight."

Martin's phone rang. "Hello? Oh yes? Yes? Oh really? Great, when can I come to pick it up? Oh right, yes, yes, I can do that tomorrow. Ok, thank you."

"Is that the sample?" asked Phyllis excitedly. "Is it ready?"

"Yes it is Phyllis."

"Finally! Thank heavens for that. Robert will be back tomorrow and then we can find out who's responsible for Emily's murder."

"I still don't understand how you can claim to find evidence like that from a blood sample."

"Wait and see Martin, wait and see" said Phyllis.

Ophelia went into the kitchen to make some tea for the group. She busied herself clearing a few things away and pottering about while the kettle boiled. What was that? It sounded like something tapping outside. Strange. She peered through the pane of glass on the door panel but couldn't see anything. There was that noise again. Where was it coming from? Should she ask Martin to go and take a look? No, that would be silly. She was quite capable of going and investigating for herself. She opened the kitchen door and went out into the garden. It was silent. She was just about to walk back in again when she heard the tapping sound again. It seemed to be coming from the side of the cottage. The problem was that there was no light there so she wouldn't be able to see anything. She strained her eyes in the darkness. There it was again. What on earth was causing that noise? She walked a bit further to see where the sound was coming from. She could see vague shapes but nothing tangible. Perhaps she should go in and get a torch ...... perhaps ....

Phyllis, Sue and Martin had been talking amongst themselves when Sue suddenly realised that it had gone quiet in the kitchen. What on earth was Ophelia doing? She'd gone out ages ago to make some tea. "You don't think she's gone to China to get the tea do you?" she said.

"I'll go and help her" said Phyllis. She walked through to the kitchen. She came swiftly back into the lounge. "She's gone!"

"What do you mean she's gone?" said Sue.

"The back door's slightly ajar and she's not there. I even went into the garden to see if she was outside but she's nowhere to be seen."

"But that doesn't make sense" said Sue. "She was only going to make some tea. Are you sure she's not upstairs?"

"No, I don't think so. I'll go and check anyway." Phyllis went upstairs, calling Ophelia's name. She came back down minutes later. "She's not here. What's happened?"

"But this is silly" said Sue, a slight nervousness in her voice.

Phyllis could detect Sue's anxiety and this only served to make her more anxious. "What's going on? Surely she can't be far away. Why would she have gone outside? I don't like this."

"I'll go and look for her" said Martin. "You two stay here and lock the door behind me."

"But we should go with you Martin" said Phyllis. "If somebody's out there and you're on your own, they could take you too."

"No Phyllis. You stay inside and lock the door. I''ll take a torch and ...... " he reached into the kitchen drawer and took out a carving knife "this."

"Oh Martin, be careful, you don't know who's out there."

"Don't worry I'll be careful. Now I'm not going anywhere until I hear you lock the door behind me ok?"

"Alright" said Phyllis, though she was none too happy at this latest development. She turned to Sue. "Sue, I don't mind telling you I'm scared."

"You're not alone Phyl, believe me. I don't know what's happening and I don't like it. What the hell is going on?"

"What if .... what if ..... somebody is out there and they ...."

"Don't think about it Phyl, Martin will be fine. He's got his wits about him."

"I hope you're right. Do you think we should call the police?"

"Not yet. Let's wait for five minutes. If Martin's not back by then we'll call them."

They sat in silence waiting for what seemed like eternity. They almost leapt out of their skin when they heard a knock on the kitchen door. They had turned the light off and decided to leave it off as they walked slowly into the kitchen. They heard Martin's voice calling.

"It's ok Sue, it's Martin." Phyllis turned the light on and unlocked the door.

"I can't see her anywhere" he said. "It doesn't make sense. People just don't wander off in the dead of night."

"But surely she can't be far away. I've never known Ophelia to run anywhere and she'd hardly leave her jacket behind and go wandering off like this. It doesn't make sense. What's happening Martin?"

"I don't know Phyllis. I could go and search in the car for her."

"I don't think that's a bad idea" said Sue.

"Ok, well lock the door again and I'll be back shortly."

"Oh no" said Sue. "We're coming with you. I'm not being funny Martin but if there's some psycho out there I don't want Phyllis and I to be his next abductees. It wouldn't take a lot to break one of the windows."

"The problem is, if Ophelia did return and there was nobody there with the door locked, she'd be stuck outside" said Martin.

"Hmmm, that's a good point" said Sue. "Ok, well go and have a drive around and call me if you find her ok. You've got my number haven't you?"

"No, but I'll take it."

Sue gave Martin her phone number and he wrote it down. "Ok, I won't be too long. I'll just take a drive around the general area. I can't honestly see how she could go any further so if she isn't there ...."

".......... then we call the police" said Sue.

"Yes we do" said Martin.

Phyllis didn't like the way that sounded so definite. "Please find her Martin, please."

"I'm going to do my damndest Phyllis, believe me."

Martin drove off in the car as Phyllis locked the door.

"I'm not taking any chances Phyl" said Sue. "Grab a knife, a rolling pin and anything else that could act as a weapon."

Phyllis didn't need to be told a second time. She grabbed whatever she felt could be used to defend herself and took the items with her back into the lounge. The two friends sat there in silence, listening for every noise, every creak of the stairs, every rustle of leaves in the wind outside. It was eerily quiet.

"I don't understand it Sue" whispered Phyllis. "Why would anyone want to take Ophelia? She's never harmed anyone."

"I don't know Phyl. It certainly doesn't make any sense."

"I wonder if we could get Grimalkin to do what

Pywackit did. Perhaps he could find her."

Sue didn't want to put a dampener on Phyllis's hopes but she came to the realisation that if Ophelia had completely disappeared, it was likely somebody had taken her off in a car and Grimalkin was hardly going to be able to trace her further afield than a hill with a ruined church on it. "I'm not sure it'll be that easy Phyl. Let's just wait for Martin to come back. God I wish Robert was here .... and Alan."

They seemed to wait for eternity but eventually they heard a car pull up outside the cottage. Was it Martin? Both Sue and Phyllis picked up their makeshift weapons and waited by the kitchen door with the lights out. There was a knock on the door.

"Phyllis, Sue, it's me Martin."

Sue peered out of the glass pane just to make sure it was him. When she saw that it was, she unlocked the kitchen door, still with weapons in hand.

"Well I'm glad I didn't try to break in. You look as though you're about to do some serious harm."

"Any sign of Ophelia anywhere?"

Martin shook his head. "None." He paused before saying what nobody wanted to hear. "I think we need to call the police."

Phyllis was trying to hold back but she couldn't help herself. She started trembling and then the crying followed. Sue went to comfort her. "Come on Phyl, we'll find her."

Martin dialled 999. "Hello. Yes, police please. Hello? I want to report a missing person. When? Not that long ago but she's nowhere to be seen and I carried out a thorough search of the whole area in my car. Well can you make sure you do please. This is quite urgent." He looked at Phyllis and Sue. "Unfortunately the only thing we can do now is wait."

Chapter Twenty-Three

When the two policemen arrived, Martin let them in. Sue and Phyllis were still sitting in the lounge. Having to hide out of sight upstairs seemed to be the least of their worries at the moment.

"So you say she went out to make some tea and then .... just disappeared?" The policemen looked at them – was that an expression of disbelief on their faces?

"Yes, that's exactly what happened" said Martin. "I went out to look for her .... initally on foot, but then when I couldn't find her, I got in the car and did a search of the wider area."

"And you're sure she hadn't arranged to meet anybody?"

"Aren't you listening to me?" said Martin angrily. "I told you she just disappeared. She didn't arrange to meet anyone, she didn't just go off for a late evening stroll, she was making tea. You don't just disappear in the middle of making a cup of tea."

"We're just asking questions sir, there's no need to get irate."

"Well with all due respect, as I'm a solicitor who has practised criminal law for several decades now, I'm pretty sure I can tell when somebody's been abducted."

"Excuse me sir, wasn't a lady arrested in this house about a week ago or so? I wonder if there's any connection."

"Yes she was, no she didn't do it, and if you don't mind, I'd rather we stick to the subject in hand. The lady you mention is still in police custody so I know she's safe, although God knows what she's going through, but we have no way of knowing where this lady is and we want to find her. As for any connection, that's for you to investigate. Oh and by the way, I have pretty much been able to prove that the lady in custody is innocent, which means that there's still a murderer out there on the loose, so when another lady goes missing, it tends to concern me greatly." There was more than just a hint of sarcasm in Martin's voice.

"The trouble is sir that if it's a grown adult ......"

"Look man, you don't need to tell me the law. Haven't you heard what I just said? I'm a criminal lawyer. I know the protocol is that an adult going missing generally doesn't tend to be taken too seriously for the first 24 hours because usually it's due to a lover's tiff and they tend to come back days later, but in this case, there is no lover's tiff, in fact there's no lover and we'd all been having a quiet evening up to that point, so there was no friction between us. Therefore, her disappearance is highly suspicious. Now I'd appreciate it if you could get some resources to start searching the area as soon as possible. We're losing time."

The policeman paused. Working with the general public was one thing, but working with a criminal lawyer who you thought was trying to insinuate that you were an incompetent idiot and you were struggling to prove to him otherwise was at best awkward. "I'll radio in to the station and take further instructions. I'll be back in a minute."

When the policeman was out of ear shot, Martin cursed him. "Bloody idiot. He's probably used to dealing with local oiks who throw things at peoples' cars. When it comes to something more serious, he obviously hasn't got the first clue."

Martin's phone rang. "Hello? Yes. Oh hello Robert." His voice sounded tired, frustrated and irritable. "I'm afraid we've got some bad news. It's Ophelia ..... she's just disappeared. Yes, that's right. She just went to the kitchen to make some tea and the next minute she was gone. I went to look for her but had no luck. We've got the police here now." He lowered his voice and spoke closer to the phone. "Although to be honest, I don't think they'd know how to make a jam sandwich with a full set of instructions and all the ingredients." Martin paused as he listened to Robert. "No, no, don't be ridiculous. You've only just got there and there's nothing you can do. I know it's not going to be easy, but try to get a decent night's sleep tonight and drive back fresh tomorrow. I received a call to say the sample's ready so I can go and pick that up. If we use it with your device, then it may give us some answers." Robert spoke further. "Well obviously Phyllis is really upset. She hasn't stopped crying and Sue's trying to comfort her but it's not easy. She even suggested we send her cat to go and look for her which I have to say I didn't think was a very sensible idea. Then again, compared to the police ......"

At that moment the policeman walked back in, leaving his colleague by the police car. "I've spoken to the sarge on duty and he's going to contact the Inspector to see if we can get some resources. In the meantime, I may need to ask some further questions."

"Ask as many questions as you like, as long as you've got people searching for her." He put his ear to the receiver again. "Look Robert, the policeman's come back to say he's trying to organise resources to go and look for Ophelia. There's nothing you can do tonight. I know it's easier said than done but try and get some sleep and then come back tomorrow with this gadget of yours." On the other end of the line Robert didn't seem particularly happy with this idea but saw the sense in what Martin was saying. They said goodbye and Martin pressed the 'end call' button.

"Look I'm quite happy to come out with you and search for her ....."

"No I don't think that will be a good idea to be honest. I think it would probably be safer if you all stayed in for the rest of the night. If you don't mind, I'll just ask you a few more questions and then we'll see what we can do about the search. I would strongly suggest you lock the door behind me once I'm gone."

Martin resisted the temptation to say "gee, I'd never have thought of doing that with a murderer roaming free, thanks for the tip." By the look on the policeman's face, he got the feeling the policeman knew what he was thinking.

Nobody slept that night. Sue and Phyllis lay on the sofa and Martin sat in one of the chairs. Robert was pacing up and down his living room 50 miles away. The only person who was totally oblivious to the whole situation was Alan.

"Just when I need him, he's not bloody here" said Sue.

"But he's flying back tomorrow isn't he?" asked Phyllis.

"Yes he is Phyl, though to be fair there's nothing he can do."

"Except give you moral support" said Martin.

"If my name was Becky he would." Was that a bitter tone in Sue's voice?

"Oh Sue, that's not fair. He's gone to pay his last

respects to her. Once he's back things will return to normal. You'll see."

Sue sighed. "Maybe Phyl, maybe."

Police cars arrived and they heard one of the policeman talking to the other men. It sounded as though they were formulating a plan.

Meanwhile, Ophelia was regaining consciousness, only to find that her hands had been bound behind her back and she had been tied to a chair.

"Ah, the sleeping princess awakens" said a low voice.

Ophelia looked at her assailant. The light was dim and initially she could only make out the shape of a face. As her eyes became more accustomed to the dim light she began to see features. "I thought so" she said.

"Thought you were clever didn't you? I guessed it had to be you that sent my little gift back, wrapped in ten layers of pretty paper."

"I bet that was quite a surprise for you" said Ophelia. "You sent out a psychic attack and were arrogant enough to presume that the recipients knew nothing about ancient magic and that they wouldn't be able to protect themselves. You didn't count on anybody else knowing what you'd done."

"You have me there and I have to admire you for your competency in this area, but you see, I now have you captive and if you don't release this curse, let's just say you might meet with an untimely demise."

Ophelia looked at her assailant and started laughing. "Oh you really are stupid aren't you?" She couldn't hide the contempt in her voice. Her assailant got out of his chair, walked across the room and struck her across the face.

"Well that was very manly of you wasn't it. Striking a woman with her hands tied behind her back. You're more of a coward than I initially thought you were. Quite a pathetic specimen."

"SHUT UP!"

"Shut up? But I thought you wanted me to talk. My my, you really are a mass of contradictions aren't you? What's the name? Darius? That's how they knew you in Australia was it?"

He looked at Ophelia and frowned, a slight agitation creeping in. "What on earth are you talking about?"

"Oh dear, you're pretending ignorance but I'm afraid your facial expression gave you away. You know exactly what I'm talking about. Some woman came hammering on the door of the cottage screaming for Darius and threatening every kind of unpleasant death on him. I'm guessing that was you she was looking for. By her accent it sounded as though she'd come all the way from Australia. Looks like you've angered people near and far. I wonder what you could have done to suffer her ire."

"None of your damn business. You just lift the curse."

"Lift the curse?" Ophelia was smiling. "I don't think so. Do your worst to me, but that curse will now be with you for as long as you live."

"Rubbish, I can lift it eventually."

"Oh really? Well in that case why did you feel the need to abduct me? Let me think now. If you know your magic like I think you do, you know the basic laws that say once a person has sent back a psychic attack and then protected themselves, there's nothing you can do. The only thing you can do is ask the person to lift the curse. Only there's one thing you forgot."

By now her assailant was becoming increasingly angry, knowing that he couldn't counter Ophelia's argument. He wanted to shut her up but she carried on talking.

"You can't FORCE them to lift it, you have to get their full consent without coercion. Well pardon me if I mistake being drugged, abducted and tied to a chair as being coercive measures, because that's what it looks like to me."

"Just shut up and lift that curse or I swear it will be the worse for you. You'll know pain like you wouldn't believe. You'll be begging for me to stop."

Ophelia uncharacteristically began laughing, almost hysterically. "Despite your build and size, you really are quite the stupid little man. You think you can threaten me with torture. NOW LISTEN TO ME!" she hissed. "When I was a young girl my parents were part of a group who shall we say weren't very pleasant. You wonder how I know about dark magic? I can tell you – through bitter personal experience. I won't go into the horrendous details, but let's just say by the time that group had finished with me, I was no more than a garment of tattered flesh. My mind was ripped apart, my body had been abused more than you could begin to imagine. I suffered a split personality for years through trauma compartmentalising my mind. I knew for certain that one day they would kill me, either as a sacrifice or just plain old constant abuse. But something inside of me had a strong desire to survive. They used to keep me locked in my bedroom when they had no use for me – windows and all. But my mother had left a box of sewing needles in a drawer. I didn't think it would work but I took several of them out and started trying to pick the lock. I had no luck at first but I persisted and eventually got the door opened. I managed to escape. I had nowhere to go, I couldn't survive on the street on my own. I remember wandering off and coming upon a fairground. Well I was attracted by all the rides and bright lights and seeing all the other children eating candy floss and toffee apples. I so wanted to try one. That's when I met Ceridwen. She was the fairground's fortune teller. She saw me looking at the rides from her tent and came out to speak to me. I shyed away at first – I was frightened of all adults and didn't trust one of them. But there was something about her that made me feel safe.

"Come here child" she said in the softest, kindest voice. "Where are your parents?"

"When I started screaming that I didn't want to see them, she could obviously see the terror in my eyes and knew that something was wrong. She brought me into her tent and tried to calm me down. Eventually I felt safe enough to take something to eat and drink from her. I didn't realise it at the time, but that was the start of the most wonderful relationship in my life. As the fairground used to travel around, people could disappear easily and she told me that if I kept quiet and stayed close to her, she would take care of me. Well a few days later the fairground moved on and I never saw my parents again. What a blessing that was. Not only that, Ceridwen was the most gifted lady I'd ever met. She knew all about magic. Not the fairground variety – she knew real magic. She taught me a lot of occult knowledge – and, bless the dear lady, she even encouraged me to learn how to pick locks properly." Ophelia smiled as she remembered. "That was the start of my journey in life." She turned to look again at her assailant. "So you see dear Darius, as you seem to have called yourself in Australia, you can't frighten me because I've already been to hell and back, and I lived to tell the tale."

Ophelia was trying to read the expression on his face. "Oh, and that's another thing. That extremely rare book you have in your collection, Samael's Grimoire." She looked at him closely, the look on her face would have been enough to make anybody's blood run cold. "I'm sure you're aware that it's one of only two in print, the other being in a German national library." She paused as if to give what she said next the most dramatic effect. "You do know that there's a curse attached to it, don't you?"

'Darius' looked at Ophelia, his anxiety beginning to rise.

Ophelia was obviously enjoying herself. "Didn't your mother ever tell you not to touch the stove in case your burned your hand?" She paused. "Well it would appear not. You see, I read quite a lot about these old Grimoires and many of them are very powerful indeed, especially the one that you are no doubt the proud owner of. But I do seem to recall that from what I'd read, I learned that if the book was obtained by means other than fair trade and consent, the owner would eventually meet a very unpleasant end. So you see 'Darius', if you obtained that book by honest means, you have absolutely nothing to worry about. But if you obtained it otherwise, well, let's just say I wouldn't want to be you."

"You're full of shit, you don't know what you're talking about."

"Oh no? Well go ahead and pick the book up. I had it confirmed to me when me and my friends obtained access to your property the other night while you were being given heavy sedation to prevent the psychic entities messing with your mind."

He couldn't hide the shock on his face. He desperately wanted to believe she was bluffing but if she was, she was doing too good a job of it.

"I'm not very good at reading the ancient texts, but I wanted to see if it was true so I turned to the back of the Grimoire when we were here and sure enough, five pages in from the back of the book, it made it quite clear that if the book was obtained by methods nefarious, the owner would pay a very heavy price. Go on – take a look." Ophelia's voice was taunting him.

"You lift that damn curse or I swear I'll kill you here and

now."

Ophelia hissed and muttered something that sounded incomprehensible. The language sounded vaguely familiar to him but he couldn't be sure what it was. Suddenly he could feel ice cold fear running up his spine. He shivered nervously. Ophelia hadn't finished though. She forced her head back and took several short snorts of breath through her nostrils. She then began to hmmm a strange tone. The room seemed to suddenly close in on him. He could feel pressure building up inside his head. His muscles began to tense – they seemed to stretch to the point of pain. His breathing became erratic and his face began to burn. He glanced across at Ophelia and her face seemed to glow and a dark green mist seemed to surround her.

"STOP IT! STOP IIIIIIIIIIIIIIIIIIIIIIIIIIIIIT!!!"

Chapter Twenty-Four

"We've got no time to lose" said Robert as he almost barged into the cottage, nearly knocking Phyllis over. "Sorry Phyllis, I didn't mean to do that, but we need to get the process underway as soon as possible."

"But we don't even know Emily's blood group do we?" she queried.

Robert looked at Martin. "Do you know what the blood group is of our victim?"

"Well that was the strange coincidence I was going to mention, she's the same blood group as me – AB negative – one of the rarest blood groups there is."

Robert almost glared at Martin. "Are you sure Martin? Are you absolutely sure?"

Martin looked back at Robert as if explaining a simple maths problem to a child. "Yes Robert, of course I'm sure. I remember the consultant pointing out that she was such a rare blood group and I happened to mention to him that I was the same."

"Right, that's made our job easier, but you're probably not going to like it."

"What do you mean?"

"Look, what I'm about to tell you might seem strange, but Phyllis and Sue will back me up as I've used the process on both of them. When we use a blood sample with the genetic decoding function on the device, we need to use it on somebody who has the same blood group. As you are the only one here with the same blood group as Emily then I'm afraid it's going to have to be you."

"Well hang on a minute, I'm not sure ....."

"Martin, there's no time to be sure or not." Robert's voice became more desperate. "We need to find out exactly what happened to Emily and this is the only way we're going to do it. Now I guarantee you that it's perfectly safe."

"He's right Martin, it is" Sue reassured him.

"Honestly Martin, Robert wouldn't do anything that was dangerous or risky. He's carried out this procedure several times now and it's always been fine."

"Well what exactly is this procedure?" Martin felt uneasy at the prospect of what he was about to undergo, but felt more than just a subtle pressure from his three companions.

"First of all I'll inject a sample of the blood into your blood stream" said Robert. "Then we attach the pads to your temples. We then plug them into the machine and you will begin to experience various flashbacks in your mind. As you go through them, I can fine tune the device to make sure we're on the right time line."

"Hang on Robert, I don't mean to sound disrespectful but what if there's any contamination in the blood? I mean I know it's been taken from a dead person but I believe viruses can survive for some time after a person's died."

"Rest assured Martin. Ian Pemberton was an exceptional man and he factored that into the equation when he created this device. The machine emits a small electrical impulse through the pads as you're going through the process. These run through your entire blood stream and kill off any viral particles. Even if she had the bubonic plague, you'd be perfectly safe."

This didn't seem to reassure Martin any more. "I'm still not very sure about this Robert."

"Martin, please, I wouldn't put you at any risk. I read through Ian's notes extensively before I used it and I can guarantee you that he did his research thoroughly before even beginning to put this device together. You have to trust me."

"Please Martin" said Phyllis. "For Emily's sake as well as Elspeth's."

With Robert, Sue and Phyllis looking at him with such expectant expressions. Martin felt there was nothing he could do but agree. "Well alright then, but I'm trusting you Robert."

"Your trust will not be abused" said Robert. He proceeded to take a syringe and pierce the lid of the sample. He extracted a measure of the diluted blood sample and asked Martin to roll up his sleeve.

Martin apprehensively allowed Robert to inject the solution into his arm and then apply the pads that were attached to the wires. He plugged the wires into the device.

"Now Martin just sit back and relax."

Although Martin was still apprehensive he tried to relax

as much as possible.

Robert continued to observe his movements and started to proceed with the instructions. "Now I want you to tune into the genetic memory that I'm transmitting. I want you to tell me what you're seeing."

Martin gradually began to relax after his initial surprise at the vivid imagery he was experiencing. It was as if he was looking through the eyes of the victim.

"I don't know if this is relevant" he said. "She seems to be a young child and she's sitting on a sofa with an elderly man." Martin paused.

Robert wasn't sure whether this had any relevance to the murder but decided to let Martin continue so that he would relax more and feel comfortable in undergoing the experience.

"He's showing her an old book. It looks strange. It's not a child's book. It looks old and as he's turning the pages, it's got all sorts of unusual symbols in it. I've never seen anything like it before. He's explaining to her what the symbols mean."

"Do you know who the elderly man is?"

"Yes, yes, I believe it's her grandfather. They have a very close bond. They're both interested in all things ...."

"All things what Martin?" asked Robert.

Martin almost jumped up from his seat. "Somebody's just come in the house. It's a woman. I think it's Emily's mother. She's furious. She's really angry."

"What's she angry about?"

"She's told her father not to show Emily these books. She says they're wicked and will lead Emily away from God."

"Go on."

"She's shouting at him that she's warned him before and that if he carries on, she'll never let Emily see him again."

"How does Emily feel?"

"She's really upset. She adores her grandfather. She feels closer to him than she does her own parents. She feels as though she can't pursue her interest in these books because of them. Her grandfather's upset as well. I think he feels that she's ..... not just his granddaughter but ..... but a kindred spirit. He feels closer to Emily than he ever did his own daughter."

"Do you know the name of the book he was showing

her?"

Martin shook his head. "No, I can't see the front of the book, but the pages are strange. Very very strange symbols, looks like quite an old book."

"Ok Martin, you're doing really well. Now I'm going to adjust the frequency on the device so that you move to the last day of Emily's life. Can you let me know when you feel you are there?"

Martin nodded.

Robert observed him closely as he adjusted the knobs on the device. Once or twice Martin let out a small gasp and twitched here and there. Eventually he nodded his head. "Yes, yes, this is it."

Robert turned the fine tuning knob back a little so that they would be able to experience the context of the situation which led to Emily's tragic murder.

"She's met a man. It's not a first date but it's the first time he's invited her back to his house. She's nobody's fool so she's just going to see how it goes." He stopped a moment.

Robert didn't want to interfere but as the pause become longer he offered a gentle push. "Go on Martin."

They're drinking wine and chatting on the sofa. He obviously likes her and she seems to like him. She's asking him about his background. He's explaining that he lived in Australia for quite a few years."

At this remark both Sue and Phyllis darted a look at each other and then at Robert.

"Does he tell her what he was doing out there?"

"No, he seems to be a bit vague. He said he did several jobs but decided to come back to England. That's strange."

"What's strange?" asked Robert.

"Emily seems to have a feeling that he's not telling her everything. She notices that his glass is nearly empty so offers to get up and pour him another glass of wine. He agrees. Oh that's interesting."

Robert, Sue and Phyllis looked at Martin, almost on tenterhooks.

"What's interesting Martin?"

"She's just walked past the bookcase to get some wine and it's caught her attention."

"Yes, go on."

"She's looking more closely at the books. She's commenting that some of them would be the type of books that her grandfather would be interested in."

Sue and Phyllis felt a twinge – was it intuition – they could hardly hold their breath.

"She's bent closer to look at the titles. She's marvelling at some of them and then ...."

Martin went silent. He had a strange look on his face.

"What's happened Martin?" asked Robert.

"She's looking at one book in particular. She's put the wine glasses down. She's pulled it out and is examining it closely. She suddenly feels a combination of anger and apprehension."

"Carry on."

"She's turned around and asked him where he got the book. He's told her to be very careful with it as it's a very valuable book. She's insisting he tells her where he got it from. He told her he bought it off a dealer. She's shaking her head. She's getting angry. She's insisting that he tells her where he got the book and he keeps repeating that he bought it off a dealer. She's taken hold of one of the wine glasses and smashed it. She's lunged towards him and cut his face. She's screaming that he's a liar. She's telling him that there are only two prints of this book. One is in a German library and the other one was owned by her grandfather. She's saying that her grandfather was murdered and when her parents went to sell his book shop, they checked the inventory and all the books were there except this one. She's pointing at him and screaming that he murdered her grandfather. She remembered her grandfather saying that somebody had come into the bookshop and had seen him reading the book. He asked how much the book was and her grandfather had told the man that it wasn't for sale as it was rare and very valuable. Oh my God!!"

"What's happening Martin?"

"He's obviously realised that he's finally been found out and can't afford for her to tell anybody that he murdered her grandfather. She's lunged for his face with the glass again but missed as he put up his arm to protect himself. She's cut his arm instead. It's starting to get extremely volatile now. He's shouting at her that he can't let her escape. She's throwing things at him. She's then tried to run for the front door but he's locked it. He's coming towards her with a knife. She's managed to kick him back and has run back into the lounge. He's followed her and she's desperately looking round for a weapon. She's picked up a small table and is lunging it at him. He's managed to pull it off her and thrown it aside. And then ... and then ....."

Martin seemed to squirm in his seat, his face twisting until ...... until .... he finally became silent.

"Martin, I'm bringing you back right now." Robert adjusted the frequency knobs slowly. He knew that to do it too quickly would cause a severe shock and do more damage. "Come back Martin, you're coming back, gently, gently, come back ......"

Martin moved his head slowly from side to side. His eyes flickered for a brief moment and then he began to open them. He looked around the room and then at the three faces looking back at him – all of whom seemed to be in shock.

"Are you ok?" said Sue.

"Hang on" said Phyllis. "I'll go and get you some water."

"How are you feeling?" asked Robert.

"I don't know. I feel strange. That was really odd. It was all so vivid. It's like I was actually there experiencing it all."

Phyllis came back. "Here you go Martin, drink some water. Ophelia and I always use it to ground people after a deep meditation."

Martin took the glass of water gratefully and drank great gulps.

"This book, it sounds like the one Ophelia was talking about the other day" said Sue.

"That's exactly what I was thinking" said Phyllis. "When he mentioned there were only two in print and one was in a German library, I knew straight away that he must be talking about the same book.

"And it all ties in" said Sue. "The tunnel under the house, the fact that the occupant came out screaming."

"Yes, Ophelia sent the curse back that was put on

Martin, only she did it tenfold so he must have had a horrific experience. It's definitely the house of our murderer."

"Hang on you two. We've got to be sure" said Robert. "Martin, would you recognise the house if you saw it again?"

"Every nook and cranny Robert. The detail was so vivid. I can see the outside as Emily first came into the house and I can see the lounge."

"Robert, we've got to get over there now" said Phyllis, urgency in her voice. "That's where our murderer is and that's where he's got Ophelia."

Sue almost didn't want to say it but it slipped out of her mouth involuntarily. "That's if she's still alive."

Chapter Twenty-Five

"Before we go, we call the police" said Robert.

"Fat lot of good they've been so far" Sue huffed.

"Nevertheless we've got to tell them they need to get over there now."

"Ok Robert. Well you'd better call them because if I do, I'd probably be inclined to tell them what I think of their efforts so far" said Sue.

"I'll second that!" said Phyllis.

Robert called the police and told them what he'd found out though he didn't disclose how he'd done it otherwise he felt they probably would have put the phone down on him there and then. When he mentioned the fact that Ophelia was probably at this address, they seemed to take a bit more notice.

"The trouble is do we go there now or do we wait for the police?" said Robert. "We don't know how dangerous he is and if Ophelia is there, we don't want to put her life at risk."

"Well the police should be there by the time we arrive" said Sue. "If not, I'll do their damn job."

"We can drive down there and park further down the road. We don't need to draw attention to ourselves. We don't want to alert him as he might do something drastic" said Martin.

"Well, that doesn't sound like a bad idea" said Robert. "But Phyllis, you've got to promise to stay in the car. If you start running out towards the house, you could make the situation worse. I know you want to get Ophelia back alive but we have to be careful."

"I promise Robert. I know you think I'm just a delinquent mad old hippy, but I care too much about Ophelia to do anything spontaneous and stupid."

Robert looked at her. "I've never thought of you as a delinquent mad old hippy Phyllis. I just know that you're crazy enough to put your own life at risk for those you care about."

The four companions got into Martin's car and he drove down the track leading to the main road.

"I must say, I don't know a lot about cars, but this is a very nice car you've got Martin" said Phyllis. "It's very spacious."

"Of course it is" said Sue dryly. "The lawyers earn all the top dosh while we lowly PAs are only given the breadcrumbs, and are then told we should be grateful for such scraps, oh unworthy beings that we are."

"Oh dear" said Martin. "If I didn't know any better Sue, I'd say you had a bit of a chip on your shoulder"

"Chip?" said Sue. "More like a ruddy great boulder!"

The car drove through the first village where the library was. It continued on the main road, heading towards the next village. As they turned into the road where the now infamous house stood, none of them could believe what they were seeing. Martin pulled the car over to the side of the road. Phyllis was about to jump out when Robert stopped her.

"PHYLLIS!! NO!! Remember what you promised."

"But Robert, look, she ..."

"PHYLLIS, I SAID NO!!" Robert's voice was more commanding.

The police had indeed arrived but nobody was expecting to see what was unfolding. Craig was standing at the front door, holding Ophelia hostage with a knife to her throat. In front of the gate a woman was standing with a gun pointing at both Ophelia and Craig. The police were trying to calm her down and telling her to drop the gun.

"DROP THE GUN???? I'LL PUT SIX BULLETS IN HIS FILTHY HEAD BEFORE I DROP THE GUN!" she screamed.

"YOU'D BETTER TELL HER TO PUT THE GUN DOWN OTHERWISE I SLIT THIS WOMAN'S THROAT!" shouted Craig, holding the knife ever closer to Ophelia's neck.

"Oh Robert, I can't stay here. I've got to help her!" Phyllis was sobbing hysterically. She was pulling at the car door but Martin, at Robert's request had put the child locks on.

"Hang on Phyllis. Just try to stay calm." Even Robert was finding this hard to do in the current situation.

"That's right, take another innocent life you disgusting piece of shit! You murdered my sister, you vile lowlife. How many peoples lives were you responsible for in that den of filth and depravity? You aren't fit to be called human and I swore that I'd get revenge for what you did to my sister. YOU'RE

GOING TO DIE, SCUM!!" The woman pointed the gun firmly at Craig, but he held Ophelia closer to him and there was no way she could get a clean shot at him.

"You'd better tell her now to put the gun down or I swear I'll slit her throat."

One of the policeman came forward. "Look, put the gun down. He's not going to get away. Can't you see you're putting this poor woman's life at risk? Do you want to be responsible for her death?"

"DO YOU KNOW WHAT HE DID TO MY SISTER?" she screamed.

The policeman was obviously trying to calm the situation down. "If you put the gun down, you can tell me back at the station what he did and we can press charges then."

"You bloody idiot, this happened in Australia. The police didn't get him there, so what makes you think you'd be any better? You're all bloody incompetent, that's why I've got to give him the justice he deserves!!!"

"Look, I'm sorry about what he did to your sister, but once we apprehend him we can start proceedings against him but if you keep pointing the gun at him, you're putting this poor lady's life at risk."

Robert decided it was time to intervene. "Right, I want you all to stay here. I'm going to go and talk to him."

"But Robert, I want to ...."

"Phyllis! No! Stay here."

Robert got out of the car and walked slowly up to the policeman.

"Sir can you go back to your car, you can see we're dealing with a very volatile situation."

"Yes I know you are, and the lady with a knife to her throat is a very dear friend of mine. Let me speak to them both."

"Who are you?" he said.

"It doesn't matter who I am. What matters is that you currently have a lady in custody for the murder of Emily Sjöberg but the real murderer is standing right in front of you holding a knife to my friend's throat. We have the DNA evidence back from the lab showing his blood on the blouse that the victim was wearing. Now first of all I want to speak to the lady pointing the gun as she is posing the most direct threat at the moment."

The policeman didn't want to admit defeat, but so far he hadn't had any luck in calming the woman down so he allowed Robert to go and speak to her.

"Look, I don't know what this man did to your sister, but the lady he's holding hostage is a very dear friend of mine and if anything happens to her, I will be holding somebody accountable. Now pointing that gun at him isn't going to resolve anything, so why don't you put it down?"

"Because the bastard killed my sister!"

"I'm assuming this happened in Australia is that right?"

"Yes that's right – and he got away before the police could get anywhere near him. Fucked off back to England, the snivelling, slimy little coward!"

"So I understand that he can't be arrested for that murder but he's already committed a murder here and very recently. We have the DNA evidence that he's responsible so why don't you let the police do their job in apprehending him?"

"You don't give a shit about my sister, you're just worried about your friend. I swore I'd get revenge on this piece of vermin and I'm going to see it through."

"Ok, so let's say you do manage to put six bullets in his head. I'm sure that would make you feel better – for a short while. But long term? Do you honestly think you're going to feel any better?"

"I'll take my bloody chances!!"

"Well let's look at it this way. If I were in your shoes no doubt I'd feel exactly the same way that you do. But I'd be a bit more strategic in getting my revenge."

"Whaddya mean?"

"One thing my father taught we was the art of delayed gratification. I wanted to leave school early and get a job straight away. He encouraged me to stay on and go to university, saying that I'd get a better job and more money if I did this. Turns out he was right."

"So what?"

"So if you kill him now, you might feel great for a day or two. But then he's gone beyond any misery and suffering while you're still grieving over your late sister. He won't be in a position to care anymore. Do you think once he's dead it'll affect him?"

"With any luck the bastard will go straight to hell."

"Ah yes, the old 'life after death' theory. Interesting, but is it true? Who knows? It's a hell of a gamble to take. Whereas if the police apprehend him, he'll no doubt be charged for the murder of the young woman who died a few weeks ago and will serve the rest of his life in prison. Now granted, I know that he won't be charged for the murder of your sister and I am genuinely sorry about that because one thing you and I can agree on is that he is a low life scum bag. But here's the thing. If he goes to prison, he will spend the rest of his life locked up, being told when to go to bed, when to get up, being given tedious chores to do, probably won't be very popular with some of the inmates. Trust me, even today there are convicts that despise those who harm women and children and let's put it this way, he might not have such a great time in prison. Now he doesn't look that old to me, possibly late forties/early fifties. That would mean, all things being equal, that he might have several decades left to sit and rot in prison, giving him time to think about what he's done. If I was in your shoes, I would be tempted to think that prison was a more favourable option. You could go to sleep at night thinking about how you got revenge for your sister knowing that he was living a miserable life behind bars."

"But I want to see the bastard bleed!"

"I'll be the first to admit I can't guarantee that if you put the gun down, but I can assure you that in prison he'll probably get plenty of opportunity to bleed out."

"You don't know what the bastard did to her!"

"I know but I'll never find out if you don't put the gun down because the police will arrest you if you shoot him and then you'll be locked away. What sort of revenge is that? Do you honestly think your sister would want to see you behind bars? That would be two lives he's destroyed. Who wins?"

The woman started sobbing. "But it's not fair."

"I know it's not fair. The sad truth is that there are many scumbags in the world like him and sadly a lot of them get away with their crimes. We just need to make sure that we bring as many of them as we can to justice. Why don't you let the police do that? I'm sure your sister would prefer to see you living your life to the full while he rots away in a cell. Don't you think that would be the ultimate revenge?" Robert paused a second. "Now why don't you give me the gun?"

"I'll go to prison anyway for possessing an offensive weapon. Isn't that how the law works here?"

"You see that car over there?" said Robert pointing to Martin's car. "The man in the driving seat is a criminal lawyer. Now I can't guarantee that you'll get off scot free for being in possession of a deadly weapon, but so far you haven't killed anybody and I'm sure that he would say that you were provoked due to mitigating circumstances. I don't think that any fair judge in the land, when hearing your sister's story, wouldn't have empathy for you. I'm sure that something could be arranged."

"I don't know ....."

Robert's tone changed from a casual voice to a more fatherly one. "Come on, don't throw your life away because of him. He's not worth it. You've got everything to live for and the best revenge you can have is to live a long and happy life. You can keep your sister's memory alive in the comfort of knowing you brought the man who killed her to justice."

The lady faltered as she held the gun, now shakily in her hands.

"Come on, you know it's the right thing to do. Don't let him get the upper hand. Hand me the gun."

She began shaking as the tears streamed down her face. "Y-you'd better p-promise me h-he's going to p-pay."

"I give you my solemn promise" said Robert. "I want to see him brought to justice as much as you do and I know three other people who want the same. They're on your side."

"B-but I-I w-want t-to ....."

"For your sister's memory, the best revenge you can have is to get him put behind bars .... just as my father told me ..... delayed gratification."

The poor woman was now shaking, crying and holding the gun tentatively. She dropped her hand and Robert gently held his out to take it. She shakily handed it over to him and almost fell to the ground, crying. Robert handed the gun to the policeman and then helped her up.

"Come on" he said. "It's going to be alright." Robert didn't feel as confident as his voice sounded as he knew that

Ophelia still had a knife being held tightly to her throat and now that her assailant didn't have a gun pointing at him, would he be more inclined to use it?

"Now drop the knife" said the policeman.

Robert looked at Craig, angry at the fact that not only had he fooled them into thinking he was trying to find the murderer, but that he now held Ophelia's life in his hands. He looked at Ophelia. Was it his imagination or did she seem to be smiling? He frowned, thinking he was imagining it, but she did seem to be smiling. She closed her eyes and seemed to lean back into her assailant. He could see her lips moving but couldn't hear what she was saying. The police stood silently by, not daring to move in case it prompted a reaction. What happened next was beyond everybody's comprehension.

The hand that held the knife close to Ophelia's throat started trembling. Robert became apprehensive that at any moment he was going to push it hard against her jugular. But as he watched ever closer, the hand seemed to be moving outwards, away from Ophelia's throat. She continued moving her mouth, her eyes firmly closed. What was happening? There seemed to be an undescribable aura around her – he couldn't see anything but she seemed to go deadly still with only her mouth moving. Craig's head started to tilt back and his arm began moving forward, the knife becoming looser and looser in his grip. The knife dropped from his hand and he began shouting – or was it screaming? He pushed Ophelia forward and she fell down the steps but managed to grip on to the post. He barged past her and the police and ran down the road like a terrified animal. The police couldn't understand what had happened but one of them started barking commands to go and apprehend him.

The next thing that happened was Phyllis running toward the house, screaming. "OPHELIA! OPHELIA! ARE YOU ALRIGHT??"

Martin had been watching all that had happened and when he realised that Ophelia was no longer at risk, he took the child locks off the door and let her Phyllis go.

"OPHELIA! OPHELIA!" She ran to Ophelia and nearly crushed her to death with the hug that she gave her.

Ophelia began coughing. "I'm fine Phyllis, just let me

get my breath."

"Are you sure you're alright? Can I get you anything? Oh thank God you're alive!"

"Oh Phyllis, you didn't honestly think anything was going to happen to me did you?"

"Well yes I did. Why? What do you mean?" asked Phyllis puzzled.

"When he abducted me that night, he must have given me something to knock me out. I awoke later and I was tied up. What he didn't realise was that I'd memorised an old incantation that Ceridwen taught me. It was used in olden times not just to ward off evil, but to place a curse on those who would harm you. The reason I didn't use it earlier was because I was afraid he'd lose control and cause the poor woman to shoot him. I didn't want her to be arrested for murder so I tried to keep the situation as calm as possible. Thankfully Robert came along and managed to persuade her to give the gun up. Once I knew it was in safe hands, I started reciting the incantation. Trust me, you wouldn't want to be on the receiving end of such a spell. I've never used it before as it's very powerful. Ceridwen always told me to never use it unless it was really necessary."

Phyllis looked at Ophelia and didn't know whether to laugh or cry. "Oh my word, Ophelia, you clever, clever girl."

Sue and Martin had by now got out of the car to join the others, but there was still a lot of commotion as the police went to apprehend Craig. He'd ran off screaming like a man possessed and the police ran after him as he weaved across the road, seemingly unaware of where he was or what he was doing.

Sue and Martin ran over to make sure that Ophelia, who was now feeling overwhelmed by all the fussing, was ok. "I'm fine" she said. "Honestly. It's this poor lady who needs help." She pointed to the woman who Robert was still comforting.

"Robert, let me help her" said Ophelia.

"Are you sure Ophelia, you've just been through your own ordeal?"

"I'm fine. Here, give her to me."

The woman who was still sobbing seemed to be unaware of what was being said, but went to Ophelia willingly. Strange that she felt .... what was it ..... comforted? ..... protected? ...... safe?

Phyllis had by now calmed down a little and Sue came to reassure her that everything was ok. It was at this point that they heard the screech of tyres and a mighty bang. Startled, they all looked to see where the noise came from. They couldn't see what happened, they could only hear one of the policeman shouting "CALL AN AMBULANCE!"

Chapter Twenty-Six

The Following Day

"I can't believe Craig would do that to me Phyllis. Why would he frame me for Emily's murder?" Elspeth looked at Phyllis bewildered, wiping the tears from her eyes. "What have I ever done to hurt him?"

Phyllis hugged her friend. "You didn't do anything at all my love. Unfortunately there are some nasty people in this world and I'm afraid he's one of them. It will be interesting to hear what Robert and Martin have found out about him when they come back." She turned to Ophelia. "Do you think he's going to be alright Ophelia?"

"From what the paramedics said, although he was badly injured, he will pull through but he'll be in intensive care for a very long time I should imagine."

"Well frankly I don't think the bastard deserves to live" said Sue. "From how angry that poor woman was, he'd obviously done something to her sister. Then he murders another poor woman here."

"Well no doubt we'll find out what the situation is at some point, but he's definitely paying some very bad karma back, that's for sure" said Ophelia. "Anyway, that's not important right now. Elspeth, is there anything we can do for you? I know it's been hard over the last month and we can't change what's happened, but if you wanted to come and take a break with Phyllis or I, you know you'd be more than welcome."

"Thanks Ophelia but to be honest, I think I just need to take some time out. Maybe just spending time doing gardening and taking walks to clear my head."

"I think you should seriously consider coming and staying with one of us sweetheart, but I understand if you just want to stay here for now. You know where I am though and all you need do is pick up the phone."

"Thanks Phyllis" said Elspeth. "I appreciate it."

"Oh there is one condition though, if you do go and stay

with Phyllis. One rule you must place strict adherence to" said Sue.

"Oh yes, what's that?" Should Elspeth be worried?

"Never, never, I mean NEVER sit on Pywackit's favourite chair! You shall NOT be forgiven."

Elspeth let out a loud laugh. Phyllis didn't mind Sue making a small joke at Pywackit's expense if it helped to lighten the mood. There had been enough darkness cast over the last two weeks and a break in the cloud was sorely needed. Pywackit looked at Sue disapprovingly from his allocated spot in the lounge.

"At least that's one thing" said Ophelia. "We won't have to keep Grimalkin and Pywackit on leads anymore." She looked over at Grimalkin. "It's ok Grimalkin, we're going home today so you don't have to wear that lead and collar any longer."

"You don't have to go Ophelia. You're more than welcome to stay" said Elspeth.

"Thanks Elspeth, but I do think I should get back and help out with the Mind, Body & Spirit Festival as they are slightly short at the moment and there's a lot for them to manage. I think Grimalkin will be more settled as well. Neither he nor Pywackit are very relaxed in each other's company."

"I know" agreed Phyllis. "I don't understand why they've never got on. I'm sure there's a strong past life link between them."

"Maybe one of them was a cat and the other a dog" suggested Sue, lightheartedly.

Phyllis didn't understand that Sue was making a joke and continued with her sombre observation. "It's just so odd, I would have thought they'd worked out their differences this time around. I just hope they don't have to take too many lifetimes to sort it out."

Sue looked over at Ophelia and gently shook her head in disbelief. "Well if there is some sort of past life link Phyl, let them sort it out between them. They've both been spoiled rotten by you and Ophelia and maybe it's time you gave them both some tough love."

"Oh I couldn't do that Sue. That would be an abuse of his trust."

Sue's phone rang. She picked it up. "Hello? Oh hello." Sue looked at the others and whispered 'It's Alan'. "Yes, yes. Well I'm still with Elspeth and Phyllis at the moment. What? Have I had a good time? Oh well if you consider following cats up to old ruined churches in the dead of night to look for where dead bodies have come from and nearly having Ophelia being murdered, absolutely. Oh and did I mention that Elspeth was arrested for a murder she didn't commit and has just found out her boyfriend tried to frame her for the murder?. Yes we've had an absolute blast up here." It was clear from the look on Sue's face that Alan thought she was making this all up. "Yes Alan, of course I have an over-active imagination. How on earth could such an outlandish story be true?" Sue continued the conversation as Phyllis went to get more tea.

"So what did he say? I take it he didn't believe a word you said?" asked Ophelia.

"No, clearly he didn't. He'll find out soon enough though."

"So when's he coming back?"

"The flight just got in this morning. I told him I was still here and he's going to get the train back home."

"Did he say how the funeral went?"

"Yes, he said it was a good service and it was nice to meet some of Becky's friends."

"Do you think he'll keep in touch with them?"

"Possibly. From what I can gather she used to talk about him all the time to them."

"Well I shouldn't worry too much Sue" Ophelia tried to assure her. "When things get back to normal, people go on with their lives. People are always saying they'll keep in touch and invariably it never happens or if it does, it soon fizzles out."

"To be honest Ophelia, I'm not too bothered about it. Despite the horrendous things that have happened here over the last two weeks, I think the time that Alan and I have spent apart has been good for us both."

"I hope so Sue." Ophelia didn't usually wear her heart on her sleeve; that was Phyllis's job; but on this occasion Sue got the impression she was genuinely concerned.

"Thanks Ophelia" she smiled. "It'll be fine."

Just as Phyllis was pouring more tea, a car pulled up

outside the cottage. Martin and Robert got out and walked towards the cottage.

"The door's unlocked" Sue called as she saw them approach the cottage.

Martin walked in followed by Robert.

"You're just in time for a brew" said Sue.

"Great, thanks" said Robert.

The two men sat at the kitchen table, with all eyes looking at them expectantly.

"Well come on, spill the beans" said Sue. "What's the latest?"

"First of all, Craig will live. He's sustained very serious injuries and it's going to take some time but they suspect ...." Robert paused.

"Well go on Robert" said Sue.

"They suspect from the tests they've done that he could be paralysed from the neck down for the rest of his life."

Elspeth shook and sobbed into her tissue. "I know I should be pleased but he's going to be a vegetable for the rest of his life."

"I have to say" agreed Sue, "even though he's an evil swine I wouldn't wish that fate on my worst enemy. How certain are they Robert?"

"Well they can't be totally certain – it all depends on how much he recovers but he's going to need a lot of help and a lot of retraining if he is going to be able to move any part of his body again."

Ophelia looked down, not wanting to make eye contact with anybody. Phyllis saw her reaction. "Ophelia, can you help me with some of these plates please, I've just got a few nibbles to put out."

Ophelia got up and went over to help Phyllis. Phyllis looked at her and whispered, "you can't blame yourself Ophelia. You had no choice. It was either do what you did or risk having yourself killed and that poor woman going to prison for shooting him."

"I know Phyllis, but I didn't intend for it to be that serious. I hoped they'd catch him before anything happened, and now this. No wonder Ceridwen warned me against using that incantation."

"Ophelia now stop that". Phyllis was trying to keep her voice low so the others wouldn't hear her. "You can't blame yourself. He brought this on himself, nobody else did. You understand the law of karma as well as I do. I certainly wouldn't wish it on him but what's happened has happened and there's nothing anybody can do about it."

"I know Phyllis. I still feel guilty though."

Phyllis touched her arm and guided her back to the table. Robert spotted that something had occured but said nothing.

"So I'm curious" said Sue. "Have they taken any blood samples from him?"

"Yes" said Martin. "I think I know where you're going with this Sue and they are indeed going to run a DNA comparison between his blood and the murderer's blood on the blouse."

"Well I wouldn't mind laying a bet on the odds that it's his" concluded Sue.

"I think you may be right" agreed Martin.

"So what happens then?" Sue looked quizically at Martin. "If he is indeed the murderer, which to be honest I think is a given at this stage, what happens in terms of sentencing? I mean the obvious conclusion would be that he gets a life sentence and goes to prison. But if he is paralysed from the neck down, I'm presuming he won't go to prison."

"That's a very good point Sue" said Martin. "Under normal circumstances, if he was found guilty, the judge would throw the book at him. The problem is, if he is physically incapacitated, then he's no direct threat to the public and he's going to need 24/7 care."

"Doesn't seem bloody fair when you think there are some poor buggers who need help and don't get it where a cold blooded murderer will have his every need tended to."

"Again Sue, I can't argue with you, but I'm afraid that's how it works. If he is incapable of movement, he'll need somebody to feed him, bath him, dress him ....."

"Wipe his worthless arse" added Sue.

"You don't mince with your words do you Sue?" said Martin.

"Martin, she's worked for a law firm for years. It sort of goes with the territory."

"I'm not sure whether to take that as an insult or a compliment Robert" replied Martin.

Robert laughed. "Well it's a bit like the joke about why won't sharks attack laywers in the water?"

"I know I'm going to regret asking this, but go on" said Martin.

"Professional courtesy dear chap, professional courtesy."

Martin said nothing but shook his head.

Phyllis burst out laughing. Elspeth followed shortly.

Sue looked at Martin incredulously. "I can't believe you haven't heard that joke, it's been doing the rounds for years."

"Sue, how long have you been working with solicitors now? You should know more than anybody that they're not supposed to have a sense of humour."

"You're quite correct Robert, how silly of me. I beg your pardon Martin, I apologise for not appreciating humour is not something that takes refuge in a solicitors head. Do forgive me."

"To think Alan's got all of this to come back to." Was that a slight shot at revenge from Martin?

Ophelia turned to Robert. "Erm Robert, I don't want to dampen the atmosphere, but I'm curious about the poor woman who tried to shoot Craig. Did you find out what that was all about?"

Robert looked sombre. "Sadly Ophelia I did. Her name is Cathy. She's being held in custody at the moment but Martin had the chance to speak to her. I'll let you explain Martin."

"From what she told me, Craig lived in Australia many years ago and apparently ran some sort of mind improvement group. He advertised in the local area saying that he could help people with self confidence, overcoming phobias and achieve their goals. Cathy had a younger sister who was a bit naive and was quite taken in by Craig, or should I say Darius."

"Darius?" said Sue.

"Yes, that's the name he went by in Australia. It turned out that this so-called self improvement group was a front for a cult. I've read about these cults before as I've come across such groups in my work."

"Oh, sounds interesting, do go on."

"Well the way Cathy explained it to me, it definitely

sounded as though he used the classic cult techniques to draw people in. First of all they use love-bombing."

"Love bombing?" Phyllis looked alarmed.

"Oh Phyl, I'm surprised you haven't heard of that before. All these cults in the sixties used to use it" said Sue.

"Sue's right actually Phyllis. The leader usually makes the new members feel very special, telling them how wonderful they are, how they can achieve anything, how nobody understands their uniqueness except for the leader himself."

"Classic cult techniques" added Sue. "I remember doing it in my psychology course."

Martin nodded. "Then once they've won the person's confidence, they begin berating them, humiliating them and telling them how worthless they are."

"But that doesn't make sense" said Phyllis.

"It makes perfect sense Phyllis" said Ophelia. "It's a way of controlling somebody's mind. First you shower them with love and then you verbally and or physically abuse them. Eventually they will do anything to regain your approval and then you are virtually their puppet."

"Couldn't have put it better myself" said Martin.

"So how does this all tie in with Cathy's sister?" asked Phyllis.

"Well by the time he had her under his control, as Ophelia says, he was physically and mentally abusing her. He would lock her in a room for more than 24 hours and the other members in the cult were told to ignore her cries. When he released her he told her it was to rid her of her impurities. This went on for some time. After much constant abuse, she became so weak and her body was so emaciated that her heart finally stopped working. If they'd got an ambulance to her in time they probably could have saved her, but it was too late."

"Oh my God, that's horrendous" said Phyllis.

"But hang on" said Sue. "How did Cathy find all of this out if her sister died?"

"One of the members of the cult hadn't felt comfortable with what was going on for some time, but didn't dare say anything as she was worried that she'd be reported to Darius, or Craig, should I say. She managed to escape and go to the police and that's how Cathy's sister's body was discovered. She actually managed to contact Cathy and tell her everything that happened.

"But didn't the police arrest Craig?"

"It was too late. One of the other members alerted him to the fact that the girl had escaped and I presume he knew the game was up. He disappeared and the other members were left to explain what happened to the police. The thing is his passport had his proper name, that is Craig, and he managed to get out of the country before they could alert the authorities."

"I feel sick" said Elspeth. "I can't believe he could be that cold."

"Suffice to say, Cathy was absolutely heartbroken when she found out not only that her sister died but also how she died. She told me she'd made it her goal to hunt Craig down and kill him."

"And she very nearly did" added Sue.

"But I don't understand" said Phyllis. "If this happened years ago, why has she only turned up now?"

"Because she thought Craig's name was Darius. She didn't even realise at first that he was English. He feigned an Australian accident and she'd already tried finding him in Australia but she managed to meet up with one of the ex-cult members years later to see if she could get any information from them."

"And did she?" asked Sue.

"Yes, she did. The person she spoke to suspected that he was English because one day he was saying something and got distracted and lost his concentration. He started talking in an English accent and it was only when he realised what he'd done that he started speaking with an Australian accent again. When Cathy heard this, she then put one and one together and realised that he'd probably fled back to England. By all accounts she carried out some thorough research to see if there were any similar groups being run in England. That's where she came across Craig's meditation group."

"That's how I met him" said Elspeth.

"She saw his photo on the website and saw that he was using the name Craig. She wasn't sure whether that was his real name but it was all she had to go on and the rest is history."

"So I wonder how she knew that you and Craig were an

item. It was obviously her that came round that night banging on the door here" said Phyllis.

"She told me that she'd tracked down where Craig held his meditation group and noticed him getting into a car with a woman. I'm guessing that must have been you Elsepth as she followed the car as far as she could up to the cottage along the main road. She didn't actually drive up the path leading to the cottage as she didn't want to be spotted. She waited in the side road and when Craig finally drove back to his house, she followed him, so she knew that he could be found at both those addresses."

"Nobody can say she wasn't thorough" said Opehlia.

"And she very nearly achieved what she came to do" said Phyllis.

"Well thank God she didn't or she would have ended up behind bars for the rest of her life" said Robert.

"What will happen to her Martin?" asked Phyllis. "I mean I know she had a lethal weapon and I'm sure there's a law against that, but won't the police take into account why she tried to do it and show her some leniency?"

"Well she has asked me to represent her and I said I'll definitely defend her. I can't guarantee she won't have to pay some sort of consequence, be it a fine or a short prison sentence, but I'm going to do everything in my power to get her off the charge. I don't think anybody hearing her story could fail to be sympathetic."

"I hope you're right Martin, I hope you're right" said Ophelia.

Chapter Twenty-Seven

"Are you sure you won't stay Ophelia?" asked Elspeth.

"I really should get back Elspeth, but thank you for the offer."

"Well thank you for everything. Thank you for helping to clear my name and for exposing that evil swine – I had absolutely no idea what he was like. It just makes me feel sick to think about what he's done."

"It'll take time, but you'll be able to put it behind you eventually" Ophelia reassured her.

"I hope so" said Elspeth, "I hope so".

Phyllis came up and as always, lunged herself at Ophelia. "Oh sweetheart I wish you weren't going. I know it's been a nightmare, but I'm sure the rest of the holiday would be absolutely fine here."

"I'm positive it will Phyllis, but I think you and Sue still need a break." Ophelia looked over to Sue to make sure she was out of earshot. "Can you look after her for me Phyllis. I think things are a bit strained between her and Alan at the moment. That's why she needs to stay here for a few more days."

"Do you honestly think I'd let one of my best friends down?" said Phyllis indignantly.

Ophelia laughed. "It's the very last thing I'd think." She squeezed Phyllis's hand.

"Goodbye Ophelia. I still don't understand what you did to cause that lunatic to run straight into the car but if you hadn't, Elspeth would probably be behind bars by now. Thank you for doing the job the police should have done."

"That's ok Sue. I'm just relieved it worked out ok."

"Oh hang on, before you go, don't forget this." Sue handed Ophelia an object wrapped in a linen cloth. "I can't help but be curious Ophelia. I haven't peeked but I am curious. Can I ask what it is?"

Ophelia unwrapped the object gently as if it was the most precious thing on the planet. "It's this."

Sue looked at it. "Isn't that the book that you were looking at the other night? Isn't that the one that Craig murdered Emily over when she discovered it?"

Ophelia nodded. "It is indeed the book. After Craig had gone running off screaming I nearly fell headlong down the stairs but managed to grip onto one of the railings, thankfully for me. Amidst all the commotion I realised that once Craig had been apprehended, the police would have taped off the entire house as a crime scene for the forensic team to go and investigate. I'm afraid there was no way I could leave this book in there – it's far too valuable and it would have probably ended up in a second hand book store without people realising how precious it was."

"So you 'acquired' it" said Sue.

"Yes I did but trust me Sue, I did it with good intent. As I explained to Craig when he held me captive, there is an instruction at the back of the book which says that if it is obtained through nefarious means, the owner will bring a curse upon themselves. I saw what happened to Craig and I certainly don't want to bring the same fate down upon myself."

"So what are you going to do with it?" asked Sue.

"I've asked Robert to drive over to Lynette's house. That's Emily's mother. As it was her father's book, she is now the rightful owner. I'm going to give it to her."

"But I thought she hated anything to do with magic? I thought you said she was married to a vicar?"

"She was Sue. But the book rightfully belongs to her. What she does with it is up to her."

"But what if she doesn't want it and tells you to take it away?"

"If she does, I will explain to her that due to the curse, I cannot just take the book without her giving her full consent and blessing. If she does that verbally, it creates a sacred contract which releases the owner from any curse."

"Well I rather think that she might take that option and I'm sure that the book would be in safe hands with you."

"Thank you Sue." They hugged and Ophelia gave Sue a smile. "Try to enjoy the rest of the holiday. I hope that you and Alan will be ok. He's a good man Sue. I understand it hasn't been easy for you recently but give it time."

"Are you leaving too Martin?" asked Phyllis surprised.

"I am Phyllis. I have work to catch up on back at the

office and as efficient as my PA is, there are certain things that only I can take care of."

"What about Cathy? Will you be able to help her?"

"Yes, don't worry Phyllis. I'm going to be in regular contact and will come up to see her if necessary but we can carry out meetings over the internet. I'm sure she's going to be alright."

"Well thanks for coming Martin. I do appreciate it."

"My pleasure Phyllis."

There was a slightly awkward moment where Phyllis wasn't sure whether she should give Martin a hug or not. She was still aware of that night back in the late sixties when she and her buddies had humiliated him and she could still feel pangs of guilt over it. Martin gave her a gentle hug but backed off quickly, or so she thought. She could feel her heart sink. Even more so when Martin quite openly gave Ophelia a hug.

"Thanks for coming up Martin, we couldn't have done it without you. Magic is my department but law and order and all things legal is definitely where I fall down."

Martin laughed. "Only too happy to get an innocent person off the hook Ophelia. I'm sure we can do something for Cathy."

Everybody said their final goodbyes. Ophelia got into Robert's car and Martin started the engine in his. Elspeth, Sue and Phyllis waved them all off as both cars drove down the track towards the main road.

"I feel so guilty" said Elspeth.

"What on earth for?" asked Phyllis.

"I've ordered a delivery of champagne that I was going to put in the fridge for all of us tonight, but the others are going to miss out."

"It's not your fault Elspeth. I know they've all got obligations, otherwise I'm sure they would have stayed to help us celebrate."

"Even so, it's a shame after all they've done. I really am indebted to them."

"Well may I suggest that when the champagne finally arrives, we all get happily pissed and celebrate your freedom?" said Sue.

"I don't usually drink alcohol, I like to keep my body

pure, but in this instance I'm happy to have a glass or two" said Phyllis.

"Oh Phyllis, I can't believe you just said that!" retorted Sue. "Your body a temple of purity – when you smoke enough weed to keep the South American drug cartels in business for decades?"

"Sue, I'll have you know I don't do that much weed these days. Besides which, they produce coke more than they do weed."

"You see, you even know what drugs they grow!!!"

"Oh come on you two. Let's go in and have a cup of tea until the champagne arrives. We can then make a toast."

"Yes indeed" said Sue. "First one to your release."

"Second one to Cathy's soon to be release" said Phyllis.

"And third – and most important of all .... to Emily's memory" said Elspeth.

"To Emily's memory" said all three.

* * * * *

Robert pulled up by the side of the road and Ophelia got out of the car. He watched as she walked over to the house of Emily's mother. She knocked on the door. Within a short space of time a lady opened the door.

"Hello, I called here a few days ago, I don't know if you remember."

The woman's expression suddenly became hostile. "Oh I remember you, you fraud. I popped over to see Alice after you'd mentioned her as I hadn't seen her for so long and I mentioned your name. She'd never heard of you. 'Friends of Jesus' indeed. Go away!" Lynette attempted to close the door on Ophelia, but she didn't count on the strengh of Ophelia's arm holding it open.

"Go away!! Leave me alone!!"

"Just let me tell you the truth and I promise I'll go away and never bother you again."

"How can I trust anything that comes out of your mouth?"

"Perhaps if I show you something, you'll believe me."

The woman looked at Ophelia cautiously. She was so

tempted to slam the door in Ophelia's face but paused for a second. "What can you possibly have to show me?" The hostility in her voice was still there.

"This" said Ophelia taking the object she was carrying and pulling the linen cloth back.

When the woman saw what it was, the look of horror on her face was palpable. "Where did you get that?" she hissed. "I don't ever want to see it again! Get it away from me!"

"Let me explain and then you can decide whether you want to keep it or let me take it away."

"I don't want any explanation, I never want to see that book again!"

"This book is the very reason your daughter was murdered" said Ophelia.

"What do you mean?"

"The man who had this book murdered your father many years ago and stole it from his book shop. I understand that you sold the shop and this was the only book missing on the inventory."

"How could you possibly know that?"

"It doesn't matter. What does matter is that I do know this for a fact." Ophelia paused. "Sadly it was also the reason that your daughter was murdered."

"How?"

"By a strange twist of fate, your daughter met the man who owned this book, or should I say she met her grandfather's murderer, though she didn't know it at the time. She went back to his house for a drink. She was looking through his library and noticed this book. She could remember your father owning it and she also remembered that there were only two copies in print."

"One in a German library and this one" added Lynette.

"Correct" said Ophelia. "She told this man that she knew this was her grandfather's book and things turned nasty. Sadly I'm sure you know what happened next."

"But I thought they'd arrested a woman for Emily's murder."

"They did, but it was a wrongful arrest. The man who murdered your daughter planted some evidence at this lady's house and called the police. The police then came and searched the house, found the garment and naturally put two and two together."

"So how do you know that she didn't do it?"

"Because they tested the garment for DNA. It had both Emily's blood and the murderer's blood on it. Suffice to say, the murderer has been apprehended and they are running DNA tests as we speak. As far as all are concerned, it's a forgone conclusion that the DNA test will come back with a match to him."

"So how did he manage to plant the evidence? I don't understand."

"He was dating the lady concerned at the time and he managed to get into her cottage when she wasn't there and planted it then. He took me captive because I had discovered that he was the real murderer. If you don't believe me, by all means call the police. My name is Ophelia – that much of what I told you the other day is true. There was an incident at this man's house where he held me at knife-point and there are quite a few witnesses who will testify to this. He also had an Australian lady called Cathy who was trying to shoot him but she couldn't as he was holding me hostage. Yes, yes, I know, it all sounds totally ludicrous, but please feel free to make your own enquiries. In the meantime, I have come to give you this book back as you are the rightful owner."

"Whether I believe your story or not, I've already told you, I don't want it near me."

"Very well" said Ophelia calmly. "You have two options. I cannot take this book away as it has a curse placed upon it that says if the owner obtains it by nefarious or wrongful means, they will be cursed. This is what happened to the murderer as he ran in front of a car and is likely to be paralysed from the neck down for the rest of his life."

The woman looked at Ophelia – was it disbelief or shock?

"Again, you can check this with the police, though no doubt it will also be in the local paper in the next few days."

"So what do you expect me to do?"

"If you really don't want the book and you want me to take it away, I would respectfully ask you to give me your consent to be the new owner and give it to me with your full blessing."

"What? I'm not interested in ..."

"I can leave it here on your doorstep otherwise, then it will be your responsibility."

"This is all nonsense."

"Madam." Ophelia's voice was now firm, almost commanding. "I never knew your father but I understand the subject that he was interested in very well and I can assure you, this is no ordinary book and as much as I would love to own it, there is no way I am taking it away from here unless you give my your full blessing and consent."

The woman looked at Ophelia – was that fear?

"Well ok, but just take it away. I never want to see it again."

"Very well. Could I ask you to repeat these words to me."

"Alright, alright." She now looked quite flustered.

"I give this book to you with my full blessing and consent and ordain you as the full and rightful owner from this moment on until such time as you pass it on to another. So mote it be."

"I'm a Christian woman, I won't use pagan language!"

"Very well" replied Ophelia calmly. "Then you can replace the words "so mote it be" with "amen."

"Alright." By now the poor woman just wanted to see the back of Ophelia and the cursed book that was seemingly responsible for the death of both her father and daughter. "What do I need to say again?"

Ophelia repeated the phrase and waited for Lynette to say it back.

"I give this book to you with my full blessing and consent and ordain you as the full and rightful owner from this moment on until such time as you pass it on to another. Amen."

Ophelia bowed gracefully. "I receive this book and your blessing with thanks. Go in peace dear lady and may your God protect you for the rest of your life." Ophelia gave another bow and took a few steps backwards. She then turned and walked back to Robert's car.

Lynette looked in wonder, still not quite sure what had happened. All she knew was that she would never have to see that wretched book again.

When Ophelia got in the car, Robert looked at her. "I'm not sure I should even begin to ask what that was all about, but I take it she didn't want the book."

"Correct" said Ophelia.

"Which I presume means it now belongs to you."

"Also correct."

"Well whatever you do with it, please don't start putting hexes and curses on people. I don't want to have to come and save you from being burned at the stake."

"Dear Robert, you have no fear there. In the meantime, I can feel studying this valuable book is going to keep me very busy."

Robert started the car. Should he be worried? He knew that Ophelia and Phyllis held some unconventional beliefs but there did seem to be a strange aura around this book. Perhaps one day, when he felt ready, he might ask Ophelia what power, if any, the book had.

Perhaps.

Printed in Great Britain
by Amazon